A Full House

FIVE SHORT STORIES

Stephen C. Porter

A FULL HOUSE: Five Short Stories
Copyright © 2013 Stephen C. Porter

This is a work of fiction. Names, characters, places and incidents either are the product of the author's imagination or are used fi ctitiously, and any resemblance to actual persons, living or dead, businesses, companies, events, or locales is entirely coincidental.

All scripture references are taken from the King James Version of the Holy Bible.

ISBN 978-1-4866-0254-4

Printed in Canada

Word Alive Press
131 Cordite Road, Winnipeg, MB R3W 1S1
www.wordalivepress.ca

Library and Archives Canada Cataloguing in Publication

Porter, Stephen C., 1951-, author
       A full house : five short stories / by Stephen C. Porter.

Issued in print and electronic formats.
ISBN 978-1-4866-0254-4 (pbk.).--ISBN 978-1-4866-0255-1 (pdf).--
ISBN 978-1-4866-0256-8 (html).--ISBN 978-1-4866-0257-5 (epub)

       I. Title.

PS8631.O738F85 2013   C813'.6   C2013-906874-0
                                              C2013-906875-9

Three Westerns, one Dramatic Transport story
and one Christian/Science Fiction tale
under one cover. Enjoy! SCP.

CONTENTS

The snow and icy road conditions often found in the Rocky Mountains can be hazardous at the best of times, but when a transport truck, loaded school bus and a late snow plow meet on one ice-covered hill... God help them.

Space Baal   101

Abraham Peters is a devoted Christian who, acting as God has commanded him, built a powerful space ship, complete with three hologram control panels he made to look like his daughters. They run the ship, Charity, through some tests to see how it works. The atmosphere, temperature and shields are controlled by Hope, another of the girl image holograms, while the fiery red head, Faith, controls the weapons and long range sensors.

Retired truck driver, Abe (short for Abraham) and his wife, Mary, test the ship in space travels and planetary excursions until the real reason God wanted it built arrives, unannounced: to battle the governments of this earth for dominance. Abe works the bugs out of the ship until the final battles, and he hopes he has the skill and power to overcome the worst enemy the world could face.

Dannie's Partner

aniel MacAulay sat on the wagon seat looking at the herd of McKinley cattle trampling what was left of his wheat field. His already low spirit slipped into his boots and mingled with the dirt between his sockless toes.

The meager harvest left from the hail and rain last week was no more.

Bart, Joe and Doug McKinley promised to drive him off his farm. They wanted to overrun the rest of the valley, but Daniel's farm was like a cork at the upper mouth between this valley and the McKinley spread in the next valley. He still had the bruises where they had beat him up every day for the last three days. The next time, they said, he would not walk away.

He had lived a useless, wandering life until last fall when he won this farm in a poker game. The old man had said he was through with it anyway, and Daniel had moved in.

A roving preacher had told Daniel about Jesus, God's son, and he had accepted Him as his lord. Daniel thought he could change his life and had worked hard all summer fixing buildings, repairing the corral and fence, plowing, clearing, planting and trying to clear the endless little green weeds that were growing everywhere. This wheat field would have seen him break even this year, and now it was gone. If he skimped, he might have enough for one more year.

Things had been going good until last week. He was reading his Bible and praying, and he had decided he needed a wife. There were no available single women near here, so he had taken a chance and sent money east for one of those mail order brides. She was sitting beside him on the wagon seat as his depression settled deeper.

She had stepped from the stage coach bundled in heavy clothes and carrying one small suitcase. Her face was all but hidden by a fur bonnet, but her high cheek bones and sharp features made him winch. She was dirty, and her hands were calloused and rough. Even the paper she passed him was dirty. It read: *"No English. German, I think."* It had no signature, but was obviously from the people who had sent her to him.

Her only word to him was "husband?" in a low, almost masculine voice. He had grunted and, motioning for her to follow, led her to the local preacher who married them. He noticed her name when she signed the marriage certificate — Olga Gunderson.

He couldn't bring himself to kiss her. *That will come, I suppose,* he thought as he helped her onto the wagon seat. They started towards his farm. His bruises ached some, but he knew he was on his own. The town men were too afraid of the McKinley's to help him.

Daniel didn't know that Olga had no family, or that the Catholic Sisters had thrown her out of their orphanage for allowing one of the local boys to kiss her. She had disguised herself as a man and worked as a seaman to get to America. There, having no one to help her, she had dodged into the office of the mail order brides to avoid the police she thought might send her back to Germany. Instead, they had sent her here to marry Daniel.

All her life she had wanted a husband to call her own — a family of sorts. She had grown up praying to the God she knew from the little Bible she was given in the orphanage, but she was beginning to think He was not there. This man had been gentle enough while helping her into the wagon, but he did not speak to her and did not acknowledge her question of him being her husband. She had a deep desire to hear him confirm their relationship.

Daniel picked up the reins and drove the small, work worn mustang team down the hill and into his yard. The cattle had come through here, and his wood pile had been scattered underfoot across the yard. He jumped down and helped Olga from her seat, but the noise of approaching horses halted their progress into the cabin.

Three large, burly men were coming toward them at a leisurely pace. Joe, on Daniel's right and facing Olga, smiled broadly and, in a louder than necessary voice, proclaimed, "He's got a squaw."

"Yeh?" Bert, the middle man replied. "Might like to entertain some real men when we finish with our friend here."

Daniel shuddered and anger started to creep into his mind. They were here to beat him to death, if they could.

The three stopped a short distance in front of the pair, smiling at their own humour.

Daniel determinedly stepped forward. As he did, he noticed Olga's foot move ahead, as if she too were moving towards the men, but her toe slipped under a piece of firewood.

Joe loosened his foot and started to swing out of his saddle. The other two made signs to do the same. Things happened fast, and Daniel had to move fast just to keep up.

Olga flipped the firewood into the face of Joe's horse, which reared back and sideways, ramming Bert's horse and making them both grab for their saddle horns. She quickly stepped in and punched the horse in the face, again driving it into Bert's horse, which lurched into Doug's mount. Joe, unable to balance the sideways motion, went backwards off his horse and landed on his shoulders, momentarily stunned.

Daniel covered his surprise and closed his mouth before ducking in front of Bert's horse and jumping at Doug, who was trying to control his horse. He slapped Bert's horse's nose to keep Bert busy fighting to stay on it.

Tired as he was, Daniel was not slow in learning a new way of fighting. Before this they had beat him because he had gone toe to toe with them and tried to out punch them. This was something different, and Daniel felt his pulse race with exuberance.

He caught Doug's half raised foot and threw it up, tossing Doug out of his saddle and onto the ground on his back. Bert was just getting control of his horse and was reaching for his gun when Daniel reached him from behind and pulled him from his saddle by his gun belt. As Bert hit the ground, Daniel kicked backwards with his foot and felt it connect. Even though he did not wear spurs, the heel of his boot did its job, making a noisy thump on the side of Doug's face.

Daniel turned to face Joe and Olga just in time to see her swing the same stick of wood into Joe's face. Blood exploded from his nose and mouth as he fell back onto the ground. Daniel's still moving foot reversed direction and met Bert's face. Daniel heard bone break as blood poured from his mouth. Daniel spun to meet Doug as he rose. All the anger gathered from their days of abusive treatment was in the vicious right he drove across his body to the point of Doug's jaw. Doug collapsed on the ground without another sound, his jaw broken and hanging.

His anger spent, Daniel looked across the opening between him and Olga. For the first time since they met, he looked into her eyes and smiled. He wasn't sure, but he thought he saw a hint of a smile back, and he noticed how pure blue her eyes were. They were light blue, like... his mind raced... *like an ice covered lake.* Shockingly pretty!

Daniel and Olga gathered the cowmen's horses and sloshed water on them to bring them around. Taking their attackers' guns, they made Joe help Bert and Doug onto their horses.

"We'll leave your guns at the line fence where you polecats cut the wire," Daniel informed them. "If you know what's good for you, don't come down this way again. I'll send your cows back to you."

"You skunk! We'll kill you next time," Joe spoke through his bloody mouth, creating red bubbles with every word.

For the first time in a long time, Daniel felt good about his future. "I don't think so. You come down here looking for trouble, we'll give it to you and add a little more for good measures. Now, git!" He slapped Joe's horse. The three rode away, hurting with each step and bounce the horses made.

He turned to look for Olga, but she was bent over one of the weeds, looking at it. He watched as she pulled it from the ground then dug in the dirt. Her hands reappeared with what looked like three good sized rocks. She repeated the process with another weed.

Curious, Daniel walked over to where she was digging at the weeds. He looked at her hands and gasped.

4

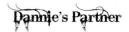

"POTATOES!" he burst out. *The field was full of them,* he thought as he looked around at his unworked back fields. They would not only have a harvest, but they could sell them for a good dollar to the town, the Army Fort in the next valley, and the rail head just twenty miles away.

He gave Olga a quick hug and motioned to the cabin. He made the motion for eating and waved her inside. Daniel bent and grabbed her suitcase as he walked by it and was surprised to find it so heavy. It must weigh forty pounds, but she had handled it so easily. He studied her back as they walked to the door stoop. Her heavy coat and leggings told him little about the obviously strong muscled body under them. His thoughts of a fat, dumpy girl were obviously wrong.

Maybe she was built like a man, he thought. *Oh well, he could live with that.* She had punched a horse for him, and he was not about to forget that.

Once inside, she put the potatoes on the small table and turned to her suitcase. Opening it, she produced a gun case, which yielded a well-oiled, new revolver.

Daniel watched as she pulled the pin on the front and removed the bullet cylinder, and he gasped when she raised the gun and pulled the trigger at the open door.

Daniel had never seen a double action revolver. His was a heavy old Navy single action. The double action clicked six times as fast as she could squeeze the trigger, and she turned and looked at him. He smiled at her and nodded. He had a *wife.* He watched the smile as it crept across her face and seemed to make it come alive.

"Home," he said, as he swung his hands wide. "Make yourself at home."

He knew she couldn't understand him, but he motioned, trying to make appropriate actions suit his words. "I must tend to the horses." He gave her another smile before turning to his chores. The horses had put in a hard summer, so he spent a little more time making them comfortable and shaking out a good portion of grain in their feed boxes. He would need their help with the potato harvest.

The smell of cooked food met his nostrils when he returned through the door. He froze. There on a chair were her coat and leggings. The inside was lined with pockets, and each was stuffed with utensils.

The table was set, and the food was on the plates. She had hurriedly cleaned up and changed into some of his clothes. They did not hide Olga's full figure and womanly curves like her coat had. She had taken her bonnet off and nervously stood facing him by the stove. Her long blond hair reached almost to her waist, and the light shone on her freshly washed face.

Daniel's mouth dropped open as he stared. She...she was "drop dead" gorgeous.

She looked longingly at him, and with her voice quivering slightly asked, "Husband?"

He realized this was important to her, and that he would have to go a long way to find her equal. "Yes, husband," he whispered.

She visibly relaxed and took a step towards him, a questioning look still in her eyes. "Wife?" she asked, softly.

Daniel's mind raced with his thoughts. Mrs. Smith, the school teacher, would love the challenge to teach Olga English, and three farms down was a German named Ben Grumman. Daniel was sure he would not mind teaching him German, not to mention interpreting for them in the meantime.

The food forgotten, he stepped toward her. "Yes, wife," he said, feeling the satisfaction of seeing happiness spread across her face like a warm spring breeze on open water.

His mind was still going and he realized that he had a rare gift here, and that she was his and that he would love her. He spoke softly. "Not husband, not wife....partner, forever." He motioned to himself with his index finger when he said husband and to her with his second finger when he said wife, then he crossed them as tightly as he could when he said partner.

At first she looked puzzled, so he walked over to her and took her in his arms. He kissed her forehead then leaned away.

"Not two, but one," he held up his two index fingers then put them together and wrapped one around the other. He was remembering the verse in his Bible where God said a husband and wife would be one.

Her eyes glistened with tears when she understood he was telling her they were one and they would never part. "Partner," she whispered happily as she leaned into his warm embrace, having found what she had prayed for.

Buffalo Chip's Wagons

Chapter 1

Chip stopped his horse, Rudy, beside the boulder and climbed up onto the saddle. He let the reins fall to the ground as his big, strong, work-worn hands grasped the rocky outcrops on the top of the boulder, and his feet found the crevasse he had used on other occasions to mount this pinnacle. His eye glass bumped against his chest, safe in its leather case that he held in his teeth by its draw-string. With little effort, he hoisted his 200 lbs. of lean, hard-muscled body up and over the rock's lip and onto the flat top lookout point.

On a clear day he could see forty miles into the dry, arid wasteland his wagon train was going into. As at other times he stayed low, lying on his stomach so that he wouldn't sky-line himself while he studied the trail ahead and the country around him.

His wagons wouldn't get here until dusk, but they were deep into Apache country and White Foot was an up-and-coming chief seeking more status. Chip and White Foot knew each other well. White Foot

...ng to kill Chip and take his wagon train for three years,
ha...men and armaments were too great for White Foot's braves...
bu...

...te Foot had somehow found out that Chip's dad had named him
...a buffalo paddy, and he delighted in calling him "Buffalo Dung."
...returned the insult by calling White Foot "Stinking Socks." He
...found out how White Foot knew his dad had abused him every
ch...ce he got, even to the extent of naming him after a buffalo chip.
H... didn't know if White Foot knew he had finally beaten his dad and
...ft home when he was just thirteen, but he suspected he did. Anger and
fighting had become a way of life for Chip, and his ugly, scarred face
with its multi-broken nose and cauliflower ears showed he had done a
lot of it. In a bar-room brawl or a bite-and-gouge dirty fight, few could
last more than a few minutes with him.

Two years ago, a roving preacher had travelled with his train and
introduced him to God's son, Jesus Christ, and he hadn't been in a good
scrap ever since. Not that he couldn't, but he had found a new thing
called "love," and, strange as it seemed, he had a warm feeling in his
stomach — or maybe it was his chest — when he thought he was loved,
and he was trying his darnedest to love others. He'd been reading his
Bible faithfully since then, too, and was starting to make some sense of
it. That didn't mean he was going to be stupid enough to let down his
guard in Apache country, though.

He had never married, because he didn't trust himself to not beat his
family. He had worked hard and his friend, Dick Clark, at the Redwood
bank where his train would end up, told him he had invested Chip's
money for him. Dick had told Chip that he no longer had to boss the
train anymore, but Chip didn't trust anyone else in Apache territory. At
forty years old he was considered a confirmed bachelor, but aside from
some squaw or one of those skinny town women, he didn't think himself
all that bad off. Besides, now that he thought he might not beat on his
family, who would have a big, ugly old man like him?

His squinting brown eyes took in the country ahead, and his experience had taught him to start right up close. Many a dead man had
looked across an opening only to have their death rise from the ground
at their feet. He scanned the ground slowly and thoroughly; one didn't
hurry in Apache country, where your next mistake could be your last.

8

He dressed like one of his mule skinners — loose, floppy wide brimmed hat, work-worn and much repaired leather shirt and breaches, and low heeled, high sided miner's boots. His old double action Navy six-shooter was tucked into his waistband, and a huge Bowie knife hung in a leather holster from his belt. He was much better with the knife than the six-shooter. Oh, he could hit what he aimed at, but he liked the close work of the knife; where he could use his hands, too.

His observations revealed nothing moving except one man leisurely dismounting in the watering pool his train would be stopping at. Lars Johnson was the new scout he had taken on in Winchester. He had begged him to take him along and bragged of his expertise as a scout. Chip could always use another good gunman, but Lars seemed to have another agenda and was proving it now. He was riding openly and unobservant in Apache country, something only a fool or a turncoat did.

He watched Lars and his horse muddy the water with dirt as he drank upstream. Chip's irritation pulled his mouth into a thin tight line. Lars had been talking around the camp and bucking his orders ever since he signed on, and Chip was just about fed up with him. He stayed low as he slipped back down onto his horse and rode back the way he had come. He'd deal with Lars later.

He had seen nothing on the flat lands nor on the valley rim on both sides, but Apaches could appear and disappear with amazing speed. They could run all day and raise little dust to tell someone they were even near. He kept Rudy on the grassy edge of the trail so that he also raised no dust. His eyes moved constantly over the scenery, looking for anything where it was not supposed to be. Searching for Indians was like looking for a needle in a haystack — the clues were small and hard to see even for an experienced bushman like Chip. A shadow on the wrong side of a bush, a boulder where no boulder should be, a moccasin toe sticking out from behind a mound of dirt or a footprint darker than the surrounding sand were sometimes the only clue you got before a bullet came buzzing your way.

Chip knew Arthur was on point, but he missed him until he heard the faint hiss of his breath through his teeth. They called him Sir Arthur because he was British, but he had fought His Majesty's tribal enemies in Africa and was the best bushman Chip had working for him. He

9

reined Rudy to a stop, and Arthur appeared from a depression he had been hiding in.

"I say, Chip old boy, you'll get yourself scalped unless you pay better heed to your surroundings." He had been in America so long his accent was being integrated into western slang.

"I'm not worried with you at my back, Sir Arthur. Been watching Lars, and I think I made a mistake with him," Chip confided.

"I could cut him open and see if he's a red man on the inside," Arthur suggested. He pulled his belt knife, which was different than any Chip had ever seen before. The blade was on the back curve, but it was as sharp as a barber's razor blade, and Arthur could handle it with blinding speed and agility.

Chip smiled one of his rare smiles and said, "Hate to ruin your fun, but I just might have to fire him."

Sir Arthur also smiled. "Who he worked for wouldn't hinder my intentions. Blighter needs a good routing if he's not committed to our cause." They were two of a kind and held a genuine friendship for each other; many a night they stayed up late debating over scripture.

"What happened to "love your enemies?" Chip chided.

"I love my enemies, old salt. I just don't turn my back on them, either," Arthur returned. Both men had been watching their surroundings for danger, and Chip knew that Arthur would be a hard man to take by surprise.

"I might not have to do anything," Chip kept on. "He's been friendly with them new wagons, and I been tellin' them folks we're going across the flats fast, but I'm going to the high side of Devil's Decision, and that new bunch will want to go straight. They sure are in a hurry to get to them gold fields. Strange about them — outfitted and look like farmers, but talk and act like gamblers. They been talking up about how there's been no danger so far and can't understand our cautious pace."

"They'll change their gab when their hair is hangin' from some buck's loincloth," Arthur commented dryly.

"Probably, but we got them new eight shot repeating Henry rifles to get to Fort Stewart, and White Foot would like real bad to have them. I'm not going to underestimate that sly fox. He's left us alone because he knows we'll give his boys a quick death, but we've got a real prize if he can get it." Chip was thinking out loud.

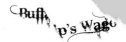

"Give us a chance to try out that new toy you ordered out east. What'd they call that thing? A Gatlin gun? What was wrong with old Betsy?" Arthur asked. Old Betsy was their six inch brass cannon they loaded with scrap metal and nails.

"We could always try both to see which is better. Want to make a small wager on them?" Chip glanced sideways at his friend.

Arthur's eyes lit up. Gambling was his soft spot, and he was always looking to bet, but he was wise enough to keep it friendly and small, often using buttons, bullets or pennies just to have the fun of the wager. "I'd like to see Gatlin workin' first, but that would be fun."

The first mules came into sight around the foot of the fading hills they had just come through. There were eight big blue Missouri mules pulling a huge prairie schooner behind them. Seven more followed, but they were pulled by horses. Twenty more low freight wagons followed, all pulled by mules. They were followed by ten two wheeled Saskatchewan carts, also pulled by mules. There were ten outriders in sight on either side of the train, and Chip knew there were ten more out of sight in the surrounding hills and valleys, along with ten men riding shotgun in the gun wagons and mixed in with the train wagons. It was a big train, but well-armed and well run. The spare mules and horses brought up the rear, again well-guarded with outriders.

Chip preferred the mules, especially when he found out that mules hate Indians and will actually attack them if they are not restrained. It was because of this attention to the small details that his trains were left alone by roving Indian bands. Most of his freight was household and farming goods and not worth the death he would deal out to the Indians.

This load was different. It had the usual household stuff, but also a commission from the Army for two wagonloads of rifles and ammunition for Fort Stewart and eight settler wagons with their women and children. This was quite a prize for any Indian band, and White Foot would want the status of taking this wealth and killing his equally famous enemy, Buffalo Chip Blackstone.

Of their own accord, Chip's eyes went to the first wagon. As usual, Sally Jones sat on the seat working the reins in her muscular hands. Very little of this large woman was not muscle. Strong as any man, she handled the best mules in the train with an expertise of a seasoned skinner.

Around and in her wagon were five kids and her demanding mouse of a h__nd. Quiet and patient, she took her husband's abuse, but dealt fair loving discipline to her children.

__e had drawn Chip's attention ever since the settler's wagons had join_d his train. He found her strangely fascinating, but he kept himself respectful because she was a married woman. Her oldest son, John, was impressed with Chip and went out of his way to be around him. The boy was smart and respectful, and Chip found his wanting to be with him rather pleasant. John was the only boy at nine, and the girls were eight, six, four and three years old. Sally's husband, Bob, would be in the wagon cursing the heat, bumps, flies and anything else he could think of.

Chip had hired John to help Big Joe, his cook, and found he was a hard worker and an eager student. Early on, John had divulged that Bob was their step-father and had only been married to Sally for two years. John and his sisters' last name was Thorn, but they were not allowed to speak it in front of Bob. John's distaste for his step dad had been obvious.

Just ahead of their wagon rode a tall man on a blue blooded, roan gelding. Dressed like an army officer, he was a striking figure and was the boss of the settler wagons who joined Chip's train. Derik Struthers was an impatient, domineering man, anxious to get west to make his fortune. He saw Chip and spurred his horse to more speed and raced at them.

"I'm goin' to look for more Indians, Chip. You know, little friendlier company. See you in camp tonight." Arthur spoke quietly, but his distaste for Struthers was obvious as he turned his horse and disappeared over the first rise.

Chip only nodded, watching the waste of horse energy approaching him. They had been pushing hard, and all the animals were wearing down. He beat Derik to the punch and said, "We'll be beddin' down at the start of some pretty dry goin' tonight by the last water for five days. Animals will have to last through some hot, arid going, so we'll give them a couple extra hours at the water."

Derik's face reddened slightly, but he held his tongue to a civil tone. "They're in good shape, but if *you* say so, we'll wet them down." He deliberately drew out the "you". He rankled at having to take Chip's orders, and thought he should have more authority in the train. "I thought this trip would be most over by now," he said it as a statement rather than a question.

"Redwood's two weeks yet, and then you folks have got another month and a half to your gold fields," Chip informed him for the first time.

"Maybe there's gold closer than California." Derik revealed he had been listening to Lars, confirming Chip's suspicions that Lars was trying to stir up division in the train. "Heard there is a big new strike in Pine Grove over Northwest of Redwood; could be worth looking into."

"S'up to you. I stop at Redwood, so you'll have to find someone else to help protect you after that."

Chip watched his words rankle and Struthers spat out. "We've seen nothing for a month; these rumours of hostiles seem to be exaggerated."

Chip shrugged and lifted his reins to head back to the train. "You're free to think as you please. I'm stoppin' in Redwood." He touched Rudy's sides, sending him towards the wagons.

The four girls were crowded on the wagon seat beside their mother when Chip rode up. They waved and jostled each other to see him better.

"We'll be resting some tonight, Mrs. Jones," he said to Sally. "There's water just over the next hill. We'll be there well before sundown, and we'll stay a little longer in the morning, 'cause there's no more water for five days. You want to start a circle just south of the pool, and you and the women can have the first chance to go upstream after we water the animals and fill the water barrels."

"Thank you, Mr. Blackstone, you are very considerate." Her smile was genuine and welcome. Her husband stuck his head out of the front of the wagon and complained.

"It's about time we rested. This traveling is rough enough to cause a man to cursing." He didn't wait for a response, but disappeared back into the wagon.

Chip had been taking the children with him to give Sally a rest from the commotion, and Jennifer, the youngest, stood up and held out her hands for him to lift over to ride with him. Chip looked a question at Sally and received an approving nod. He lifted Jennifer under her arms to a seating position behind him. These trips with these well-mannered and eager children made him regret not marrying. Touching his hat in respect to Sally, he rode away with little Jennifer happily hanging on to his waist.

13

They made the rounds of the outriders, telling them about the stop and designating positions for each wagon. The Gatlin and cannon were each in one of the Saskatchewan carts, so they could be easily turned with only two wheels. These he ordered placed away from the water one on each end of the camp. He had every man learn to shoot the cannon, and now they were learning to handle the Gatlin gun. He always put a trainee with one of the men who had handled it before.

His reputation was that of the most dangerous and best wagon trains to hire, and the Army was paying for the whole trip just to get their rifles through to the Fort. The freight money would be extra and give him a handsome profit. Because he did well, he hired the best fighting men and bush men in the country and paid top wages. Every man he had working for him was a crack shot and a tough man in any fight. All but the most desperate or largest Indian tribes left them alone. Those that did choose to attack them usually left empty handed and carrying many dead braves.

Derik Struthers and his wagons were Easterners and inexperienced with the western Indians. Without Chip's men, the Indians would have probably attacked them by now. Derik did not realize this and would probably end up getting in trouble somewhere in the west unless he learned quickly, which was unlikely with his attitude.

They met Lars just before the camp site. Chip could tell he had been sleeping by the puffiness about his face and the wrinkles in his clothes. This bothered Chip more than he wanted to admit, because Lars did not impress him as a stupid man. This meant he was involved with White Foot and would lead them into an ambush if he was given the chance.

He had still not fired Lars Johnson when the darkness of night settled over the peaceful scene around the water pool. The wagons were circled, the mules watered, the people fed and the night guard was sent out when Chip stepped down from Rudy at Big Joe's cook wagon after dropping Jennifer off at Sally's cook fire. Big Joe was a retired army sergeant Chip had hired as his cook seven years ago. Chip found he was as good a cook as any man, but he could also hold his own in any fight they got into. He had taken a liking to John, working with the pots on the fire, and was teaching him about Indian fighting as well as cooking.

Big Joe had a rifle tucked into a cubby hole so he could pull it out and start shooting from the back of his wagon, but his secret was a greener cut down to pistol size in a home-made holster under his apron. A greener is a twelve gauge, double barrelled shotgun cut down to be easily handled in tight places. Two loads of double O buckshot cut a mean path through any advancing Indian band and had the unsettling effect of size on their enemies.

"You still callin' them boot soles steaks, Joe? I thought you told me you bought a cow at that last stop?" Chip chided his big friend and noticed a newly made knife sheath with a small bone-handled knife hanging from John's belt.

"Well, Chip, I never seen the like of it. That cow done walked all that muscle off in the last couple days and left us with nothing but bone and tallow. Hardly enough left for a good soup, but if you strain it through your moustache you might find a sliver o' meat there somewhere," Big Joe said with a straight face and convincing demeanour. He reached his fork into his frying pan and plopped a huge steak on top of three cups of beans on a plate and passed it to Chip. "Might find an old, mouldy biscuit or two I cooked up way back half an hour ago on the wagon tongue."

"Dang, Joe, if you weren't the only man I got that can stand to be near a fire all day, I'd send you out to be Apache bait." Chip also kept his face straight, but his eyes twinkled with mirth.

A look of hurt appeared on Joe's face. "You wouldn't do that to them poor Indians, would you? You know I'd give them the worst case o' lead poisonin'."

Almost laughing, Chip relented. "Ok, ok, I have to agree with you. You can just stay here and poison us, I guess."

Without missing a breath, Joe smiled and said, "Thanks, Chip. I been trying real hard to do that. Your boys are tougher than them Missouri mules you keep buyin'." He turned back to his cooking while more of the hungry crew came to his fire. John had paused to listen to the banter, but jumped to work when there was more to do.

Chip was late bedding down after a busy evening getting the camp secure and organized.

He and Sir Author had sat with the teamsters and listened to the range talk. The boys described the country they were traveling through and the draws and outstanding landmarks. The visual description helped each one form a lay of land in their minds and mapped the countryside for future use.

As they listened, Chip and Author watched Lars at the Easterner's camp fire. They were trying to be discreet, but Chip could see the jug they passed among the group. There was more than one jug, and the camp was not too sober when they bedded down for the night. They would be hung over and cranky in the morning. That was none of Chip's concern, but Lars was his employee and that was his concern.

He also didn't want to admit it, but he was also concerned for Sally and her kids. John let it slip that Bob took to beating them if he thought he had a cause, and a drunk could always find a reason to abuse some-one else. Sally was the only woman of the train who didn't look like a hooker. There were five other women with men in the train, but no other kids, and those women had eyes that challenged a man to stare at her every time they looked at him. Their clothes hung too loose and open, and Chip had warned his men about going too near the wagons for fear they would get ideas and end up in trouble.

He had changed Rudy for a tough little mustang he called Chance. He was as brown as dirt with two sandy coloured socks, one front and one hind leg. He loose-saddled Chance and tied him to the wheel on the Gatlin gun cart. He would sleep under it with three of his men tonight. Two of the night guards sat atop the cart. He kept ten men on guard all night, rotating them every four hours. That way the guards were fresh and alert most of the time, and everyone still got a good sleep. The mules he didn't worry about. Any Indian stupid enough to go near them would either be trampled or they'd cause such a commotion they could easily be shot before they could get away.

Chapter 2

Sir Author was up and gone, even though Chip rose well before daylight. He would be making a scouting round just outside their perimeter and would report to Chip before the end of breakfast.

The two of them had watched Lars palavering with Derik Struthers most of the evening and had made some plans of their own. Chip was going to send Lars ahead just before the split at 'Devil's Decision' point and take the train up the mountain the long way. They were hoping they could be too far to turn back when Lars caught up with them.

John had brought his oldest sister with him to the chuck wagon this morning, and he walked out to meet Chip as he strode up.

"Betsy would like to help out at the chuck wagon if you could use another hand, Mr. Blackstone. She's strong and could do some of my chores, and I could help out at the Ramada if you like." His look was almost pleading for a yes answer. "I talked to Joe and he thought it would be a good idea."

Puzzled, Chip looked at Big Joe. His gaze was almost physical with intensity when he looked at Chip, and he was closing and opening his large hands angrily.

"Joe runs the kitchen, John. If he says he could use the help, Betsy can travel along with you two and help out. It'll maybe give your mom a break from having to drive team and watch kids at the same time. She's probably a good cook and worth ten dollars a month and found, and you should get fifteen if you're going to learn to handle those jug headed mules we been buying to haul our wagons." He was hoping to lighten the atmosphere, but everyone nodded seriously and, after a mumbled "thank you," they turned to their work.

Joe stepped over beside him and opened his mouth to speak, but Chip had seen the bruise on Betsy's cheek before she hastily turned away. His eyes turned hard as he listened to Joe tell him what he was going to do to *Mr. Bob Jones.*

Chip let him talk off his anger and controlled his own then said, "I know, Joe, and we'll deal with him, but it has to be later. We're in White Foot's country now and need to keep peace in our camp until we're out, but we'll watch the other girls and head off any more of his cowardly abuse." He was clipping his words through clenched teeth as he finished.

Joe gave him a knowing look before he said, "I want to get him first for about five minutes when we reach Redwood, that's all I ask." He turned back to work, gently helping Betsy gather up the morning utensils and showing her the cleaning routine.

Sir Author rode in and reported to Chip before they ate breakfast together. Chip filled Author in about the situation with Betsy and her step-dad, and asked him to help John with the mules. He also told him to run them close to the Jones wagon and keep an eye on the other kids.

Sir Author's eyes shone wickedly, and he fingered his knife as he reassured Chip that the wagon would encounter no problems today.

A long, thin cowboy with a distinct Texas drawl strode up from morning watch and hankered down beside them. "Saw some smoke ova' No'th o' here an' Tiny's sayin' that White Foot's on the prowl."

"Thanks, Tex," Chip said. "We'll put Lars on point, and you and Tiny travel together out about half mile and cover the North flank. John?" He raised his voice to get the youth's attention. "JOHN! You travel with Sir Author and keep the ramada close in to our South flank. Big Joe, we may be in for a little red company, so you travel in close just ahead of the ramada. Tex? You want to put Toby and Luke on the Gatlin and have it bring up the rear?"

He thought for a few minutes while his mind went over the trail ahead, then he continued. "It's open country ahead, so we'll double the wagons up two apiece and put Old Betsy on the North point with Slader and Pop. Everyone rides with their rifles loose. Ten miles out we hit Devil's Decision; we'll cut to the mountains and push on after dark to the breakers. Clear night should be no problem seein' to circle on the mesa. We'll rest in 'til noon and push through tomorrow night and the next day to Clearwater Pool. White Foot will be expecting us to move at daybreak and camp at sundown."

He paused again and everyone waited. They trusted his leadership and ability to think of his opponent's moves. "Maybe the Army will have a troop out this way we can meet up with. They're probably expectin' these Henrys," he finished.

Breakfast over, they filtered away to their work, and the train prepared to move.

They moved out just short of midday. Lars had come out about ten, obviously hung-over and cranky. He didn't complain when Chip sent him out on point. He obviously wanted to hide somewhere out on the prairie and sleep his headache off. Chip took the short point position himself to cover for Lars lack of usefulness, and from where he could keep an eye on the Jones wagon travelling just behind him. He saw nothing out of the ordinary, but was not lulled into complacency. He moved constantly from point to side and back again, watching the country, sky and horizon.

They were making good time; as they reached Devil's Decision, Chip dropped back and told Sally to bear to the left and follow him unto the open desert. Anna, the six year old, asked to go with him, and he swung her onto the horse behind him.

He pulled away and crossed Lars' tracks as he turned and angled hard left into the open country. The sand looked soft and dry, but was baked hard as rock here and held the wagons up so they could make good time.

They had only gone about a mile when the dust from a hurrying Lars could be seen behind them. Derik Struthers was riding beside his wagons and looking back while he slowed his wagons down. As Lars came pounding up, Derik and his wagons stopped and they met in conversation.

Chip rode back to them, knowing what he was going to hear. They were in heated emotional conversation when Chip rode up.

"The other way is faster, so you shouldn't be going here," Lars was saying. "Obviously, Chip wants to slow you down so he can get to the gold fields first."

"That's preposterous," Derik shouted. "If that other way is faster, we'll just turn around and take it."

"You're already on this trail. Might as well not lose the time and stay on it. We're all going to get to Redwood at the same time that way and this way is safer." He had surprised them and they turned suddenly to face him.

Derik's face reddened. "See here, Mr. Blackstone, you have needlessly taken us out of our way, and we are going to go back to the faster route. We're not women and children and can travel faster if we weren't travelling with your freight wagons."

Lars had really poisoned their minds, Chip saw. "Well, you have the Jones with you, and they are women and children. White Foot would love to capture some white women and children for slaves in his camp."

Derik scoffed. "Hah! Lars tells me there are no Indians within thirty miles of here, and we haven't seen anything of this red menace you talk about. We're going back." He raised his hand and waved the wagons to turn around.

"Have it your way," Chip conceded. "Why don't you let the Jones come along with us? They're just women and children, and they would slow you down."

Derik hesitated, and finally said, "I don't think you could talk Bob into traveling slow with you. He wants to be on the start of any gold field we come across with the rest of us."

"But you have to think of the kids. They are young and not used to this country. You wouldn't make a very good impression coming into the towns ahead with sick or dying children on your hands." Chip spoke softly, convincingly; trying to play to the man's greed and ego. He saw Derik's brain mulling over what he had said.

Chip knew he had lost the Easterner's wagons, but he was playing for the Jones kids and Sally. He watched Derik think about his situation as his wagons were already turning back.

Sally sat her seat, letting her mules advance away from the other wagons and along the trail Chip had picked. The freight wagons pulled aside to let the prairie schooner's pass back the way they had come.

Lars was openly giving Chip a bold stare, and a smirk played across his lips. "I'll guide you from here out, Mr. Struthers." He spoke to Derik, but he was watching Chip.

"Thank you, Mr. Johnson," Derik said. "And *thank you, Mr. Black-stone*. We'll be moving on now. Bob can go where he pleases; it just means more for us. Good day, Sir." He turned his horse and galloped after his departing wagons with Lars beside him.

Chip breathed a sigh of relief, but was soon turned around as the Jones wagon stopped and a commotion could be heard coming from the front.

Bob Jones' head popped up over the top of the canvas, and his mouth was going in a tirade of swearing and curses. Chip felt Anna's small arms tighten spasmodically on his waist. His mouth tightened into an angry thin line. The Eastern wagons had stopped to watch the fracas, and Bob's wagon was making a slow turn to come back.

Chip could make out what Bob was saying as he came around the wagon. "Don't you do that again, you stupid woman. You never learned to read or write and can't think your way out o' the rain."

"Bob!" Chip interrupted him as he was raising his hand menacingly. "You're our lead wagon and Sally was doing a good job. What's your problem?"

"You!" Bob blustered. "You're trying to separate us from the rest of the wagons so you can get to them gold fields we told you about ahead of us. Well it won't work." He raised his voice. "WAIT! WAIT FOR US, DERICK!"

"Wait," Chip said while his mind raced. "What about the kids? They can't travel fast or they'll get sick." Sally was watching him with a pleading look in her eye.

"Kids? Where are those brats? Here, Anna, get up here on the wagon. Where is Betsy?" Bob threw orders as he moved around on the wagon seat looking for the children.

"She's working with Joe on the cook wagon. I hired her and John," Chip informed him.

A strange, greedy look appeared in Bob's eyes. "You hired her? You got work for them kids?"

Without thinking, Chip hastily said, "Yeh, I got work they can do and more. Always looking for workers, and they can earn top dollar if they want to." It was a desperate ploy, but he wanted the kids with the freight wagons where they would be safe.

"And you're going to Redwood where we can pick them up later?" Bob was calming down with the thoughts of monetary gain.

"Yep, they can come through with me, and you can pick them up later." Chip had never encountered greed and selfishness like this before, but he knew these kids needed help right now.

"Jennifer! Hope! Get down over that wheel," Bob said as he disappeared into the wagon. Sally stopped as the two girls scrambled down. She was looking at Chip with the saddest but most relieved look Chip had ever seen. This was the strangest outfit Chip had encountered, and he began to wonder what the real story was behind their travelling west.

Sir Arthur rode up as the children's possessions were dropped from the back of the wagon. Their clothes were stuffed into burlap bags and lay in a pile on the prairie when Bob shouted for Sally to start away.

Sir Arthur growled and reached for his six-gun, but Chip hissed and stopped him. "Think, Arthur. Wait. At least the kids will be safe." He could tell it took a huge effort for Sir Arthur to settle back in his saddle and reined ahead to pick up the burlap bags.

The two girls stood wondering on the ground as their parents drove away with the wagon. Arthur stepped down beside them and threw their bags over his saddle. Then he picked up Jennifer and put her on the bags. He swiftly picked up Hope and, leading his horse, started for the cook wagon. Big Joe was hurrying to meet them; Betsy sitting beside him, craning her head to see what was happening. Anna had wanted down and was running to catch up to her sisters.

The Jones' moved into place behind the other wagons moving to return to the main route.

Chip's freighters moved into form and proceeded on by him across the desert. The first wagon drew up beside him and paused for a minute. It was driven by a gristly oldster dressed in buckskins and looking more like an Indian than a white man.

Chip looked up at the mountain man curiously and watched him spit a huge stream of tobacco juice over the wheel of the wagon before he drawled, "Done the right thing, Chip." He motioned his chin after the departing wagons. "They won't last long. The West is a real nasty place for mean people. Patience, Chip; they won't last long." He chucked his reins, and the mules leaned into their harness as the wagon moved on.

Chip watched him go, and said under his breath, "Thanks, Buck. I needed that."

The train made good time and formed a protective circle just after midnight on a flat mesa with a good clear field of fire that could be easily protected. The night was clear, and the Moon was full and bright.

Everything had been quiet through the trip, but Tex had seen more smoke signals just before sundown. Two smokes were talking to each other, one directly north and the other ahead of them to the west.

Everyone could feel the tension and knew this would not be an ordinary, quiet trip. The children took up chores Big Joe found for them to do, and the rest of the men doted on them as if they were their own children. Aside from missing their parents, the kids never lacked for attention or safety.

Chapter 3

They rested the next morning until noon then started out following an old trail Chip had discovered three years earlier. He had never used this trail with a train, but had travelled it a couple of times alone when he was scouting and going east to order more mules. Two days longer, it was smoother and easier with a good hard bottom to travel on. There was also better protective cover and areas to fort up in and water. The next water hole at a spring called Clearwater Springs came right out of the rocks, and was the best water Chip had tasted for miles around. It was in a basin and high up for water, but easily protected because everything dropped off around the basin but a couple of trails in and they could be covered by a few good men with rifles.

The day was quiet and uneventful, lulling them into a false sense of security, but Chip knew his men would not let down their guard and be taken by surprise. The children took to their duties willingly and proved to be normal, happy children when their abusive step-father was not around.

They saw nothing of the Indians, but occasionally saw smoke signals off to the north and either ahead or behind them. They moved consistently west through the heat of the arid desert. There was going to be a little cloud cover tonight, but the desert sand here was a bright yellow and would give them enough light to travel in comparative safety. Dusk found them pushing forward with little sign of stopping.

They had stopped for a short meal and rest at supper time, but would eat sandwiches and beef jerky tonight without stopping.

Sir Arthur rode point well out in front and would report back occasionally. He came across signs where the Indians had waited for them but had left before they arrived. The late start had thrown the Indian's battle plan off, and they were not quite sure what these white freighters were doing.

He also had some disturbing news of large bands of Indians moving north towards the other trail. No one had to tell the freight wagon train that the eastern wagons were the center of the Indian's attention. It was just a matter of time and place when the Indians would decide to attack the smaller, unprepared prairie schooners.

The night travel proved to be a good idea, and they arrived at Clearwater Springs early in the afternoon. Everyone was tired from a long hard night, but no one complained or shirked his duties. Everyone's life depended on everyone else being alert, and no one wanted to let their friends down.

Chip had Hope with him when they arrived at the camp site. She had nervously talked continuously, and he suspected she missed her mother. The night and day had passed quietly, and everyone settled in to rest, but before dark there came an angry, dark smoke from the north and the sound of rifles cracking could be heard on the wind. They were about ten miles from the other trail and could not get there in time to help the wagon train. It would be dark, and anyone trying to go would have a difficult time finding anything in the night.

Chip and his men listened to the faint noises until they petered out just after dark. Whatever had happened was over, and they knew it was not good for the wagon train.

"Darn shame the world has to keep lettin' people walk around being dumb," someone commented.

Chip moved over beside Arthur and, speaking in a subdued voice, said, "We'll have to go see what we can do for anyone that might have gotten away."

"Yep," Sir Arthur said, not looking at him but keeping watch on Jennifer, Hope and Anna playing with some dolls the men had made for them.

"I want you to go with me, and I'll get Tex to put together a group of fifteen men to follow a short ways behind us. They will fort up if we run into trouble and be a place we can run to. The rest can hold this high ground until we get back. We'll leave after midnight and should get there just before daylight. You and I will each take an extra horse for anyone that's left alive or to switch off if we have to run," Chip laid out his plan.

"Sounds about right to me, old chap. Most of them don't deserve that, but there are some I would like to see alive." He was referring to Sally and some of the other women while he continued to watch the girls play.

"I'll talk to Tex." Chip got up and moved to explain his plan again to the other men.

Tex came up with the idea to break out some of the Henry rifles and load two apiece for each man, so everyone had three loaded long guns.

All of Chip's men were given a Winchester Yellow boy six shot when he hired them. The Henry rifles were eight inches longer and could carry another quarter of a mile farther than the Winchesters. They would be carrying a lot of firepower if they ran into trouble, which they were expecting to.

Chip also ordered each man to break out his extra hand guns and carry at least two loaded pistols each. He saw Sir Arthur heading for his bedroll when he was done talking to Tex, and he did the same. By midnight they rolled out of bed rested and fresh, ready for the trip to the burning wagons.

Chip chose Rudy for his own mount and picked a big black mule named Snake for his second mount. Snake was the biggest, meanest mule in Chip's ramada, and he hated Indians. His black coat hid him in the dark, and he was deathly silent travelling through the night. He was too tough to kill and could carry 400 lbs. all night and still be the first one up in the morning. He'd tried to bite most of the freighters, but when he tried to bite Chip, he had punched him and knocked him down. Now Chip was the only one Snake would let work with him without any trouble.

His men were gathering beside the circle of wagons when Chip came up, ready to go. Everyone knew this would be a dangerous trip, and everyone there would gladly volunteer to go out and try what they were about to do. The small figure standing by Sir Arthur drew Chip's attention. He drew up beside John and looked angrily over his head at Arthur.

Arthur smiled and nodded. "Funny about family, isn't it Chip? One would gladly die to help.....oh, say...their mother, for example, and nothing anyone could say would stop them. I just figured that I'd stick close to young John here and lend him a hand if he happened to not kill all the Indians we meet tonight."

Chip opened his mouth then closed it again. He did not have the advantage of a good family relationship to know, but what Arthur said made sense to him because he would do the same for any of his men, and they knew it.

John stood nervously wringing the brim of his hat he was holding, waiting for Chip's response. Chip remembered the hardships he faced alone when he left his home, and knew that John would have to face trouble and overcome it if he was going to amount to anything. He sighed and thinking out loud said, "We could use someone with us to

25

run messages back to Tex and to lead anyone surviving back to the men. He'd have to stay close and be ready to run in a blink."

Turning to John he said, "Take Chance; he's a good, tough little mustang and will get you home if you can stay in the saddle. Can you tell the mules apart?" At John's nod he continued. "Put a lead rope on Satan; he's the blue with half an ear, and Bella, the mouse coloured mule. Satan won't give you any trouble as long as Bella is there to chew his other ear off. Put a slip knot in the lead rope, and if any Indians get too close to you, pull the leads off them. They'll kick enough Indian behinds long enough for you to run for it."

John was all smiles. "Yes, Sir, Mr. Blackstone," and he hurried away to follow Chip's orders.

Sir Arthur watched him go as he said, "You know, Chip? I've known you a long time, and it still amazes me how quick you catch on and how efficient your brain works. I never would have put Satan and Bella together with him, but you know, that's the best protection that boy could have. The only thing Satan hates worse than Indians is Bella, and he's more afraid of her than any other animal in God's little green earth. Them poor Indians will be so busy dodging teeth and hoofs, they won't remember to chase one little boy."

Chip couldn't stop himself and chuckled in spite of the seriousness of their mission. "You must figure he's got sand, Arthur, or you wouldn't have stuck by him. I hope his mom is still alive, for his sake."

The three left the protective circle of the wagons a half hour later with a full Moon to help them make time. The fifteen man troop would leave in twenty minutes, traveling slower, and would keep moving until one of the three met them.

They traveled silently over the hard desert floor. The Indians would not be expecting them to come at night and would be off guard. They threaded their way through the occasional rocky outcrop and down. Chip figured the wagon train was ambushed just short of Salt creek. It was a small river running through the valley, but was too acidic to drink.

They were still two miles short when Arthur hissed, "Stop."

They pulled up, eyes straining to see what had spooked him. "Motion over to the left, by that clump of boulders."

They waited and watched.

"Too much movement for Indians," Chip said. "Drop back and ride towards them, Arthur. John and I will move ahead over there, as if we're riding by. If they hear us and start shooting, we'll be just out of range. That way we can maybe get a closer look at them before they know we're here."

Arthur moved without a sound and John followed Chip at a slow walk. They had not gone far when Chip was sure the strangers were white men. These men stuck their heads up over the boulders to look around for trouble, while an Indian would look around the boulder, keeping his head low and off the skyline.

They moved up opposite the men without being spotted. Once they were close by, Chip started to circle back. He knew that Arthur would go right in among them if they were not good bushmen. He would scout them out and be back out without them knowing he was anywhere near them.

They waited a few minutes when a whippoorwill call shrilled from in front of them.

Chip motioned for John to follow, and he moved ahead cautiously. The whippoorwill sounded again just in front of them, and Arthur materialized from the dark. He was horseless and moved to Chip's side.

Chip leaned down and listened as Arthur told him of eight soldiers and three horses bedded down in the circle of the boulders. They were travelling light with no supplies, and some had dirty bandages on them.

"Go in and warn them not to shoot us, and we'll see what their story is," Chip told Arthur, and the man disappeared into the night.

Chip and John moved in more slowly and were met by a group of badly beat and harried soldiers. The leader was a well-seasoned army sergeant named Dutch Mercer. They were all that was left of a troop from Fort Stewart sent out to meet Chip's train.

Sergeant Mercer told them about being ambushed by Indians and how only ten had escaped — these eight and two wounded. They were cut off from the Fort and had been hiding in the desert for four days. The wounded had died, and they were just about done in from hunger and heat.

"We're some glad to see you, Mr. Blackstone," the Sergeant finished.

Sir Arthur had been outside scouting and keeping guard. He moved in beside the men just as the sergeant finished. "Tex is just back of the ridge coming this way, Chip," he said.

Chip thought for a minute then said, "John, you take these men back to Tex; use the extra animals to carry them. Tell Tex to send three men with them back to the train and look after them. Tell him to get the men on fresh mounts and back here. They're to feed and care for these men and arm them. They can fill in at the train as they are able to. Arthur and I will wait for you there." He pointed to a high knoll ahead and to their right. "Come straight to it unless you hear shooting, then skedaddle back to Tex and stay with him."

John nodded and moved away to obey, moving as Arthur had shown him and with as much stealth as he could.

Chip sent Arthur an approving nod, and they helped the men mount and move out.

After the troop left, Chip turned to Arthur. "We're close to Salt Creek, so you go round this side of that knoll and I'll take that side. We'll see what's on the other side and be able to see the Creek from the top. Any problems go right to the top, and I'll do the same."

Like he taught John, Arthur didn't say a word as he turned and disappeared into the night.

There proved to be no-one around the knoll, and John found Chip and Arthur studying the dark riverbank at the top of the knoll. They could make out a few dark objects on the desert floor that looked like burnt wagons, but nothing moved.

It was the total darkness that came just before dawn when they moved in among the burnt shells of the wagons. The Easterners had tried to run for the river and been picked off one by one. The wagons were spread over half a mile, and they hankered down by the first wagon to wait for light.

Chip kept John with him as Arthur roamed through the death scene. He didn't want him to see what the Indians had done to their bodies while and after they died.

"Indians want white women and children, John. They'll kill the men and what you are going to see will not be pretty, but women and children can be assimilated into the tribe. If we don't find their bodies, the women are probably alive." Chip hated to talk about John's mother like this, but it was reality and he would have to face the truth when daylight came. He found himself hoping Sally's body would not be here for personal reasons he would not own up to.

28

The sun poured daylight over the horizon, and the scene gradually revealed itself to them. The wagons were burnt and the horses killed or taken. Personal belongings were scattered over the area; papers were blowing away, furniture was smashed, food stuffs were broken into and trampled in the dirt. The human remains were badly mutilated and scalped. All Chip saw were men, and there was not much left. The buzzards had been at the remains yesterday and the coyotes last night. It was a grisly scene.

"Hurry, John, this way." Chip started following Arthur, who was already two wagons away.

They found what was left of the Jones wagon. It was the first one attacked, and the mules were killed before they could hurt the Indians. All the men were dead, and Bob's body was beside his wagon. He had died hard with an arrow low in his back; he had lasted long enough to be tortured and scalped.

Casually tossed aside beside his body was a small storage box with a padlock on it. John kicked it away in anger. When he saw Chip watching him, he said, "It was his." He waved his thumb at Bob's body. "He wouldn't let anyone else touch it, and he carried the key for it around his neck." He spat into the dust.

"Okay," Chip said softly. "Only one woman died here, and there were six, so they must be alive somewhere. Arthur will tell us where they've gone when he gets back."

Arthur appeared a few moments later and told them the Indians had taken hostages and booty and traveled straight west. "I think their drunk on their success and may try to ambush us later on."

Chip looked a question at his friend with a raised eyebrow.

"No," Arthur growled. "No Lars. He sold them out."

Human deceit was a strange idea to John, who could only stare at Arthur while he digested his comments.

"We haven't time to bury them," Chip told them. "Those buzzards overhead should be landing if there was nobody here. Long as they stay up there, they're telling everyone around someone is here. We don't need company from our local Apache neighbours. You two start for Tex on the knoll. I'll catch up to you."

As the two mounted and started away, Chip hurried to Bob's body. He pulled back his shirt and found the key John said was there. He cut it from the leather strap and found the box.

29

Glancing over his shoulder, he saw the other two deep in conversation and moving swiftly away. He unlocked the box and glanced at the papers inside. One news clipping caught his eye. It was a wanted news article from a New England paper about a murdered wealthy landowner named Ben Thorne and a search for the suspected murderer; his wife and their five children.

As he stuffed the contents of the box in his saddle bags, a folded piece of official looking paper fell to the ground. He picked it up and opened it. It was a letter to a Mr. Bob Jones from the manager of some bank, instructing him to disappear with one Sally Thorne and her children. He was paid 2000 dollars and given drugs and a fake marriage licence. It informed said Mr. Jones that the woman and her children had to disappear, but they or their bodies could not be found anywhere near the Eastern seaboard.

Chip was stunned. The answers to Sally's situation had fallen into his hands, and she might not even live long enough to know it. He settled into his saddle, deep in thought; there would be time enough to tell the others after they were safe.

Chapter 4

Chip conferred with Arthur and Tex on the knoll.

"If we hope to save the women, we have to act now and follow White Foot to his camp," Chip informed them. "Tex, you go back to the train and move it to the next camp. Arthur and I will follow the Indians and meet you tonight. We'll take Buck and Tiny with us. The Indians are ahead of us, so keep a sharp lookout. John. You did a good job last night, but you'll have to go with Tex for now."

After the men moved to go, Chip spent another few minutes giving Tex extra instructions, and then they all moved out. The troop headed back to the train to break camp, and Chip with his three men and the extra mules moved to follow the Indian band west.

They crossed the battlefield where the Apaches had ambushed the Fort Stewart troops. It had been a massacre, and Chip wondered at the ability of the survivors to escape.

Two victories, Chip thought. *They will be drunk with pride and celebrate for a day or two. Then they'll hit us sure. They'll think their medicine is strong enough to take on our train.*

Sir Arthur was tracking, but the trail was fresh enough and bold enough for a child to follow. They followed it all that day at a gallop, and by sundown knew they were close behind the Indians. The trail had made a gradual curve, which put the Indians directly in the path of the freight wagon train. Chip's orders to Tex would see the train stop just short of the narrow pass through the next mountain range. Chip had told Tex not to attempt the pass that night and wait for his orders before moving in the morning. He suspected the Indians would camp at the back of the pass and be ready for Chip's wagons either that night or the next day.

Chip had also scouted this pass and had found a few other ways of getting through it for a few men on horses and now he turned his small group towards one of those trails that would be out of the way and probably not guarded.

The trail was narrow and they made their way slowly up the side of the mountain and along the top to another narrow trail on the other side. Dusk was settling over the desert when they stealthily moved into a position to leave their mounts.

31

Leaving Tiny with the animals, Chip, Arthur and Buck moved to the lip of the valley and found the Indians at the base of the valleyside, and spread so no one could come through the pass undetected.

There was enough light to detail the village and get an idea where the hostage women were being held. There was a heavy presence of many guards on the trail through the pass, but this back end and the village itself were fairly unguarded. White Foot was overconfident and expecting an easy victory and had celebrated and feasted for these two days.

The Army and wagon train horses were kept separate close to the edge of the valley wall so they would not escape and run away. The Indian horses were kept between them and the open desert, and they were effectively penned next to the camp.

Seeing this, Chip hatched an idea. They had brought their mules as added protection and as mounts for the women, but if they could get horses, they could use the mules as a diversion.

Chip explained his plan to Arthur and Buck while they watched darkness close around the camp. A tall, dignified figure detached itself from the Indian village and walked up the rise to an outcrop of rocks. Chip recognized White Foot as he watched him settle on a boulder and smoke his pipe contentedly. He marked that boulder in his mind for later reference.

The three men slipped back down to their animals and lay down in a clump of bushes to nap for part of the night.

Chip awoke at two o'clock by the Moon's location and sat up. Instantly the four were up and had a light meal of beef jerky and water before rising to the rim looking over the Indian village. Tiny would bring their animals along the wall and behind the Indian horses into the herd of captured animals. Buck was to round up enough horses for everyone to ride and loosen the rest. Then he and Tiny would wait for Chip's signal to advance towards the camp where they figured the captured women were.

Chip and Arthur would sneak into the camp and free the women as quietly as possible. If the camp was aroused, Tiny and Buck were to stampede the animals into the camp, and Chip and Arthur would catch a mount and run for it. If not, they were to advance slowly to the very edge of the tents and wait for the women that Chip and Arthur would bring to them.

The three men started down the side wall toward the village. There was enough Moonlight for them to see, but they had to advance slowly and carefully to not attract the attention of anyone awake in the village, even though most of the guard Indians' attention was on the pass expecting the freight wagons to try going through tonight.

The going was slow, and they had to pause many times as the occasional Indian woke or tossed in their sleep. Buck separated at the bottom of the wall to move down and meet Tiny with the animals, while Chip and Arthur continued to move towards the captive's tent.

They were sure the hostages were there, because there was little activity around it except for the bathroom duties of the occasional captive woman. They only had two Indian women guarding the hostages, because they didn't think they could escape with the village there.

Chip dropped to all fours and scurried through the sand to the first tent. He could hear the heavy breathing from inside as he inched by the outside wall. Arthur waited until he was under cover in the shadow of the tent then slipped across the open space.

The two crouched in the shadow waiting for a cloud to cover the Moon. The hostage tent was the next one across a short open space. The dark shadow of a cloud made a dark line in the sand as it advanced towards them. They rushed together into the darkness and across the space to the side of the tent. They could hear the occupants' heavy breathing and moved to the doorway under cover of the darkness.

"You watch here," Chip whispered to Arthur. "Open the tent flap when I tell you to then guard the door. I'll handle the two Indian women and get the captives." Chip was going to have to work fast and rough, and he could work best alone in tight quarters.

Arthur squeezed his should to confirm he had heard and moved to one side of the door. He reached across and grasped the door flap and pulled it aside.

Chip rushed into the tent and flopped on the two figures rising from under his feet at the opening. He wasted no time, and swung his rock hard fists one each way. The first connected with a thump on the forehead of the Indian, knocking her down, stunned. The second struck the woman fairly in the face and Chip felt a sickening in his stomach as he heard bone break as the woman collapsed soundlessly at his feet.

33

The first was struggling to rise, and he pushed her face into the dust to keep her from screaming as he struck her again behind her ear with his fist. She went limp and stopped struggling. He was not taking any chances; he lifted her head enough to cause her pain if she was still conscious, but she remained motionless, out cold.

The scuffle was done silently, but two of the remaining white women gasped and would have screamed except for the light of a small fire in the center of the room, Chip tossed the Indian women's blanket over their heads and shushed them. He saw the others open their eyes, and he held his finger up to his lips, hoping they saw and understood before making a noise.

His heart was pounding as he waited to see if they would understand or give them away. One by one they realized he was a white man. Sally was the first and reached out to shush the others. He motioned for them to gather around him while he checked to make sure they were not tied. They gathered around him closely and listened as he told them about Arthur outside the tent and Buck and Tiny bringing horses along the wall.

"We must be absolutely quiet as we go outside and over to the wall," he whispered. "You first, Sally, and take one other with you. Follow close to Arthur and do exactly as he tells you." She nodded her understanding and reached for another girl's hand.

Chip pulled the flap back a crack and whispered to Arthur. "You take two with you, and I'll follow with the other three. We'll wait until you get to the wall, then we'll make our way to you. Don't wait there for us. Move down the wall towards Buck and Tiny."

Arthur hissed a low "Okay" as he moved away from the entrance. Sally and the next girl slipped out and followed him. Chip watched them move stealthily to the next tent and past it to the valley wall, where they disappeared into the dark shadows.

Turning to the remaining three he whispered, "Take each other by the hand and follow me. Don't fall or make a noise, just move as swiftly as you can." He took the first girl's hand and led them out of the tent door and across the open area to the wall. The Moon came out from behind the cloud just as they reached the shadow, and they scurried into the dark safety.

Chip wasted no time but moved along the wall following Arthur. He almost stepped on the woman Sally was holding hands with. The three werc stopped at a slight bend in the wall, and Arthur was motioning for him to move closer.

"There's something on that boulder." He pointed to a boulder part-way up the hill. It was the boulder White Foot had sat on last night.

"Wait here, and when you see me sit down up there move the women on to the horses. I'll join you as you make your way back along the wall," Chip whispered to him. He turned and found a way to climb up the side of the valley, hidden from anyone watching from the boulder.

It was a slow and strenuous climb, but he succeeded in getting behind the boulder with no sound and could see the man sitting, facing the camp. He recognized White Foot's silhouette and quietly moved up behind him. There was space enough for him to move to a seat just out of reach of the Indian, who had his eyes closed in meditation.

As he sat down he softly said, "You are careless, Stinking Socks." He was ready in case the Indian tried to warn the camp, but he had to try to buy Arthur and the women some time.

The Indian started and sucked in his breath. His eyes flew open, and he stared at Chip calmly sitting beside him. He glanced to both sides then stared straight into Chip's eyes. "You sneak in the dark and kill me like a coward?"

Chip shock his head. "No. Why would I kill an enemy that sleeps the sleep of the foolish while I walk up to him and sit down?" He was watching the base of the wall out of the corner of his eye, but, with Arthur he was not expecting to see anything. A flicker of movement did tell him they were on their way, however.

"Foolish! It is you who are foolish, Buffalo Dung. You are surrounded by my camp, and you are now my prisoner." White Foot spoke, though his voice did not sound convincing.

Softly Chip drawled out his words. "Or maybe all of you are my prisoner." He was leaning ahead, hiding his hands. He could see the whites of White Foot's eyes as he thought about this and nervously looked around him.

Time was slipping by, and Chip was trying to guess how much time the group would need. Suddenly, White Foot sprang at him, pulling a knife from a sling in his belt.

Chip was ready for him and slipped his hand in beside White Foot's knife hand and guided it past his stomach while he brought his right fist crashing into his chin. White Foot dropped without a sound. He did not have to check to see if White Foot was unconscious. Few could take that hit and stay awake. White Foot would be missing a few teeth, and if his jaw was not broken, would not be able to eat right for a week or two.

Chip crouched and slipped down the hill to the valley floor. He turned along its dark edge and made his way towards his group and the horses. He only travelled twenty yards when he heard the horse's hooves as they moved towards him. He hid in a darkened indent and hissed as Buck led the group by him.

Buck was leading Rudy and passed Chip the reins. Arthur and Tiny had the women mounted between them, and Tiny was leading the mules and spare horses. It seemed the night guards were concentrating on the pass, expecting the freighters to try to get through in the dark, and they were not expecting any movement from behind them. Chip and his group made it through the camp undetected and stopped a few hundred feet from the perimeter of the Indian village.

As the group closed about him, Chip said, "Buck, you and Tiny wait here with the women until you hear a commotion in the camp, then you hightail it for our train. Arthur, you and I are going to drive the mules and spare horses into their camp."

There were only a few nods as everyone moved to obey. Chip and Arthur drove the animals ahead of them back towards the camp. At the edge, they slapped the hindmost animals with their hats and spooked the herd into the village. The camp exploded as the mules got a good scent of the Indians and trampled their way through and over the camp, kicking and biting anything that got in their way.

The guards on the pass saw the commotion and, leaving their posts, jumped on their horses and rode back to the village.

Chip and Arthur knew that Buck and Tiny would be on their way and kicked their horses into a run down the pass. The Indians were not long in figuring out what had happened and were soon on their trail.

It was a dangerous ride for both sides in the dark valley, but the sky was already turning grey in the east. Chip could see the two men and the women racing for the desert as he and Arthur gained on the group. Behind them was an angry hoard of Apache Indians bent on vengeance. The wind whipped through his hair and curled his hat brim up as they worked with their horses to gain every ounce of speed out of them. It was a life or death run that could only end badly if they lost.

The group broke out of the pass and into the breaking dawns light with the Indian gaining ground. They would soon be in rifle range and already were starting to try a few shots that fell short of their targets.

Chip and Arthur were side by side and had just reached the group of fleeing survivors. Chip was directly behind Sally, and she turned her head and smiled at him just as her horse tripped in a hole and fell. She sailed over its head and landed rolling on the desert floor.

Chip pulled hard on Rudy's reins and stopped just short of running over her. She sat up stunned, and Chip jumped down beside her. "GO! GO!" he screamed at Arthur, who was trying to turn around.

He grabbed Sally and bodily threw her on Rudy and jumped up behind her. The Indians were gaining more ground and were coming in rifle range. Bullets started dropping and hitting beside and around them. Chip looked ahead at the line of boulders still a half mile away. The group of men and women were almost there.

Rudy stumbled but picked up and ran on. Chip saw a red blood stain appear on his side. The Indian rifles were firing steadily now, and the bullets were angrily buzzing by his ears. He was riding behind Sally as she urged Rudy to give his all. Chip couldn't help himself. He held Sally and felt a surge of warmth and protection for her overwhelming him.

Rudy stumbled again and just recovered when another red stain appeared by his ear. His head dropped, and Chip kicked free and landed on his feet running as Rudy went down. Sally tried to land on her feet but tripped and again fell rolling in the desert.

The rest of the group had almost reached the boulders and were looking back over their shoulders at the massacre the Indians were anticipating. Chip spun on his heel and pulled Sally back and down behind the now dead Rudy. He pulled his rifle and prepared to make their death as expensive as he could. His first shot emptied the horse nearest them. He knelt on one knee with Sally in the dust before him behind Rudy. His next shot emptied the next horse, but the bullets were tugging at his sleeves and hat brim.

The sound of an angry bee went by his ear, and the next Indian went backwards off his horse. More bullets came from behind him and started emptying Indian horse saddles before and around him.

Chip glanced over his shoulder and saw puffs of smoke from more rifles come out over the boulders. The Indians pressed on, feeling sure they were at least going to get him before they were driven back by the rifles in the boulders. They were so close and closing around them.

Suddenly, the hammer of many bullets driving statically into flesh filled the air, and Chip made out the steady snap of his Gatlin, sending the Indians a death chant they could not hold up against.

Chip had given Tex orders to move up ahead of the train with half the train freighters armed with the new Henrys and the Gatlin. They were set up in the boulders and were well within range of the attacking Indians. The steady rain of lead drove into the Indians, and many fell dead from their horses before they turned and fled.

Chip blinked as he watched them turn and hastily retreat from the deadly barrage. He turned and watched as his freighters advanced from the boulders, riding army style in a straight line and firing as they advanced. Sergeant Mercer was at the head of his men, and Tex was with the advancing Gatlin gun wagon, which was still firing over the heads of its mule team.

He let his breath out as he looked at Sally. That had been too close for comfort. She was looking at him with a strange watery look in her eyes and a small smile playing on her lips. Chip realized he had much to tell her, and he was eagerly looking forward to their future conversations. She was not married and a very sensible and good looking woman. Maybe Chip would find a reason to not remain single anymore; he could always hope so, anyway.

Golden Valley

Chapter 1

Ryan Bower and Gene Porter had been best friends all their lives. They had grown up as neighbours in southern Maine. Their families had been farmers and gone to the same church. They had teased each other's sisters and dated the same girls.

They had been there for each other through thick and thin. Had each other's back when there was fighting to do, and dragged each other home when one or the other got into too big a pickle to make it home themselves.

They had learned to ride together, shoot together and went to school together.

They had both had the same dream — to come west, find gold and go home wealthy.

At twenty-three and twenty-two respectively, they were sure they couldn't be far from their dream. An old prospector they had befriended had told them about some ancient gold treasure hidden in this valley by the Spanish soldiers. They had taken the gold from the Incas and were transporting it to the Mexican coast when they were waylaid by Apache Indians. They had fought fiercely but had been pushed back into this valley in New Mexico and had put up their last stand here. All the soldiers had died, but they had hid the gold before they were wiped out. The last man had drawn a map using Inca signs, Spanish words and land marks long since eroded and worn away. The Indians had found the map and pawned it to Eastern traders for beads and knives.

The map had been passed from one person to another until it ended up in a traveling peddler's wagon, and Gene and Ryan had bought it for only fifty dollars. Their families thought they were crazy, but they had set out with their last summer's wages and travelled and worked their way to New Mexico, where they stumbled across the old prospector in a little town called Chico, just one hundred miles north of the valley.

That had been last year, and it had taken until this spring to earn enough money to outfit them for a summer's hunt in the valley. They called it Golden Valley because they were sure they would leave it rich men.

They had found an old Inca house built right into the rock wall that surrounded the valley. There were only a few places one could get into the valley, and most of them had to be traversed on foot or by horseback. The one room house faced east, and the morning sun shone right through the front door and onto the back wall. It was a large room with plenty of space for their beds, gear and modest furniture they built. A fireplace was cut from the rock wall and took the smoke up an old sandstone tunnel made from rain erosion. There was even a stone hovel they used as a barn and a rock wall corral.

The first day of August found the two friends up with the sunlight. The back wall was warmed by it and showed the wall covered with spider webs, bat droppings and blown in dust. The edge was wearing off their enthusiasm after four months of searching the valley for the cave of gold the map said was here. They turned the map on the table they made and looked at what obviously must be an X.

"It's got to be the head of the valley," Ryan was saying. "Any normal person would make the X at the North end of a map, especially when it's the only big entrance to it. It doesn't help that this valley is as wide as it is long and all looks the same from any angle."

Gene smiled; he did that a lot. "You're just anxious to find the gold and be rich. It wouldn't be worth being wealthy if we didn't have to work for it." Silently he studied the map, twisting his head first one way then the other.

"It could be where the river runs out under that rock cliff at the south end. That would mean the gold treasure is on the other side of the valley. Hmm...I would still like to know what those lines under the treasure box mean. If it is a treasure box; maybe it's a building, like this one, and the X is the treasure," Gene speculated.

"Stop that," Ryan spat out. "You keep coming up with any more ideas and we'll never figure this map out." He was getting a little testy and snapped his words out more often. He was slighter than Gene but five inches taller and considered the handsomer of the two. He kept his black hair neatly combed and liked his clothes to be clean and unruffled. His low-slung black holster sported a pearl handled six-gun and a row of shiny brass cartridges and matching high-top black leather boots.

Gene smiled again but said nothing. He wore his gun tucked into his belt and dressed in a flannel shirt and blue jeans. He preferred the brown high-top low heeled miners' boots for easier walking and climbing. His dusty blond hair always seemed to be tousled and a big cowlick hung down over his forehead.

He looked down at the map again and put his finger on some wavy lines in the center. "This has to be water, but the river is even here. Maybe we can try to recreate the history of the valley by the erosion and weather signs and locate some of these marks. Lord knows we haven't done very well so far."

Ryan gave him a hard look. "That would take too much time. Look, we've covered the upper part of the valley on this side; let's take a look on the other side?"

"Alright," Gene answered. "I'll get the horses, but I'm going through the middle to see if I can locate any old lake or swamp markings."

"Yeh, yeh," Ryan said absently, still studying the map.

Gene brought his tough mountain bay and Ryan's long legged black to the front of the rock house. He noticed that, set into the wall the way it was, it also could be considered a cave. He had picketed their five pack mules in the meadow encompassing ten acres of lush, waist high grass in front of the house and ending up at the river, which shone and sparkled from the light reflecting from the still rising sun over the far valley rim. He turned after calling Ryan and marvelled at the beauty of this valley. "Our Golden Valley," he murmured, drinking in the scene.

Ryan's boot steps brought him around and he smiled again, but it was lost on Ryan, who was still frowning at the map. "Those lines may be a ladder or steps," he ventured. "Look." He held the map out to Gene and continued, "This hump must be a rise in the ground, and these images might be rocks that look like animal who look that way. Memorize these other marks and look for anything similar."

He had only told Gene this a dozen times, but the hunt was wearing on him. Gene liked the outdoors more than Ryan, who liked the city and the girls more.

"Yes, Sir," Gene snapped to attention and saluted, drawing a hard look from Ryan. If they didn't find that gold soon, Ryan was going to turn into an old grouch.

They mounted and rode across the meadow towards the river. Ryan studied the far rock wall, looking for any sign of a hole or cave to start this day's search, while Gene started looking over the river erosion, looking for signs of an ancient lake or swamp land. He spotted the first clue just short of the cut-bank of the river.

He was turning to look back at the rock house when he noticed the ground dipped here, and he couldn't see the house doorway. It was almost hidden in the grass, but when you looked from the back, you could see a visible rim well back from the cut-bank.

"You go on," he said to the preoccupied Ryan. "I'm going to look at something here."

Ryan looked at him and grunted, then turned to continue across the river and up the other side. As he disappeared into the trees, Gene started riding parallel to the river, following the faint rim he had found.

The map showed a body of water almost heart shaped with the point at the bottom where the water ran out, they figured. Its position on the map put it at the top end of the valley, too.

Gene spent the morning mapping out the first real clue they had with the pool of water, and when he stopped for a sandwich at noon, he was frowning at the image of the pool he had formed in his head. According to the pool, they had the map upside down. The point was where the water came into the pool, and it exited in two streams that ran under the rock ledge at the bottom part of the valley.

That would put the gold over there on the same side of the valley as the rock house, but lower down than where they and been looking, he thought.

They had ridden in from the upriver side where it had been obvious the river ran a lot lower than it had in the past. He looked around, picturing the map's details as he studied the terrain.

That would put the three hills over there. He looked to the northwest. The valley was covered with a thick growth of trees over that whole area.

"Well! No wonder we couldn't find those hills. They're in the trees." He felt himself getting excited. He turned and rode up into the trees.

As soon as he entered the thick foliage, he started to noticeably climb. It was hard going in the trees, but his horse, Buckshot, was a tough mountain horse used to trees and rough ground. Gene let Buckshot work his own way through the forest, and he concentrated on not being swept from the saddle by the low branches.

It took him the rest of the afternoon to work through the trees and over the three hills, but he had definite bearings and a good idea of how the map was supposed to be positioned in the valley when he was done. *This changes everything,* he thought to himself. *Now we have a real starting point.*

It was too late to meet Ryan by the rock wall, so he turned Buckshot towards their house and headed in for the night. He didn't hurry, even though he was excited. He liked this valley even at night. The Moon displayed a white Moonscape when it came up and threw a dull white light over the scenery.

Ryan was waiting for him when he rode in just after dark. It was obvious his mood was becoming worse.

"Enjoy yourself lazing along by the river?" He asked sarcastically.

Gene's excitement wore off, and Ryan's tone irritated him. "You bet," he replied. "Caught up on my sleep."

Ryan gave him a hard look. "Maybe the gold should be split more evenly than fifty-fifty; seems the one who does most of the work should get more of the reward."

Gene's mouth dropped open in surprise. He was used to being accused of being lazy or something similar, but this was the first time Ryan had mentioned anything about changing the division of what they found. He looked hard at his boyhood friend and wondered if seeking wealth had affected his outlook.

He shook off the feelings that were building between them and slowly said, "I found the pool of water and the three hills. We had the map upside down. The pool is at the bottom of the valley and the hills are covered by that forest to the nor'east of here."

Ryan's mood changed instantly and he stammered, "Wha....what? You found them? That's great news. Come in, and you can show me."

Gene did notice Ryan did not offer him food first, even though he could see Ryan had eaten already when he entered the house.

Ryan laid the map out on the table. "Show me," he said excitedly.

Gene reached and turned the map so it mimicked the valley from where they were. Laying his finger on the map, he pointed while he talked. "Here is the top of the valley, and here is where the pool of water is. The hills are over here, overgrown by trees so we couldn't see them."

Moving his finger over to the X he said, "This starting point must be this house, and the cave is down here by that rock wall we haven't looked at because we had the map wrong."

Ryan looked at him. "Are you sure? You can show me in the morning. It's about time we caught a break. We've worked too hard at this. Just think what we could do with that gold. We would be rich and could have whatever we wanted. A house in the city would be great, and so would a business with some good farm land. We could hobnob with the rich folks, and women would be scratchin' to be near us."

Gene looked at his friend. This was a new side to Ryan that he had not seen before. He thought they were looking for the gold to go home and help their families as well as start a business together. He had no desire to be hobnobin' with the rich folks. They had done him no favours.

Gene fixed himself a bite of lunch while Ryan poured over the map, making plans for tomorrow. He wanted a walk outside to think and talk to God for a spell. He had heard that wealth corrupts, but he had never seen it before now. He didn't like what he was seeing in Ryan.

Chapter 2

The morning broke with a flash of lightning and the crash of thunder. They had become complacent by two weeks of sunny warm days and mild nights, but dark storm clouds moved in through the night and woke the two adventurers.

They lay in their beds listening to the thunder move in, and the wind picked up to an angry howl. The rain started before dawn and prolonged the morning light.

They had taken the time to make some much needed repairs when they had set up camp and were protected from the storm by a solid wooden door and canvas shutters that they could unroll over the window openings. The animals had the rock barn that still stood solid against the valley wall a few short yards away to also protect them from the elements.

They roused late and ate a leisurely breakfast. There would be little searching today, and Ryan's irritation showed in his pacing.

"Good day to repair equipment and get some climbing gear ready," Gene ventured.

"Huh? Oh, yeh," Ryan said on the way by, gulping his third cup of coffee. "Yeh, maybe it will let up later and we can have a quick look around." He made no move towards their gear stashed in the back corner.

Gene settled in to sewing the holes in his pants and strengthening the leather straps in their packs. Ryan watched from his chair and finally moved over and helped him. By noon they had run out of things to repair and were going over their climbing gear for what might be a busy time after the storm.

The rain let up shortly after noon, and they went outside to tend to the animals and do a few chores around their yard. Gene saw the strange horse first and went to investigate it at the edge of the woods by the river where it stood quietly, with its head down.

The horse didn't look up until he was almost beside it, and it started nervously. As it sidestepped, Gene could see a person lying on the grass beside it, not moving. He hurried to the figure and rolled her over. He could tell right away it was a she, as her hat fell off and her long brown hair fell over her face.

She was dirty, and her clothes were torn and hanging off her. She had obviously had a rough time wherever she had been before she came here.

45

Gene knelt beside her and felt for a pulse. It was weak and hard to find, but she was alive. He checked her over for cuts and broken bones, but all he found were a lot of bruises and some minor scratches.

He looked around for Ryan, but he was nowhere in sight, so he picked her up and, leading her horse, carried her to their camp. He dropped the horse's reins and kicked open the door. He placed her on his own bed then built up the fire to warm the room more.

He felt a little strange and swallowed hard, but he had to get her out of those wet clothes and warm her up. He tried to avert his eyes from her naked body as he worked and finally succeeded in getting her undressed and under the covers. He was glad Ryan was not here to see his embarrassment, because Ryan was the one who really liked to be with women, especially if they were a little loose and friendly.

He couldn't help noticing how pretty and young she was. He figured she must be about sixteen, which left him with a lot of questions. She was travelling light, with no supplies or weapons, and her horse was worn out from a long hard run.

Gene put the cook pot near the fire and built a good healthy stew from the locally found vegetables and fresh deer meat. He slid the coffee pot close to the fire on the other side, figuring she would need some warm liquids when she woke up.

He was heading out to tend to her horse when he met Ryan at the door.

"Whose horse is that?" Ryan asked suspiciously. "And what do they want in our valley?"

Gene waved at his bed and said, "Little girl was passed out in the meadow, and I carried her in here. Looks like she's had a hard go of it." He didn't like the way Ryan's gaze went instantly to the girl at the mention of her, and he didn't take his eyes from Gene's bed when he asked.

"You…ah, you undressed her?" He licked his lips.

"Yeh, she had to get warm and her clothes were soaked. I hung them by the fire, but they're a little worse for wear. We got anything smaller that she could wear?" He was thinking of his clothes, trying to think of some articles that might fit her.

"Sure. Sure, we can find something for her. She looks young." He had moved closer and was looking her over.

Gene answered, "Yeh, too young to be out here alone. There must be someone searching for her right now." That brought Ryan out of his imaginary world, and he turned to face Gene.

Gene continued, "I'm going to put her horse away and rub it down. If she wakes up, I got stew on the fire and the coffees warming, too. She'll need to eat and warm up. You want to keep an eye on her while I go out?"

Ryan nodded, coming back to his senses. "Yeh, you go ahead. I'll make sure she's looked after."

It took Gene about an hour to make the horse warm and comfortable, but no one showed up looking for the girl. The storm had picked up again, and the rain beating on the side of the house muffled his approach. He opened the door in time to catch Ryan replacing the covers over the unconscious girl.

"Hey!" He hissed, startling Ryan. "Leave her alone. What were you looking for, anyway?"

Ryan looked at him and hesitated. "Ah....I was checking to make sure she wasn't hurt or anything." He quickly looked away and moved over to the fireplace.

Gene had not thought about it before, but now it dawned on him that Ryan was not taking this solitude as well as he was. He loved the outdoors and could be alone in the bush for months and loved it, but Ryan was more of a social person and wanted to be around cities and people. The stress of not finding the gold and being alone in Golden Valley was wearing on his nerves and his senses. Gene determined to keep a closer eye on him, just to keep him safe.

"We're not going to get much done with this weather. How about a game of cards?" Gene asked Ryan, who seemed preoccupied with his thoughts again.

"Sure......sure, I guess so." He moved to their packs and returned with the cards. He took the seat facing Gene's bed, where he could see the girl as Gene stirred the stew and moved the steaming coffee pot away from the flame. They had eaten some beef jerky and cheese earlier and were not hungry, but Gene poured them both a hot cup of coffee and returned to the table.

All the time they played, Ryan's eyes kept turning to the girl. Gene didn't want to think about what he was thinking of and tried to keep up a running conversation, but they had been alone here too long for lengthy conversations, and talk dwindled out.

It was deathly silent when the girl groaned and stirred in the bed. They both jumped and hurried to the bedside. Gene reached and held the covers so she would not uncover herself, and was leaning over her when she opened her eyes directly below him.

Her eyes went wide with fright, and she tried to bolt upright as she screamed.

"Easy, girl. We won't hurt you," Gene consoled, and he gently held her down.

Ryan was looking over his shoulder and added, "Yeh, just relax. You've had a rough go of it."

She frantically looked around her and back at them again as she flailed her arms about and tried again to sit up.

"Please, stop, girl. You don't want to uncover yourself," Gene again counselled her. He watched as her eyes stopped roving and looked into his, then at Ryan. She settled back, clutching the covers up to her chin and cowered.

"It's alright. You're safe here." Gene's voice was soft, convincing. "My name is Gene Porter, and this is Ryan Bower. You wandered into our valley, and I found you unconscious out by the trees. Your clothes were wet and.......well, they're dry now and, if you have the energy, I'll bring them over here, and Ryan and I can go outside for a time."

She watched him gather her clothes and put them on the foot of the bed before he and Ryan went outside.

It was still pouring down rain as they made their way to the stable. They gathered enough straw and framing to build another crude bed, and made their way back to the house. The girl was dressed and eating a bowl of stew hungrily. She looked up anxiously, but they went about putting together the bed for Gene.

"You just take your time, Miss. You look like you've had a time, so just relax; you're among friends," Gene assured her. Ryan kept passing sideways glances at her and smiled reassuringly whenever she looked his way.

Finishing the bed, they made their way to the table where the girl was finishing her third bowl of stew and fourth cup of coffee. She rolled her eyes as they sat down at each end of the table.

"You'll feel a whole lot better after a good night's sleep," Ryan commented, patting her wrist. She flinched away from him, but stopped when she saw it was a friendly gesture. "You got a name? We can't keep callin' you girl or Miss."

"Susan," she whispered softly. "Susan Shepard. I was held by Indians and escaped. They were chasing me. Please, don't let them find me."

"Indians!" Ryan exclaimed. "They won't bother you here. This is our valley, and they don't come here." Gene glanced at his friend, curiously. They had seen no Indians but had heard there were some wild Apaches around. They had stayed in the valley and made no trails in or out for anyone to follow, but that didn't mean they wouldn't come if they had reason to.

Ryan continued, "How did a pretty little girl like you end up with the Indians?" Gene couldn't believe Ryan was making up to her, but maybe that was what she needed to get comfortable with them.

"They attacked our wagon train and......and...." She broke down and cried great, sobbing tears. Through the sobbing she said, "they k...k...killed the men and ...it...was...horrible. We tried to find a man called Buffalo Chip Blackstone, because they said he had the safest wagon trains around, but we missed him and had to travel with someone else. The Indians came out of the ground and were everywhere. They killed the men and captured most of the women and children. My... my...dad was dead and they...they killed my mom, too."

She paused for a breath, and Ryan shook his head and exclaimed, "Tsk, tsk, such animals. Murdering heathens; they should be chased down and hanged." Susan seemed reassured by his attitude.

She continued. "They made us work and married us off to the men. It came my turn, but I had not been making trouble and secretly making plans. I still had my horse, so I left in the night. They chased me, but I hid in the day and moved at night. I don't know how I got here. I lost track of where I was and where I could go. I just sat in my saddle and hung on while my horse walked."

"You got a smart horse. Your safe now; we'll look after you. Don't you worry about a thing," Ryan said confidently.

Susan stared at him for a moment, and then Gene saw her body starting to relax as she turned to him. He nodded in turn and said, "Yeh, you can stay here with us and be safe enough, I guess. We've seen no Indians in here, but we'll keep an eye out and protect you."

They spent the rest of the evening telling stories and learning about each other. Susan delighted in the clothes they found could fit her, and she seemed to take a keen interest in Ryan. Gene mostly watched, but he pondered Ryan's smooth talking and Susan's swooning. He busied himself putting up a makeshift curtain to give Susan some privacy.

It was late when they finally all went to bed. Morning would come all too soon, and they had to plan their next move. Susan's arrival changed everything. They would have to take her out, and they would have to start watching for Indians. Their days would no longer be the same.

Chapter 3

The changes started the next morning. The two men could not get out of bed and scratch their itches or walk around half naked as they were used to. The presence of a female made normal daily occasions change into polite, but hidden, necessities. The first thing Gene noticed was how Ryan hovered around Susan. His comments were aimed to flatter and impress her. With Gene he became more distant and critical.

The rain had stopped through the night, but fog hung low over the valley at sunup, making everything seem unearthly. The far mountains were hidden in the fog, and the trees looked like shadows walking in clouds.

They discussed how they could search the valley and look after Susan, until she suggested that she could go along with them. They didn't tell her what they were searching for.

After breakfast, the three saddled up their horses and moved carefully through the fog towards the lower western wall of the valley. It was too foggy to think about climbing the wall, so they decided to ride along the bottom and scout the base.

Gene found Ryan's antics amusing as he tried to entertain Susan and see every trace of evidence along the wall. He was oblivious to the fact that Gene and Susan noticed his preoccupation with both as he talked to Susan while studying the wall and smiled out of turn at the serious things she said.

Gene watched as he rode behind the two but did notice Susan occasionally turn and look back at him. He would wink or give her a smile while he lifted his shoulders, letting her know he didn't know what Ryan was doing.

On the pretence of scouting, Gene would take a ride to one side or the other as they rode further along the rock wall. His reconnoitring had two purposes; he was watching the valley for signs of Indians or anyone else who would follow Susan into it, and he was looking over certain prospects for evidence he saw along the wall's edge. He made notes of anything he thought might be useful later.

The lines below the box, which they thought must be the gold, occupied his mind, and he looked for similar markings in the ground or rocks about them. Like the hidden hills, they might be covered with growth or eroded away by now, but they were all they had to go on for now.

The rock wall rose straight up from the valley floor in this part of the valley, making it a very unlikely place to find golden treasure. They did find and catalogued a few caves to investigate later, but the valley floor was strewn with fallen boulders and edges of cliffs that had long since fallen from the heights above.

By noon, they had made it to the foot of the valley and, after a lunch that Susan had packed, they started back. The day had brightened and cleared somewhat, and Gene told the others he was going to ride out from the base so he could get a bigger look at the wall. Ryan's face brightened at the thought of being alone with Susan while she looked seriously at Gene.

"Don't worry," he reassured her. "I'll just be out there about a quarter of a mile, and if I see any Indians I'll hustle right back and tell you. Ryan's a fair decent shot and can look after you fine."

"Yeh, yeh, I am. You go on, Gene. We'll be fine," he said, not looking at Gene but glancing at Susan and the rock wall.

Gene winked at Susan to reassure her and turned Buckshot away towards the valley.

As he rode, he kept looking back at the rock wall and the hillside around them. He had found the old lake bed by looking back and thought he might be able to do it again. He was not disappointed when he noticed rocks shaped like the animal shapes on the map dotting the valley wall and outlined on the rim.

Gene stopped and studied the shapes; in his mind he placed them in the proper place in the map and guessed at the location of the box. Looking ahead to its approximate location, he found himself looking at a huge expanse of solid rock wall, top to bottom.

He rode on, still looking for a hill, mound or hump that was also marked on the map. He kept a watch on the two as they rode along the wall and kept pace with them. They occasionally stopped and explored any opening they came to. He also noticed the playful attitude they seemed to be sharing.

Well, score another one for Ryan. He sure knows how to play up to the girls, he thought, and found himself a little disappointed. He had to admit to himself that he was rather fond of Susan.

Gene almost rode into the sharp-sloped depression while his attention was on Ryan and Susan. He managed to pull Buckshot up before he took the first step down the sloping walls. He had just come through a clump of thick brush and was looking for the pair along the rock wall when his attention was taken by the lack of anything in front of him.

Gene stared down the slope to the bottom of the depression. It was in the shape of a bowl and dry as a boot. They had not found it before as it was surrounded by a thick growth of alder bushes that only a rabbit or a searching treasure hunter would go through.

Gene realized he had found the map's marking for what they thought was a hill; instead, it was a depression. If it were not for the bushes, according to the map, he should be able to look right into the place the gold treasure was hidden. He couldn't see a thing through the brush.

He circled the hole and forced Buckshot into the brush towards the rock wall. The horse valiantly pushed into the brush and forced it to part and bend, but it clung to his saddle and bridle and grabbed at Gene's boots and upper body. He slowly backed the horse out, realizing it was too dangerous for Buckshot. He would have to go back the way he had come, because the brush was just as thick in front of them.

Gene gathered some dry branches and made a small fire pit. He lit the branches and banked the fire, hoping no Indians were around to see it. The smoke went start up in an even column. He quickly back-tracked through the brush and worked his way around the outside until he was directly opposite the rock wall and in front of the pillar of smoke. He was lower here than by the edge of the depression, but could see he was again facing a solid rock wall for several hundred feet in each direction. It looked formidable, but he advanced to its base and looked up.

Ryan and Susan appeared at the far edge, coming his way. They did not notice him sitting there, and were eagerly talking and waving their hands. Gene frowned; after the way Ryan had snapped at him, he was beginning to take on the same grumpy spirit.

They noticed him there by the wall and hurried to meet him. They were excited and smiling broadly. "We were just spending our gold and having a high old time," Ryan commented, riding up facing Gene.

"Harrumph!" Gene ejected. "Better find it first," he continued, cynically. Susan gave him a curious look and stopped smiling.

"Oh, we'll find it alright. It's our gold and we're not leaving without it." Ryan kept smiling, but it turned cold. He was facing away from Susan, and she didn't see the cool look on his face, nor he the surprised look she gave the back of his head.

Ryan's look became thoughtful as he continued, "I thought you were riding farther out to look at the wall from a distance. We can look in close; two sets of eyes are better than one."

"Sure!" Gene exploded. "If you could take your eyes off each other long enough. I saw the way you two are "looking" for the gold. It would have to fall on your head or jump into your hands for you to see it." His own jealousy surprised him.

Ryan's look became colder. "And you are doing better, riding around in the brush spying on us?" He had noticed the leaves and twigs caught on Buckshot's rigging.

Hot with guilty anger, Gene blurted, "As a matter of fact, I have. I found what we thought was a hill on the map, and it turned out to be a depression. That smoke is from the edge, and I was lining it up with this wall. Those animals are actually boulders and humps along the edge of the rim, and everything points to this rock face." He was sweating and breathing hard.

Susan was staring at his face with apprehension, her mouth half open. She looked more womanly than Gene wanted to admit.

Ryan looked up and, taking his time while Gene stewed, carefully studied the rock wall. Inwardly, Gene cursed his emotions that had betrayed him. He hadn't intended to say anything until latter while they looked over their map.

The sun was edging close to the horizon, and shadows were starting to appear out from the rocks.

"Ah, shucks! We can't do anything more today. I'm for heading home for supper. We can prepare to hunt this cliff in the morning," Gene said, dejectedly. He looked pleadingly at the two, hoping to make amends and appease their animosity.

"I am hungry," Susan said, hopefully.

Ryan scowled at Gene, but smiled as he turned to Susan. "Sounds like a good plan to me. Let's eat." As they turned to go, Gene noticed Ryan glancing back at the cliff face and fingering their map.

Gene led the way back to camp while Ryan and Susan rode together and kept up a lively conversation. Gene, overhearing, thought they spent most of the gold before they reached the house.

The evening meal was eaten with little change in atmosphere, but ended with them sitting around the table and Gene telling all the clues he found and where they were. He could see Ryan paying close attention and, whenever he looked into his eyes, they shone with the light of heated anticipation.

Finally, Ryan spoke with an exaggerated authority and said, "It's getting late, and we have a lot of work to be done tomorrow. Go to bed! We are going to start early and have a long day. I have plans for that gold, and we need to find it."

Susan yawned and made to head for her bed, but Gene waited and, after she was across the room, whispered, "You have plans? What about *our* plans?"

Ryan jerked his head around to stare angrily at Gene. "Sure, sure, whatever you say. Get to bed; it's late." He rose and moved to his bedside.

Gene was not convinced of his sincerity, and felt like he had been dismissed. Fuming, he undressed and crawled into his bed. He lay awake staring at the ceiling and wondered where they had lost their usual good humour. He finally gave up and figured they were stressed from the summer's hunt and Susan's arrival. She was the first female they had seen in months, and their male egos were starved for an approving glance.

They were up well before dawn and were ready to travel as the eastern sky turned light with the sun's soon arrival. They found Susan some appropriate clothes for walking and digging around the rocks, and carried their picks, shovels and lanterns for any cave or cave-in they might encounter.

Exploring the rock face proved to be hard and strenuous work. It was not as smooth as it first looked. The wall rolled as they moved along in front of it, and was honeycombed with natural caves, cracks and ledges. The rock wall was rotten, and much of its face had fallen to the bottom, making walking very difficult and the search along the base hazardous as the trio combed through the rocks and boulders looking for clues to the hidden gold.

The caves and rock cracks they found had periodic cave-ins, especially if they leaned on the walls or bumped an outcrop. The caves were full of rocks from cave-ins, and these had to be moved with great care not to cause another fresh cave-in while they were in them.

By noon, they were dirty, scratched, tired and worn. They were all in an angry and sarcastic mood as they stopped to eat. They had found nothing to indicate the presence of anything other than rock, so far.

Gene leaned on the wall and said, "Let's rest a bit before we eat. I could lie in a sunny spot and soak up some warmth right now." His hands were bleeding from cuts received from the sharp rocky outcrops and, when he wiped his brow, spread a crimson streak across his forehead.

"You go ahead," snapped Ryan. "Susan and I will find the gold ourselves and hire you to care for the pack animals."

His sharp retort not only hurt Gene, but it drew Susan's attention.

"Stop it," she snapped. "We're tired and hurting. Maybe this gold is not here."

"Don't talk like that!" Ryan said. "Of course it's here, and we'll find it."

Gene sat down and leaned his head on the wall. He closed his eyes and rested them. He felt the tension ease from his body as the sun's heat soaked into his muscles. Ryan's and Susan's conversation seemed to get farther and farther away and he dosed lightly in the warmth.

He was suddenly awakened by a sharp blow on his boots. He bolted upright, fists ready to strike, while he tried to clear his fussy brain. Ryan was standing over him, having kicked his feet. "Slacking again, are you? You can sleep all you want when we find that gold." His hands were up, expecting Gene to swing at him.

"Go ahead," he taunted

"Will you two stop?" Susan asked in frustration. She was eating a sandwich they had brought with them.

Gene shook his head, half to clear it and half in disbelief that Ryan would do what he just did. Ryan seemed to be getting worse, and it was making Gene more irritated. They had been friends a long time — too long to be acting like this.

"I...I don't know you anymore, Ryan," Gene said quietly. Without waiting for an answer, he picked up a sandwich and his canteen and moved off along the wall. "I'll go lookin' over here," he said over his shoulder.

Susan sat in stunned silence and watched his back. "Do you think that was wise?" she asked Ryan.

"Aw, Susan. He'll get over it. We been friends a long time, and he always acts this way when I have to push him," Ryan blustered.

"Do you?" she asked, eyes wide with question. "Do you always have to push him?"

"Yes. Yes, I do," Ryan said convincingly. "You watch. It won't be long before he hops on his horse and takes off for a ride to cool off."

Susan looked again at Gene's still moving back and shrugged. Maybe she was wrong, but Gene seemed like a nice guy. She looked at Ryan. It was obvious he was making plans that included her, and he was handsome.

They finished their lunch and went back to searching the rocks at the base of the wall.

By mid afternoon, Ryan and Susan came upon a white cloth on a stick left by Gene. He was almost to the brush at the end of the wall and was walking back to meet them. They reached the stick at the same time.

"I left that there for you, in case I found something else further along, but it's scattered all along here. From the edge of the woods," he pointed to where he had just come from, "to here." He swept his arm down over the spot at his feet.

Susan and Ryan looked down at the rocks, puzzled, and seeing nothing new.

"Here, look." Gene bent and moved a rock. "Under the rocks back there was sand and pebbles, and it was dry. Here there is dead grass and dirt, some broken limbs and.....smell! Smell that!"

They took a deep breath and Susan caught hers, "What is that horrible smell?" she asked.

Slowly Ryan said, "Death. I remember it from the gut pile after the snow went off."

Gene looked at them and said, "Yep, and if there were a massacre here like the old man said the Indians did to the Spanish soldiers, there would be a lot of rot and decay piled up. The smell would hang around for a long time and be fertilizer for plants and trees."

Excitedly Ryan said, "So, we're close. The gold must be here somewhere." He stared around him as if he could spot the hiding place. He didn't notice Gene staring past him at the sky, but Susan saw and turned to look at what he was looking at.

A thin stream of smoke from a single small fire was rising in the air from the north entrance to the valley. As they watched, the smoke stopped, then puffed in a ball and stopped again, and another ball followed by two more balls of smoke.

Smoke signals! Indians!

The thought raced through their minds, and Susan shuddered.

Gene commented, "I think we best be going back to the house and den in for a while."

"Wha...what?" Ryan ejected. "No you don't. We're so close, and you want us to leave." He turned on Gene as he spoke.

Gene thrust his chin towards the smoke and said, "OK, you stay and talk to them."

Ryan turned and saw the smoke. His face turned white, then red with anger. "This is our valley and my gold, and they can't stop me. We'll come back in the morning and find that gold."

They gathered all their belongings and tools and made their way back to the rock house. There they put the animals in the stone barn and hid their presence around the area as best they could. Gene knew it would not fool the Indians, but they had to try.

It was dark when they were done. They had a cold meal and went to bed without showing a light.

Chapter 4

The three were up well before dawn. It was decided that Gene would head to the entrance to scout out the Indians, and Ryan and Susan would try to find the gold before the Indians moved into the valley. By sunup, Gene was well up the valley looking for signs of Indian travel, and Ryan and Susan were at the rock wall looking for a cave or trail near the massacre site. They dug under rocks and dirt at every likely looking site, and came up with Spanish armour, old rusty swords and muskets. These were strewn over and around the skeletal remains of the Spanish soldiers. Indian spear-heads and arrows were mixed in with the carnage.

By midmorning, Gene reached the entrance and scouted the trail into the valley. The Indians had camped at the top of the divide, but had returned without coming into the valley. Gene let out a low sigh of relief and turned back to help the others.

He stopped as he looked out over the valley towards the rock wall. There, in sharp relief and visible to the naked eye, were horizontal lines across the face of the wall, identical to the lines described in the map.

Gene hurriedly took out his eye glass and, looking through the single lens, studied the lines. They were rough and broken, but visible enough to tell him how they were made. The rock had ledges running across it where layers of rock had fallen away from the face, leaving the jagged edges of what remained there. It would no doubt be weather worn and where erosion had taken away most of it he could see where the ledge had been when the sun shone directly on it. The heaviest wear was lighter than the newly made naked parts, so even though many of the ledges were gone or worn down, Gene could still see the outline of them under the revealing glare of the morning sun.

The map had three lines under the box, and Gene counted up the rock face three distinct lines and followed them both ways with his eye glass. One end curved down almost to the valley floor, but the other disappeared out of sight into a fissure crack in the wall.

Gene felt his pulse quicken as he put his glass away and made his way back to the house. His mind was going over the wall, and he knew there was no easy way to climb up that face.

At the house, he gathered their supply of rope and rode back up the valley to another climbing spot they had found. He made his way up the difficult climb to the rock wall's upper rim.

It was afternoon when he appeared above the ledge. As he looked down, he could see Ryan and Susan working the massacre site below. He took the time to study the valley with his eyeglass, but saw no sign of Indians or hostiles.

The sun was past this point and, even at this early hour, the wall was shadowed and dangerous as Gene laid the rope on its edge and fastened the different pieces together to make it longer. He found a strong, healthy tree to anchor the rope to and started down the rock face. It was slow, strenuous going, but he made it to a good ledge just above the trail he had seen and was heading for. It took him some time in the fading light, but he found a solid boulder that would not move by their weight. He anchored another rope around it and let the rest fall to the valley floor below.

It was the best he could do, and he hurried to climb back out before darkness made the climb impossible. Each hand and foot hold was dangerous going back up, but he succeeded with only a few slips and near misses. His arms were weak and shaking and he was out of breath, but he was happy they were getting so close to their goal.

It was another slow and agonizing ride back down the trail to the valley floor. He let Buckshot pick his own way down. He was a mountain horse and completely at home on a narrow steep trail.

Gene heard them before he arrived at the house. Ryan and Susan were arguing loudly, and there was the occasional bump of violence. He hurried to the door, concern making him not think about announcing his presence. He burst through the door to find Susan sprawled on her bed and Ryan standing over her, anger written all over his face.

"Whoa, hold up there, Ryan. What are you two doing?" Gene asked quietly, not wanting to escalate the situation.

"Well, well," Ryan sneered. "You decided to wake up and come home." He turned his anger on Gene.

"Of course!" Gene snapped, "There were no Indians, and I found map signs up on the wall where I hung some climbing ropes." He looked narrowly at Ryan. "I pull my weight around here, too, and you're not the boss."

Ryan's face turned a deeper red and he spat, "You, too?"

He stared at Gene while his anger grew. "I have to do the thinking and planning while you two idle away the time. Someone has to be the boss, and if you don't like it you can pull out now." His eyes narrowed and he tensed.

Gene straightened and looked from Ryan to Susan. He saw the bruise on her cheek and the fright in her eyes. *This is not right, and I best go careful here,* he thought.

"Just what do you mean? We have always done everything together, and now you want to take over. What's the difference now?" Gene asked.

"I've worked too hard keeping you going this summer," Ryan grated. "Now Susan comes along and makes up to me and you disappear while we do all the work, and she decides she has to leave when we're so close to my gold."

He saw Gene's mouth drop open and he continued. "That's right. I've seen you looking at her and thinking that if you could get us out of the valley, you could get Susan and come back for the gold without me." His eyes were large and glassy. "That's why the both of you want to slack off and leave. These imaginary Indians are just the excuse you need. Well, it won't work. We stay and find the gold, and when we leave, Susan is marrying ME!" Ryan stabbed his thumb into his chest. He turned on Susan. "And no more talk of being scared and tired and wanting to leave, understand? "

Susan sat shocked and could only nod her head.

Gene tried to reason with him. "Look, Ryan, I found where the Indians camped up on the entrance, but they left again. They could come back at any time, but we still might have time to find the gold. I found the lines on the map and climbed the ridge to attach some climbing ropes and let them down into the valley. They're hanging there now for us to climb in the morning."

Ryan blinked. "Wha....what?" he stammered. "You found it and wasn't going to tell me unless I forced you?"

"No, no!" Gene said. "I was just...ah...concerned when I saw you and Susan talking so loudly." This was not going well. Ryan seemed to be obsessed with the gold and not thinking right. He continued, "I hurried in to see what the problem was. I didn't think I would startle you, and only now had time to tell you how close we are." He smiled gently, hoping to ease the tension.

"Close. We're close." Ryan rolled the words around in his mouth and walked into the center of the room, thinking.

Susan sat up and looked desperately at Gene, but as he edged closer to her, he kept watching Ryan. "Yeh, tomorrow we should find it. Of course, it could take a few days to get it all down and back to the house."

Ryan turned, and Gene stopped moving. Ryan said, "A couple of days? Yes! Yes, there must be a ton of gold in that treasure. We may have to make more trips out to get it all. I'll be rich and won't have to grub in the rocks and dirt anymore. I can hire others to work for me and live the way I was supposed to live."

He looked at Susan. "You'll be married to the richest man in the country and can live in our mansion." He looked at Gene again. "Where did you say it was?"

"I put the ropes down by that big rock cut in the middle. The ledges are eroded, but the ropes will hold us while we look for a cave or hiding place." Gene spoke while he edged between Ryan and Susan.

"Good, good. We'll start first thing in the morning and fill this room with the gold. We can hide what we can't carry until we get back." Ryan turned and slowly walked to the doorway, head bowed in thought.

Gene knelt down beside Susan and whispered, "Are you ok?" She nodded and whispered back, "Only bruised, but scared."

Gene looked at the bruises on her face and didn't notice Ryan turning to look at them. Ryan's quick movement drew Gene's attention back to him.

"What are you two talking about?" Ryan asked, loudly.

"Nothing," Gene answered. "Just that Susan has to go outside, and she's afraid of Indians. I thought we could check the brush for her."

Ryan jerked to a stop. "So you can get me outside and do what? Trying to get rid of me now we've found the gold?" His hand rested on the butt of his gun.

"No, no," Gene quickly exclaimed. "It's just that we have to use the toilet and eat, and I have to put Buckshot away." He was edging towards Ryan as he spoke, but Ryan saw him coming and backed a step, grasping his gun-butt.

"Stay back! I know what you're up to. Get me out of the way; that was what you were telling Susan. Well, she's mine and so is the gold." Ryan's voice was rising on each word.

Gene stopped, but his foot rolled on a pebble and his hand went to his middle, next to his gun. Ryan saw the action and thought he was going to draw. He pulled his gun, pointed it at Gene, and shot.

Gene never heard the shot. The bullet slammed into his head, and he fell into the darkness that rose up to meet him. Susan screamed as she watched Gene fall limply to the floor and a pool of blood eddy out from his head.

Ryan and Susan looked at Gene for a few seconds, then Ryan rushed and grabbed Susan as she rose to run to Gene. "No you don't." He found a rope and tied her hands to the bed posts, and then he turned to Gene's body.

The pool of blood had stopped spreading, but Gene was not moving.

"Serves him right for trying to take the gold and Susan away from me," Ryan mumbled.

He emptied Gene's pockets and took his gun. Then he lifted the dead weight by his shoulders and dragged him outside. Gene had left his horse ground-hitched by the door, and Ryan struggled to lift his body into the saddle. He finally succeeded in throwing him face down over his saddle and led the horse away towards the river.

Ryan found an overhanging bank beside the river and dropped Gene's body over the side. It landed beside the bank, and Ryan jumped on the rim until the bank collapsed, covering Gene's limp form.

Ryan returned and put Gene's horse away and made his way to the house. They had eaten before Gene showed up, so Ryan just checked Susan's bonds before getting ready for bed himself.

"He was going to draw and shoot me," he said to Susan in the dark. "I had to defend myself. You'll understand and it'll be alright. Once we're married and living a high life, this will just be something to laugh at as a silly experience we had when we were young. Good night, Susan; sleep well, and I'll see you in the morning."

Susan lay awake shivering with fear and staring at the dark room. *How long before he killed her, or worse, made her marry him and live the rest of her life as his wife?* she thought.

She could hear Ryan's deep breathing and knew he was asleep. She struggled with the rope, but only succeeded in making it tighter until her hands were numb with the restricted blood flow. Her mind raced with every horrible thought that could happen to her and what had happened to poor Gene. She had liked him; he was gentle and had been kind to her. Even the Indians seemed to have been better than this.

A thunder storm moved over the valley in the night, bringing a sudden downpour of rain. It rain hard for some time then moved off, leaving Susan shaking with a damp chill. It was almost an ominous sign of things to come. Even the early morning was overcast and dark, but Ryan was up before dawn.

He let Susan loose to do her morning toiletries and eat some breakfast while he ate and made preparations to assault the mountain. The sky was turning grey when he tied her hands to the bedpost again.

"Don't worry, my love. You'll calm down when you rest, and life will be back to normal soon." He kissed her forehead before leaving for the rock wall.

Susan hung her head and cried for some time until she heard a shuffle and scrape on the outside wall. It was still early dawn, and she had visions of Indians finding her tied and helpless. She looked around, hopelessly trying to find someone or something to help her.

A dark figure appeared in the doorway and cast a shadow over her. She screamed helplessly, knowing the only help she could expect would be from Ryan, and even though he was too far away to hear her, she was deathly afraid of him, also.

Chapter 5

ene's head was a throbbing mass of pain, and his breath was restricted by his shirt sleeve where his arm lay over his face. He tried to move, but his body did not want to respond. He remembered the evening before and how Ryan had shot him, and he forced himself to shift his arm. He had to move, he had to get up, and he had to find Ryan and help Susan.

He managed to move his arm from his nose, but dirt fell onto his face, smothering him again. It was wet and slippery, and he was damp with moisture that was covering him. He moved his head lower to breathe, and a wave of nausea swept over him as stars exploded in his head.

Panic set in, and he tried to roll over. He met resistance one way but, when he tried to the other way, he managed to roll onto his stomach and found a pocket of air to breathe in. He gasped at the air, filling his lungs, and then he gathered his strength and pushed upwards and outwards away from the restriction.

He pushed up into the dark until his head came out of the dirt and he could breathe. Rain was pouring from the sky and washed his exposed head. The cool water helped clear his mind and eased the ache in his head. He gathered his strength and again pushed up into a sitting position. The movement brought a throb to his head and stars again went off in his brain, but the rain was reviving him. It was too dark to see where he was, but he could hear the roar of the river and realized he was very close to it.

Ryan must have dumped me over the bank, he thought. His mind refused to admit that his boyhood friend had just tried to murder him for the gold and a girl. Even so, he realized he had to be careful not to be seen, because Ryan now considered him dead and would be totally unpredictable if he knew Gene was alive.

He rolled over and pushed himself up on all fours and crawled out of the dirt before falling at the edge of the river. His head and one shoulder landed in the water, but the sudden cold shocked him and revived him. He pushed himself up again and crawled back to the bank where he could rest before climbing out of the river bottom.

He dozed fitfully until he forced himself awake. He had to get to his horse or somewhere under cover before daylight, in case Ryan came to check on him in the morning. He crawled up the bank and managed to stagger through the meadow and into the barn. He collapsed into a pile of old, musty hay and passed out again.

When Gene woke again he struggled to the door and saw the faint light in the east announcing the coming dawn. He checked his belt but found no gun, and his pocket knife was missing. Everything was in the house, and Ryan would be waking up and coming out soon; he had to hide. He watched as Ryan and Susan came outside and did their toiletries, then he hurried out of the barn and hid in the surrounding brush until he saw Ryan saddle his horse and start for the rock wall.

He had to move now. He knew Ryan would be at the wall all day, but he had to get Susan and get away far enough to outrun Ryan when he returned and found them gone. He staggered through the grass and brushed against the house wall before he found the door and pushed inside.

Susan screamed from her bed and Gene hurried to her side. "Susan......Susan, it's me, Gene. Stop screaming; you're alright," he called. She stopped screaming when she recognized his voice.

"Gene? You're alive! But......but...I saw him shoot you in the head. Oh, my go...you're his ghost. Please, don't hurt me," she whimpered.

"Shush now. I ain't dead, though I do have a whopper of a headache. I still can't believe he shot me," he said while he untied her hands.

She sat up on her own and looked at him. The long red gash above his eye and running back his temple showed her that he had only been grazed. The rain had washed the blood and dirt away, leaving him pale and haggard. Overwhelmed, she reached out her hand and touched his face. He stopped and turned to look at her. She kissed him lightly on the lips. "I'm glad he didn't kill you."

"Yeh, me too," he said awkwardly, trying to hide his embarrassment and the surprising excitement of her kiss. "We got to get out of here before he comes back."

He left her to gather her things and went to the back wall, curious about the bullet that almost took his life. He found it flattened against the back wall. Taking his knife that Ryan had left on the table, he pried the bullet out of the wall.

Just then the sun came over the horizon and shone through the door, lighting up the back wall and showing Gene a shiny yellow hole where the bullet had been. Curious, he dug the point of the knife in and made the hole bigger. The bigger the hole became, the bigger the yellow glow became.

"Well, I'll be," he exclaimed excitedly. "We been living beside a wall of gold all this time, and lookin' everywhere else but here for it. Come see, Susan."

She walked to him and looked over his shoulder. "I've never seen gold before. It looks like shiny butter."

They busied themselves getting ready to leave, but Gene determined he was going to take some gold with them. It was a rich wall, almost pure gold, and it came away easily with little effort. Gene worked while Susan watched for Ryan, and by noon they had four of the five pack mules loaded with their things and 400 pounds of gold in burlap bags. With Ryan in the valley, they had no intention of ever returning for more gold, so they took most of the pack animals. They left one for Ryan to take some gold out, knowing he would return for more later.

By taking the gold out they had made a large circle in the wall, which was still showing pure gold.

Ryan had not returned but, just as they mounted to leave, they heard a shot from the direction of the rock wall. Gene drew his hand gun, but no one appeared. He led Susan and the pack mules out over the narrow trail he had found while making his way to the top with the climbing ropes.

Ryan rode up to the rock wall just as the sun was coming over the horizon. It didn't take him long to find the ropes and scout out a way up the cliff. He worked half the morning combing the cliff side, trying one trail after another, always to dead ends.

The more he failed the angrier he became, and his thoughts became more violent as he thought of all the things he would do to Susan or, if he could, to Gene.

It was almost noon when he followed a thin, precarious ledge into the rock crack. He came to a wall at the end and was about to turn back when he spotted an indent in the rock between his feet. He balanced himself and bent over to look at it. It was a fossilized footprint pressed into the rock. It had been made by a boot while it was still soft from the sun's heat. Excitedly, he knelt down and studied it, looking in the direction it was going. He noticed an overhanging lip he couldn't see while he was standing. It was knee high, and by crawling he could go under it to a dark hole on the other side. He scrambled through into the hole and found he could stand up inside a large cave. He lit a match, and the light showed him a pile of old wooden crates and canvas bags. On top of the bags was a pile of shiny gold coins.

His hands shook excitedly as he gathered some of the coins and bit one. It was soft and obviously made of gold. He found an old pitch torch on the floor and lit it. He shoved it into a crack in the wall and dug into the bags, revealing more gold coins, gold bars and gold ornaments.

Here is my gold fortune, Ryan thought, *and I'll finally get to live the way I deserve.*

He stuffed as many of the coins into his pockets as he could and gathered up what ornaments he could get on himself. He found a heavy, thick gold necklace and put it on around his neck. The last thing he picked up was a beautiful ornamented gold crown that he slipped on his wrist before crawling back out to the ledge.

He was admiring the crown when he stood up and only noticed the movement on the facing rock wall after taking a step to the edge of the ledge. An Indian was on a similar ledge across the opening, holding a bow and notching an arrow.

Surprise slowed Ryan down, and he was late getting his gun out. It went off pointing at the ground as the arrow impaled his chest. He took a staggering step forward and his foot came down on open air. Slowly, he leaned out and fell from the ledge, turning as he fell to land behind a large boulder blocking the crack from the rest of the world. Totally hidden, he died looking back up to his cave of golden treasure.

The Apache scout, sent to check on this valley for their escaped white girl, lowered his bow and smiled broadly. *He would be praised as a warrior for this kill,* he thought as he turned to go back down the ledge. The rock gave way beneath his feet and he slipped, losing his balance. His grasping hands caught a rock outcrop, and he placed his weight on it while trying to swing back in against the wall. At the crest of his swing, the outcrop broke away in his hand, and he sailed out away from the wall. He turned in the air as he fell and landed on a rock pinnacle, right side up so it impaled him and left him dead, staring at the valley ten feet below him.

The next morning, a shadow appeared in the doorway of the rock house, then another and another. They moved around the room, studying the living arrangements of the white men and the girl. They were totally engrossed when the sun burst over the horizon and the back wall of the house was lit up with a shiny golden orb of light.

The Apaches had never seen such light and fell on their knees, thinking it was the son of the sun god. The chief decided the white man who had captured their white squaw had to be the son of the sun god to live here in the sun god's house, and he quickly sent runners to call his braves back from chasing the white man and woman, hoping to stop them before the sun god became angry with them.

He declared the valley sacred ground and, when he found his dead scout, brought gifts and offerings to the house. He left the obviously god- killed scout on his pinnacle and offered gifts there, also in the hopes of appeasing the sun god.

Chapter 6

Susan rode beside Gene as they rode away from the house. The pack mules were well rested and followed willingly. Gene made for the steep and treacherous path he had descended after placing the ropes yesterday. Weighed down with Susan's tired horse and the heavy packed mules, he didn't want to take the chance on the old familiar trail where Ryan could catch them. Crossing the valley, Gene held the group down to conserve their strength for the climb. They were going to need it.

The morning birds sang, and the small animals rustled in the underbrush, making small sounds that mixed with the wind and gave the day a surreal feeling of peace and safety. It belied the danger Gene knew they would be in if Ryan knew he was still alive. It's one thing to murder your best friend with no one to know; it's quite another to have that best friend escape alive and tell others.

Gene had no disillusions about how adamant Ryan would be to kill them both.

They made their way across the valley with no sign of Ryan and arrived at the narrow trail leading up the side of the mountain. Gene had no idea where the trail went or how they would get over the mountains and back to the town, south of them.

Buckshot remembered their climb of yesterday and laid his ears back on his head, not wanting to repeat the ordeal. Gene urged him up to the start of the trail and dismounted. He unlashed his lariat and walked back to Susan's horse. She watched him apprehensively, glancing up at the steep climb doubtfully.

"Is...is there no other way," she asked hesitantly.

Gene shook his head and immediately regretted it. Pain shot through his brain and down his neck, reminding him he was wounded. He waited for it to subside and said, "I found this way out yesterday. We have come across no other ways in or out, and we have been looking at this valley all summer. We don't have the time to search. If Ryan finds us, he'll kill the both of us."

He looped the lariat around her horse's neck while he talked and, giving her a small grin, said, "Don't worry. God looks after the innocent and the fools, and that means us. I didn't see him losing his mind over gold until yesterday."

Sadly, he stopped his work and continued, looking at her while a tear slipped down his cheek. "We were best friends since we were toddlers growing up together. We were inseparable and always had each other's back. The lust for gold and wealth poisoned him inside, and he finally snapped yesterday. I should have seen it coming. He's been getting crankier all summer, but I missed it. I should have done something to stop it."

His plight tugged at Susan's heart, and she softly said, "I've only been here a short time, but I didn't see anything wrong with him until he turned on you. You couldn't know what he was thinking, and he was your best friend. You trusted him, and he failed you as well as himself. You can't take the blame for his thoughts."

He looked at her intently and shuddered. He said, "You're right, I guess. I don't know...." His voice trailed off as he stood staring at the ground.

Susan glanced back nervously and softly said, "Maybe we should try to get up this trail and onto a better path."

Gene looked up at her blankly, and she watched reason clear his vision. "You're right," he said as he turned back to his horse with the lead rope in his hand.

He mounted and looked at her over Buckshot's rump and said, "Buckshot has been over this yesterday and knows the trail. I'll keep a tight pull on the lariat and keep your horse from slipping. The mules will follow. They're as sure footed as Buckshot and won't have any trouble, but your horse is tired and may need a little tug."

He turned back around before she could see the worry on his face. He was not sure her horse could make it at all, but it had to, even if he had to drag it over the top. He urged Buckshot onto the trail, and they slowly started their assent. The surefooted mules crowded Susan's horse and helped encourage it onto the difficult climb.

Buckshot put his nose close to the dirt on the trail and dug his toes into the trail, scrambling up like a dog with his belly close to the ground. Susan's horse saw his efforts and did the same. The mules close behind did not give her horse any room to fall back, and it struggled valiantly up the incline. It seemed to take forever, but they climbed one foot at a time, inching their way to the top.

Gene kept his head down, concentrating on helping Buckshot climb the trail, and only knew he was at the top when he suddenly saw it appear before Buckshot's nose. He thrilled with exhilaration and turned to tell Susan they were at the top — just in time to see her horse go down.

The brief warning was enough for him to throw a loop of his lariat over his saddle horn and throw his weight ahead on Buckshot's neck before the down horse's weight hit the end of his rope. The floundering horse started to roll sideways and back towards the long fall hundreds of feet below. The mules bulked behind it and scrambled to get out of its way so they would not be swept off the trial and the mountain.

The horse slid and rolled as Susan screamed and grabbed desperately for anything to keep from falling off the horse, her only hope of escaping the long drop to the valley floor she hung over. The rope tightened and strained with the combined weight of horse and rider. The horse's head snapped upright, and its shoulders rolled and stopped, hanging out over the drop off by its rump and the tight rope. Susan hung by her legs and one hand on the horse's bridle while her other hand flapped wildly out in the open air.

Gene was practically climbing up Buckshot's head while the tough little pony dug its toes in and held the great weight from falling to the horse and rider's crushing death. His weight helped balance the horse, and he inched his way up the trail dragging the floundering pair back onto the trail. Susan's horse gathered its feet back under it and lay on the trail, quivering while Susan lay across its head and shoulders to distribute her weight on the uphill side.

"Beat him!" Gene said through clinched teeth. "Beat him. He's got to get up. If he doesn't get up now, you'll both start slipping back down the trail and go over the drop off."

The rope was vibrating and humming with tension as Susan kicked her horse's side and screamed in its ear. The horse struggled to rise; its knees buckled, and it slipped down the trail, loosing precious inches of safe ground and getting closer to a sure death.

Susan screamed hysterically and used her fists to strike at the horse's head. It lurched onto its knees again and heaved a ghastly sigh as it flung itself up on its toes and over the top behind the surging Buckshot. The mules crowded up behind the exhausted horse and gathered safely over the top on a small level clearing.

Gene loosened the rope and let it fall as he bounded back to Susan's horse and helped her down. He smiled reassuringly and left her clinging to his saddle while he took the rope off the horse's neck so it could take great gasps of air and he started walking it in a small circle. If it didn't stay moving now, it would overheat and die a slow, lingering death as its heart cooked itself.

He spent a quarter of an hour moving and rubbing the horse while it regained its breath and cooled down. At the same time he was glancing back down the trail, looking for signs of Ryan coming after them. At least here he could shoot it out with Ryan, having the advantage of high ground, but he was not sure he could actually pull the trigger on his former friend.

Susan remained silent, watching him work with her horse. She was not as familiar with Ryan as Gene was, and did not know what he was capable of doing or not doing. She did know she didn't want any more to do with Ryan.

Gene stopped walking her horse and said, "We had better walk with them for a while until he regains his strength. It's still a long ways back to town, and we don't know how soon Ryan will find out we're gone and come after us."

Susan nodded her assent and reached for the reins of her horse.

Gene held them back and said, "No, you ride Buckshot, and I'll walk. You're still weak from your ordeal, too." He reached in his saddlebag and found his moccasins. They would be easier on his feet than riding boots and give him more sure footing in this high ground.

Susan mounted Buckshot, and the group started off, following the only game trail in sight as it wound around the top of the hills and along the dizzying heights overlooking their Golden Valley far below.

By noon, Gene was foot soar and blistered, so they stopped to rest. The going was slow and laborious through dips and rocky outcrops. The air was thin at this height, and he was breathing raggedly, as were the horses. Buckshot and the mules were holding up, but Susan's horse was struggling badly.

They had to ride and make up some time before night caught them with its cold grip on the heights. Gene motioned for Susan to ride her horse. She was the lightest and would be the easiest for the horse to carry.

The afternoon sun punished horse and rider alike as it seemed to laugh at their pitiful struggle to find a way down the far side of the mountain. The game trail moved steadily along the top with no side trails branching off either side. They had to find a way down soon, because they were getting no closer to the town travelling parallel to it. Occasionally they could look through gaps in the surrounding hills and see far enough to make out the dust cloud which constantly hung over the town, three days journey away.

Gene found himself pulling harder and harder on Susan's horse's lead rope as its energy failed. They had switched three times, riding and walking with Gene leading Susan's horse while she rode Buckshot. He and the mules were rested and fine, but her horse had been through a lot and it was failing fast.

By nightfall they came upon a faint game trail leading out and down to the side of the mountain, where they needed to go in order to make the trip to the town. Gene and Ryan had not scouted the area for more towns or dwellings, so Gene did not know if any place was near to provide shelter. He knew where the town was and set his mind to reaching it for safety.

They couldn't get down the steep sloop in the growing dark, so they watered the animals from their canteens and picketed them on a grassy knoll before bedding down behind some boulders to catch whatever sleep they could. Gene lay listening to the night sounds, unable to sleep in spite of the exhausting day he just had. He rolled the thought of Ryan's betrayal over and over in his mind, but failed to understand the deadly worm that was eating at his brain. Greed, power, selfish lust... he had heard all these things preached about back home in church, but they never seemed real until now.

How does one go and let these evil ideas and wicked thoughts take away their reason and sanity, especially one's best friend? He looked to the heavens where he had always heard God lived and whispered, "Lord, God. My pastor said you were always within hearing distance of those who pray and.....well....I guess I'm prayin' to ya. I don't understand the worm or devil that took Ryan, but I don't want it to happen ta me. I don't think I'm strong enough to fight off no spirit or any of those things, so could you help me? I need your help, and Susan needs your help. We ain't strong people like some are, and I heard you take kindly to the weak, so I'd like to have you on our side, please."

He thought about his prayer for a few seconds and added, "If there's any hope of Ryan gettin' sane again, could you help him with that? I miss our friendship and hope we can make amends. Thanks for listenin', Lord. Amen."

He hadn't known Susan could hear him until he heard a soft 'amen' come from her bedroll beside him.

"Thought you might be sleepin' after the time you had today," he said softly.

She replied, "I tried, but the things you prayed about were bothering me, too. I don't know how God could let someone go crazy like that. Isn't He supposed to love us?"

"I always heard that, but does love force someone to love them back and make them into kind, caring people when they got other things they want to do? Ryan fell in love with the thought of havin' all that gold and forgot the important things. He just acted out his wants and forgot to stop himself, I guess," Gene reasoned.

Susan rolled over on her elbow and looked at him. They were not too far apart, and he could see her eyes were wide and staring. She asked, "How come you didn't want the gold and go crazy, too?"

Gene thought for a while and then answered. "I just couldn't feel right hurtin' anybody for a yellow rock. We'uns back in Maine alus worked hard for what we got, and me and Ryan was workin' for that gold but hurtin people is not work; it's wrong."

"If you didn't want it, why did you take that gold out o' the wall then?" Susan pushed him.

Gene hesitated again before answering. "Well, when we come out here, we wanted to get rich so we could go back home and start a business to help our folks get by easier. That map said the gold was just layin' there waitin' fur someone to come along and pick it up, but we was still workin' for what we got. We had to search around and spent time crawlin' over rocks and climbing cliffs and such; but, when you take somethin' at the point of a gun, you're forcin' them out of what they worked for, and it ain't honest work anymore."

Susan said quietly, "Like you said, God don't force love at the point of a gun, because it won't be honest."

"Yeh, I guess. If it ain't right, why, I guess it ain't worth the gettin'," Gene summarized.

Susan quickly leaned over and kissed him. The kiss was a lingering, meaningful statement, which Gene returned.

When she pulled back she said, "Well, you got me out o' that valley safe, and I hope I ain't wrong for appreciatin' it."

Gene quietly said, "No, Ma'am, That didn't feel a bit wrong. Thank you for your appreciation."

Susan laughed softly. "You're welcome, and don't call me "ma'am." My name is Susan, and you get used to callin' me that."

The trip down off the mountain and across the plain didn't seem nearly as long as Gene thought it was, and it ended all too soon for the pair. They were married as soon as they found a preacher who could perform the ceremony, and they went back to Maine to start a business to help their kin folks and community prosper and grow.

The gold they took out of the wall was gone all too soon and turned into industry, community and society, but the gold they found in their hearts lasted through the generations, passed down from one generation and taught to the next in an ever-growing spread of wealth.

Epilogue

The growl of the tough little motor as it finally made its way through the meadow and up to the front of the rock house was the only sound heard in the valley. The birds and animals all stopped to watch this strange vehicle that had invaded their territory.

Chaplain, Major Douglas Gene Porter, wearily stepped out of the Jeep he had driven from the nearest town. He turned and admired the tough little four-wheel drive vehicle.

These Willys Jeeps will be a great asset to our boys on the front, he thought. *I would never have made it in here with any other vehicle.*

He had spent all day on the short drive and hard climb getting into their family's Golden Valley. His namesake, Great Great Grandfather Gene Porter, had started the family businesses and, in his will, specified that Golden Valley was to remain a family heirloom forever. They were never to sell it or change it. It was his and Great Great Grandmother Susan Porter's Christian faith that had inspired Douglas to become a Christian and join the Chaplain Service. He was making his first visit to their precious valley before being shipped out to the Second World War in Europe.

He grabbed his duffle bag full of supplies and headed into the house, cut into the rock wall of the side of the valley. It was already late, and he had to prepare a meal, so he watched the beautiful valley go dark while he leisurely ate his evening meal. He took an evening walk after sundown and enjoyed the quiet valley while talking with his God. He went right to bed afterward and slept soundly, waking just before sunup.

As was his habit, Major Porter was up before dawn, had a fire going and his breakfast cooked. He seldom hurried, and thought it a waste of time to worry, so breakfast was a leisurely luxury, enjoyed while he read his Bible.

The Eastern sky was a dull gray when he packed his last utensils away for the trip home, and he strode to the doorway and leaned on the door jamb to welcome the coming daylight.

His last cup of coffee was sipped while he watched the sun drench the valley in a golden glow in the morning fog, oblivious to the dull yellow glow on the wall behind him. The bat droppings, spider webs and dust faded the yellow to a dirty grey in the daylight hours.

"Golden Valley indeed; it's beautiful. God, you've made a golden treasure here, and I won't change a thing." He spoke familiarly to his God. "I wish I had the time to explore its wonders and learn its splendour, but it will take me too long to return from here, and I must go to Europe."

An hour later, the roar of the Willy's motor told of his departure. He was happy he had learned the true value of the golden wealth in his valley, just like his grandparents had before him.

He Knew How to Drive Truck

Chapter 1

Abby Waite, short for Abigail, sat in the front row of the large auditorium. She was staring at the smiling face of her husband of fifteen years, Sheldon Waite, on the podium in front of her.

Their children sat beside her on hard metal chairs: fourteen year old Denny, twelve year old Gail (Abigail too, but Abby disliked her nickname and had been determined there would only be one Abby, much to her husband's teasing delight), and the eight year old twin girls, Brie and Anne. It sounded like one person when she called them both at the same time. Her husband was a hero and was being honoured at the school auditorium in Benton, British Columbia.

The auditorium was full to capacity, with the center aisle looking like a biker gang as her husband's trucker friends all thought dressing up was done with black leather, ball caps and western boots. The home town of Benton filled the auditorium's right side, and the visiting town of South Flats filled the left. The front seats on the South Flats side were full of young children who attended this school. Their school bus driver and his wife sat with them, occasionally wiping away the odd tear that trickled from their eyes.

The silent crowd sat listening to the owner of Millennium Overland Transport Company as he said some wonderful things about Sheldon. Abby had a hard time believing him when she heard words like *serious*, *dedicated*, *on time* and *professional*. She was remembering a teasing, fun-loving man who always seemed to be tangled in a group of wrestling children and getting the worst of it.

Sheldon had slept in. The rest had felt good, and the house was quiet with the kids on their last day of school before the Christmas holidays. He could hear Abby in the kitchen cleaning up after the kids. He smiled playfully and threw on his robe while he hurried to the kitchen. He slipped quietly through the door and crept up behind his wife.

"Don't even think about it," she said without turning. "Don't you dare tickle me this morning!"

She jumped away as his fingers touched her ribs, and he laughed while she tried hard to frown.

"You faker," Sheldon chided. "You know you like the attention."

"Not when you tickle me," she replied, slowly backing away.

"Give me a hug then and I'll be happy," he conceded and she slipped into his embrace.

"No morning-breath kiss, either; not 'til you brush," she murmured, snuggling closer.

"You're just so mean," he laughed and hugged her closer.

"When do you have to leave?" she changed the subject.

"Soon, I guess. They're calling for bad snow squalls and wet flurries starting this afternoon, and I have to be in Vancouver by midnight. They have me on an express post load with some deliveries for tomorrow. We wouldn't want those Christmas presents to be late," he said, soberly.

"You be careful," she chided him. "You know the mountains can turn treacherous very quickly."

She had travelled with him often enough to know the dangers he drove through, and she always worried when the weather was going to be bad.

"You're going to get all wrinkled up worryin' about me. Hey, I'm the best there is, and I've got God looking out for me to boot. He and I can bring it through in one piece and on time, too," he blustered, but Abby knew he was a good driver and would be cautious in the bad weather.

An hour later he fired up his Freightliner truck and filled in his log book.

His run took him over the Rocky Mountains, but he'd equipped his Columbia style Freightliner with a small block Detroit set at 460 horsepower with an eighteen speed double over transmission and heavy duty 430 rears with the triple lock ups. His tire chains hung on the frame behind the cab, but he also ran winter deep tires that grabbed the road and hung on for good traction.

He'd run this truck five days every week for five years, and he knew every nut and bolt personally. The only thing he couldn't do with it was fly, but he made good time by being consistent. It was a comfortable truck to handle; it rode like a car due to the setback front axle softening most of the bumps and potholes before the impact got to him. He hadn't spilt any coffee in a long time. Sheldon smiled at this thought. He liked his coffee; even if he drank it weak it still tasted good.

He arrived at the Post Office by noon and was pre-tripped and ready to go by one o'clock. The snow was just starting when he pulled out onto the street and pointed the loaded transport towards the mountains. He couldn't see them three hours away, but he had been doing this run for most of his driving career and knew it almost as well as he knew his truck.

Once outside the city limits, he locked up the cruise control at sixty-five mph and took another sip of coffee. The prairie was flat all the way to the foothills, and he could see for miles.

A chorus he made up when he was newly saved came back to him, and he started humming its tune.

I'm going home, I'm going home, I'm going home soon to be with my Lord. I've run...hummmmmm, hum, hum.

'Well, well. I've forgotten a few lines, Lord. Maybe you could help me remember them," he said to God.

When he was saved, they told him God was his heavenly father. He knew he could call his earthly father on the phone and have a conversation with him, so he thought he should be able to do it with his heavenly father. He started talking to God and learned to hear Him talk back.

They had long talks every day, especially when Sheldon spent so much time alone with God.

He snapped on the radio to get the weather forecast while his eyes constantly scanned the road looking for dangers. He never failed to check his mirrors every few seconds for fast approaching cars. He'd had many problems overtake him from behind, so he'd learned to spot them and be ready to avoid those bad drivers. The snowflakes were getting bigger.

Ken Murphy was late. He was a semiretired truck driver and drove school bus in the winter. He picked up the younger elementary school students in South Flats and bussed them to the school in Benton, halfway through the Rocky Mountains.

His bus had mechanical problems, and the spare was out of service, so he had had to limp around with his sputtering bus to get the kids to school for the last day before Christmas break. He had arrived an hour late to deliver his children at Benton Elementary and made his way to the shop. He'd been asking for new tires and was hoping to get them at the same time.

His day was not going well. Mack had been too busy to get to him in the morning and had only found the problem a short time ago. His phone call to the auto parts store was no help. The parts Ken needed for his bus wouldn't be here for another hour, and it would take a couple of hours to put them on. His new tires would have to wait until the New Year.

Ken slumped dejectedly into a chair in the waiting room. He would have to call the school and see if a couple of teachers could stay and care for his kids until he could get the bus going and pick them up. He had no doubt some of them would stay. They were good teachers who loved their kids.

Ken noticed the snow while he was frowning over his problems. It was getting heavier and falling faster. There must be almost six inches on the ground now, but he saw the town snowplows moving quickly to keep the streets open.

It would have started as rain in South Flats, Ken thought, *but Danny Taylor will be salting the mountain long before I get there.*

A devoted Christian, Ken also drove the church bus on Sundays to take those who could not drive to Sunday school. He had made many half-hearted attempts to get all the children on his school bus to Sunday school, but most of their parents wouldn't send them. Most attended the church for the Christmas and Good Friday services, but had other things to do the rest of the year. Their comments to Ken rang in his ears: "they're young and have all their lives ahead of them to come to God and attend church" or "they can go to church later" or "I'm not going to push religion on my kids." Oh, he'd managed to get a few going to Sunday school, but most always found reasons not to go. His wife, Beth, taught every Sunday, and Ken would help her or one of the other teachers with their class when there were too many students for one person. All the school kids and their parents knew he was a Christian and respected him for it, but they just could not see a need for Christ in their lives just yet.

Mack was finished with his bus by five o'clock, two hours late, and he hurried to the school for his sixty-two children as the sky darkened with sunset. The heavy, wet snow was piled a foot deep where the snowplows hadn't gone but he knew the roads would be well cared for.

The maintenance garage manager, Doug Banks, had told Danny Taylor to sleep in, and he had done just that. The snow would start as rain here in South Flats but would freeze on the mountain road and change to wet snow and then blowing snow as it got dark and the night turned colder. It would be a long night of driving, salting and plowing.

There would not be a lot of traffic this close to Christmas, though. Everyone would be staying in town to shop, and most of the mountain towns would be doing the same thing. Around here everyone knew a snow storm could be a treacherous thing in the mountains and would stay home until it was over. The only thing moving in a bad storm would be the mail and a few delivery vehicles.

Danny looked in on his sleeping twin five month old girls on his way by to his breakfast. He stood for a few minutes admiring them.

I suppose this means Jane will be pestering me about going to church, he thought, as he reached in one crib to recover one of the girls.

Jane, his wife, was a quiet and dedicated church girl. He used to attend church regularly when they were first married, but had let his attendance slip for sleeping in and sports games. They were young, yet, and had the rest of their lives to get ready for God and heaven.

He would have a long time to help his girls with their Sunday school lessons, he thought as he turned and headed for the kitchen where he heard Jane setting the table for his meal.

She looked up and smiled at him from her place by the stove. "Good morning, Sleepy Head." Her voice was so gentle and soft that many who met her thought her meek and fearful, but Danny knew how firm she could be.

"That bacon and eggs sure smells good. I'll need it tonight. Doug thinks it's going to be an all-nighter," he said, reaching for a coffee mug and the fresh pot of coffee.

Her smile disappeared. "I know you will be careful; you don't need me to remind you, but the girls and I could not go on without you, you know."

Danny laughed. "I'll be around for a long time yet. I'm only twenty-three; don't put me over the hill just yet."

"I know," she responded, "but scripture says we have no promise of tomorrow, and I worry when you're out there on the mountain at night."

Danny shrugged. He avoided talk of scripture as much as he could, because he felt guilty. She was a devoted Christian and had married him thinking he was also. It disappointed her that he was not a faithful church attender and not be interested in Bible study like he used to be.

It was starting to rain when Danny arrived at the maintenance garage to start his truck. It was a monster six ton Mack with dual steer axles. It had a V front plow and a wing plow on either side. Where he travelled between rain, ice and snow in every trip, the province had put "live" chains on the truck's back tires. A switch on the dash put them down under his tires in a second even when he was moving fast.

He had personally put four lights across the top of his cab that gave off one hundred watts of light each. With the truck's normal high/low headlights and the blade's high/low lights, he could light up the night and see better than in daylight.

Doug was standing in the doorway to his office when Danny punched the clock. "You'll be on your own tonight. Dick's truck is down and won't be out of the shop for three days, and Red has to watch everything in the valley. He'll be out west of town all night. You got the mountain all to yourself."

Danny grunted and took another sip of coffee. He looked at the spare truck that was in pieces all over the garage floor. "We can handle it," he said confidently.

He was swinging out of the yard an hour later, full of fuel, salt and sand and ready for his first run. He normally made one run over the mountain road laying down a center strip of salt while he winged the snow back at a fast clip. On his second run, he would plow the snow back on one side at a time, while the first salting spread over the road. After that he would salt and plow as the road needed it for the rest of the night.

Danny was remembering his sleeping girls and feeling good about his life. *God will come later,* he thought to himself, content for now just to be having everything else that life could offer.

He looked out at the mountains past the beating windshield wipers. It was hazy with low clouds and rain mixing with snow higher up.

An hour from the base of the mountain, where the road took a turn and hid it from view, the Mack's motor went silent and died.

"What the..." he exclaimed. He pulled to the side of the road and cranked the motor over, trying to restart it. It burled busily but refused to fire.

Danny grabbed the two way radio and called. "Doug, you got a copy on me?"

A second later Doug answered. "Yeah, Danny boy. S'up?"

"I'm dead in the water, Doug. She just died. You want to send Bobby out with the shop truck and get me rollin' again?" Danny said.

"Shoot!" Doug exploded. "Bobby is out to Red's truck. He's broke down on the other side of town. Any idea what could be wrong? Can Dick fix it if I sent him out in the pick-up?"

"Give me a minute and I'll take a look. I'll get back to you." Danny slid out of the truck and opened the hood. He reached in and started moving hoses and pulling belts, looking for anything that was not right.

Fifteen minutes later he found the broken fuel line hose.

Back in the cab, Danny radioed the garage. "Doug. Doug, you copy?"

"I'm here, Danny. What do you need?" Doug radioed back.

"Could you send someone here with a half inch hose joint and some ether? I found a cut in my fuel line. Did Bobby get back?" Bobby was a good mechanic, but Danny knew he would have to repair it himself if Dick came out. Dick was a nice guy, but he didn't know squat about mechanics.

"Sorry, Danny. It will be a couple hours. Dick had to run some parts out to Bobby. As soon as he gets back, I'll send him your way. Should we call the RCMP and have them close the mountain road, or do you think it will be alright until you're going?" Doug's voice was heavy with concern.

"Hold off for now," Danny replied. "Not much traffic out here, and everyone knows it's going to get worse. They'll be driving slow and careful."

He hung the mike back on the dash and settled in to wait.

The rain turned to snow before Dick arrived with his parts.

Chapter 2

Abby looked at Denny's girlfriend sitting beside him. Sharon Blackhawk was a tall, thin native girl of thirteen. She had grown up beside them, and she and Denny had bickered with each other constantly until she reached the age of twelve and matured into a beautiful young girl. She sat close to him now, quite respectful and far more mature than most other young teenage girls.

Sheldon had teased the two of them mercilessly, but he had often commented to Abby how proud he was of them both. Her father was a trapper and an honourable Christian man, and her mother was a beautiful, dedicated wife and mother to Sharon and her five brothers and one sister. They were good neighbours, even though the town looked down on native people.

Sharon was a top athlete, and she had drawn Denny from his studies and into a more physical world. Together they went hiking, canoeing and trapping with her dad. Denny had reciprocated by helping her with her schoolwork. He was a straight A student and was bringing her marks up in the hopes she could get an athletic scholarship and take nursing. Denny was going into medicine, and they wanted to be a team as well as a married couple.

They smiled as they endured the constant teasing of not only Sheldon, but their brothers and sisters as well. Both families were very happy the two had decided to be with each other. Their involvement in the church youth group had brought many more of the local teens to their activities.

Abby had seen more than one heated Bible discussion with Denny, Sharon and the girls around their kitchen table. She again looked at the smiling face of her husband and knew he had a great pride in how his kids were serving God in their lives. He had been the greatest influence on them, and Abby murmured a small prayer of thanksgiving to God for having Denny in their lives.

Sheldon was still trying to remember the words to his song while he drove across the flat prairie towards the mountains. He couldn't seem to get them, even though he remembered the tune. The snow was clogging up his wipers occasionally, and he had to reach out his side window and catch the driver's side wiper as it reached its peak and give it a quick snap to clear it of snow balls.

He met the snow plows clearing away the heavy wet snow and was following them, making good time. By the time he reached the foothills, the snow was closing in his vision, and he had to drive carefully because of the cars travelling close to the center of the road. The snow was starting to get a little deeper here as the snowplows were having a more difficult time keeping up with it.

He was still making good time when he hit the first climb into the mountains. The traffic was getting less as more people went home early to avoid the storm. The snowplows had dumped a lot of salt on the hills, and it left Sheldon a clear center strip to put one side of his tires on when he climbed them.

Benton was only an hour away, and he hoped more people had left early there, too. He was going to go through just about supper time and didn't want a lot of traffic around him in this snow. The higher he climbed up the mountain, the deeper the snow was on the shoulder of the road and where the snowplows had not gone. It was turning into a bad snowstorm, and Sheldon was thankful for the dedicated and punctual snow plow drivers.

"You got everybody in place to keep your people save, haven't you God?" he said out loud, confident in God's constant presence.

Sheldon snapped on the radio to the weather channel and listened for the news on this snowstorm. They warned everyone to stay off the roads if they could. It was going to be heavy wet snow all night. In some places it had rained first and frozen as the temperature dropped with approaching night. The ice was quickly covered with snow, but the snowplows were out, so everything should be fine.

He reached the edge of Benton shortly after five o'clock. The snowplows had been busy clearing and salting the town's streets. He'd run with his lights on as he always did in a snow storm, but the night darkness was closing in and he needed them now to see. On the far side, going out of town, Sheldon came upon the tracks of another big vehicle with duel tire marks, so he fit right into those tracks and followed them as the snow became deeper. It was nice to know that someone else thought the roads were okay to go.

By the time he reached the Rooftop Inn, he was following only one set of tracks, and the Inn's parking lot was full of the cars of people who had decided to stop and wait out the storm.

Must be a local driver or a delivery truck in front of him, Sheldon thought. *Anyone else would have stopped for the night. He must not think it will be too bad, though, if he's still goin'.*

He continued following the tracks, a darker grey in the snow as it got deeper and deeper. Benton was almost the halfway point through the mountains, and it was mostly downhill from here. He was content to trust God and this other driver, so he hummed to himself as he drove.

Ken took the time to count every one of his beloved children as they boarded his bus. He wanted to make sure he had them all before he closed the doors and started home. Their parents had been contacted and knew they would be late.

The windshield wipers thumped rhythmically as they cleared the snow and gained a clear vision of the fast approaching snowflakes and the ever increasing snow banks. It was swiftly growing darker, so Ken snapped on the buses lights. By the time they reached the edge of Benton, he was relying more on the headlights to see the road ahead.

The streets of Benton had been well cared for by their snowplows, but outside of town the roads showed deeper drifts and a heavier snowfall. By the time they reached the Rooftop Inn, just before the long twisting trail down the mountain, the snow was almost a foot deep, and there were fewer vehicle tracks for Ken to follow. The parking lot of the Inn was almost full of cars, as the owners had decided to stop and wait out the storm.

Ken started down the first hill, gearing down to let the heavy back tires drag and keep the bus's speed down. The snow was deep here, which puzzled Ken.

Danny should have had this cleared and salted by now, he thought. He grabbed the steering wheel as the drive tires locked temporarily and the bus slipped sideways. The children were watching the snow through the front window and screamed as the bus slipped sideways. The noise quickly subsided and turned to excitement as Ken straightened the bus and it proceeded down the road.

Shoot! That was ice. Where was Danny? Ken worried as he concentrated on the road. With a start, he noticed there were no more tracks in the snow in front of them. Everyone else had stopped, and they were alone pushing through fresh snow banks.

The snow helped, but a fully loaded school bus was not an easy thing to hold back on a hill. They were gradually picking up speed as they descended into the valley below. Turning the corner on the last steep hill, the bus' motor was straining at a high rev, and they were traveling slightly over the speed limit. Ken was sweating and began to pray. *Lord, we need your help here. Just one more hill and then we're on the level. Just one more hill, please? If you get us through this safe, I promise I'll work harder to get these kids and their parents to church so they can hear your word.*

This last hill was three miles long and had two turns close together in the middle. On the driver's side, the mountain lifted right out of the ditch and went straight up. A guard rail close to the road on the other side kept vehicles from leaving the road and going over a sharp drop off into the valley 500 feet below.

Ken's hands were wet with sweat when he arrived at the first turn. The kids thought it was fun and were cheering him on.

We're going too fast, he thought as he started around the turn. It looked like they were going to make it, but as he tried to straighten the bus in the short straight area before the next turn it refused to stop turning, and the back of the bus slid towards the guardrail.

The children screamed again as the bus slid faster into a skid and shuddered as the back end impacted the guardrail. Ken knew the back of the bus was now hanging out over the drop off as it scrapped and bumped on top of the guardrail.

"Please, Lord. We need your help. I meant what I said. I'll twist their parent's arm, if I have to, to get them to church." Ken whispered his prayer. Some of the children had fallen to the floor and were crying with fright, but the rest were watching the swinging lights and shaking bus with wonder.

The next post brought the bus to a sudden stop and reversed the back end's motion. It was now swinging back into a straight position, and Ken started to hope that God was bringing it out of its slew. He was sadly disappointed as the bus kept on going around and he watched the guardrail come into the headlight's glare.

The only thing he could do was lock up all the brakes on the wheels and hope they didn't roll them over the guardrail and off the cliff. Slowly, almost agonizingly, the bus kept turning. It missed the mountain wall behind them by inches as the back now hung over the small ditch between the road and the mountain. The front was sliding slowly, almost gently, closer to the guardrail in their headlights. It disappeared out of Ken's sight under the hood.

Ken's hands ached from holding the steering wheel so tightly, and sweat was running into his eyes. Slowly the bus continued to turn until it was rolling backwards in the downhill lane. Ken unlocked the brakes and pumped them vigorously to bring the bus to a complete stop.

Ken closed his eyes. *Thank you, God.* He heard a loud voice in his ear say, "I will expect you to keep your word."

"I will. I will," he promised and opened his eyes. His heart skipped and he caught his breath. He was looking back up the road they had just slid down as he watched a transport truck round the turn and barrel towards them.

Dick arrived with the parts he needed just as it was starting to get dark. Danny was ready to jump out of his truck when the radio squawked. "Danny, Danny. Is Dick there yet? What's the road like? Should I call the RCMP and get it closed at Benton?"

Danny grabbed the mike. "No. Dick just got here, but it should only take me about twenty minutes to fix it. I'll get back to you if there's any problem, but there is no traffic comin' off the mountain now."

He threw the mike on the dash and scrambled out to take the parts from Dick. He slid under his truck to repair his fuel line. He was sliding back into the truck twenty minutes later, to the minute. Dick stood by his raised hood with a can of ether ready to give the breather a shot when he turned the motor over.

Danny hit the key and, as the motor whirled, Dick sprayed the air filter. The motor roared to life and sat quietly idling while Dick started back to the pick-up and Danny called on the mike.

"Doug, we're going again."

"Good, good. I called the RCMP anyways and they're going to block the road at the Inn until you get it ready," Doug responded.

"Ok. Tell them to give me two hours and I'll get back to you," Danny shouted into the mike as he put the truck in gear and started away. He watched Dick turn and leave in his rear-view mirror.

The snow started by the time he reached the bottom of the first hill, but he had had to turn on the salt a mile back. The rain that had fallen before it turned to snow had frozen, and the road was covered with ice. Danny lowered his plow and wings while he drove and was taking the whole road in one pass. He snapped on his four top lights. With his regular lights, he could easily see everything for hundreds of yards in front of him. He was alone on the road; he shifted up another gear, hoping for a little more speed. He listened as his 600 horsepower motor lugged down and started torqueing under the load. His side blade lights showed snow billowing out from both wings.

Danny had to down shift as the hill got steeper, but he kept going as fast as he could. It wasn't like him not to be on the mountain and have it clear for other vehicles, but he saw no one. He rounded the first turn and froze. His heart jumped as he looked at the back end of a school bus staring at him from the downhill lane. Heading straight at it was a transport truck.

"Oh, God, they're all going to die!" he said out loud. He stopped his truck and, out of habit while meeting oncoming traffic, grabbed the left blade lever; he lifted the blade up and into the side of his truck. That's all he could do as he watched the tragedy unfold before his eyes. He completely forgot about his bright lights as he held his breath, waiting for the impact.

Chapter 3

bby let her eyes slowly move around the room. These people owed her husband so much for what he had done. She knew Sheldon would not consider himself to be a hero, but he would think that any other driver would have done just what he had done.

They sat stonily in their chairs, listening intently to Sheldon's boss speak about him.

The room was eerily quiet except for the CEO's voice, and it grated on Abby's nerves. She shook her head and tried to concentrate on what was happening. It would soon be over and they could go home.

Sheldon followed the tracks of the heavy vehicle as it went down the first hill, his Jake breaks rattled nosily as they added drag to his forward momentum.

"Strange the snowplows hadn't cleared this hill yet, Lord," he spoke to his God. "The driver who does this side of the mountain is always very good at being around before it gets this deep."

He shrugged and worked his truck down the hill and around the turns. He saw lights flashing back and forth just as he was getting to the last turn before going down the last three mile hill, and he braced himself to face the oncoming car's lights as he drove around the turn.

The sight in front of him froze his hands and made his blood run cold. A school bus was facing him in his lane, with its high beams shining right at him.

He pumped his brakes before the truth dawned on him; he was on solid ice and couldn't get stopped. While he watched, a snowplow came around the next corner and stopped, which meant extra bright lights shining straight into his eyes. He knew that everyone had panicked and forgotten their high beams. He concentrated on his job.

As the sweat broke out on his forehead, he scanned and evaluated the situation. If he tried to sacrifice himself and go through the guardrail, his angle wouldn't let him break through the steel rail and he would probably slide down it. The trailer would jackknife and swing across the road, taking the school bus and the snowplow over the cliff with him. He did the only thing he could do. Sheldon turned his steering wheel slightly to the left and gently pulled on his trailer spike. At the same time he let his Jakes grab his drivers, causing them to catch and skid slightly.

"Jesus, let me save those folks, please?" Sheldon prayed out loud while he made his calculations.

His truck slowly folded up into a jackknife. His front end slowly moved left out of line with the bus, leaving the nose of his trailer aimed straight for the front of it. If he stayed in this position he could survive the crash, because the trailer would hit the bus, but everyone on the bus would die.

Continuing to sweat profusely, he kept his hands busy turning the wheel back and to the right. His eyes were studying the fast approaching collision and his brain did the necessary calculations for what he was about to do. He reached for the spike again and applied gentle pressure, putting a drag on his trailer wheels.

Ken watched his and his children's death fast approaching as the truck's cab gently swung sideways, out of the way. The truck driver would at least survive the crash, because where he was in the cab would break away and miss the impact point. The trailer would come straight into the bus, killing him and many of the children instantly. Then it would probably push the bus over the side of the road and into the waiting void of the long drop to the rocky valley bottom.

He watched as the driver calmly and slowly moved his hands over his controls to escape the collision. Their lights were shining into his cab, and Ken could see his calm demeanour and confident movements.

At least he'll save himself, Ken thought. *Danny came too late.* He could see the snowplow's revolving lights in his mirrors.

Danny watched horrified as he saw the truck jackknife with the trailer pointed straight at the front of the bus. *God, the truck driver is saving himself, but he's going to kill all these children.*

Danny knew most of those children and their parents. He knew Ken and had gone to church with him. *And now they're going to die. So young, and maybe never having known Jesus. Oh, God, help.*

Danny couldn't take his eyes off the impending collision. His bright lights let him look right into the truck's cab and see every move the driver made. He watched as Sheldon turned the steering wheel back to the right, aiming it straight at him.

"Nooooo," he said aloud. "He'll kill me too turning that way." Panic was in his voice. He had not been to church in quite some time, and he didn't think he was ready to go yet.

Jesus! Jesus, help! If you'll save me, I'll get to church and go faithfully. I promise. He prayed in his mind. Then the thought struck him. *My girls! Who would teach my girls about Jesus and heaven?*

He knew Jane would try, but he wanted to do it. He had never had this urgency before, because he had never thought of death being this close before.

Ken saw the trailer getting closer and closer and knew the driver had saved himself. He turned and looked at the kids. They were staring out the front window, spellbound by the approach of such a large truck coming at such an unnatural angle.

He turned back just as the truck cab was about to reached the bus. He stared as the cab missed the bus and was amazed to see the trailer swinging towards the mountain. The front of the trailer missed the bus by mere inches and travelled by the bus so close he could have touched it from any of the windows.

"Remember your promise." He heard the voice as plain as anything and knew that God had saved them. He turned in his seat and looked at the children as they watched the truck go by. His children; and he had to get them to church. God had performed a miracle, and he had to keep his promise.

That lucky truck driver probably didn't know he was saved from this crash by God and thought it was dumb luck. He looked out through the back window and his mouth dropped open. The driver was doing the same manoeuvre to try to miss the snowplow. He was already starting his jackknife.

This was not a dumb, lucky truck driver; God had sent them a professional when they needed one badly. No driver Ken knew could pull this manoeuvre even once in that short time, but this man was trying to do it twice, back to back.

This driver....he knew how to drive truck.

Danny was panicking as he watched the truck miss the bus by mere inches. He was now directly in front of the truck and was the impact point. He could look right into the cab and saw the driver still turning the steering wheel.

What a lucky fluke. He missed the bus but he's got me. He's not even upset that he's going to die. Danny thought, as he watched Sheldon calmly turning the wheel and reach for the spike. He watched as the front of the truck started to move to his left and the trailer followed, again going into a jackknife.

He's....he's doing it again! He missed the bus deliberately and he's trying to do it again with me, Danny thought, amazed. *Buddy, you've got to be good, real good, to pull that one twice up here.*

He watched, spellbound, as inch by inch and fraction by fraction the truck cab moved sideways away from the point of impact. All the while it was coming at him way too fast.

Danny felt faint and realized he was holding his breath. He took a large gasp of air and stared as the truck succeeded in moving far enough to miss the front of the plow. The front of the trailer was now aimed directly at the front blade.

He watched the man as he reached for the trailer brake spike and turned the steering wheel back towards the center of the road. He continued watching with his mouth hanging open as the trailer slowly started moving away from the front of his truck. Inch by inch and fraction by fraction it moved away while it still barrelled towards him.

The transport missed the corner of his blade by mere inches. He could have reached out of his window and touched it as it went by him. Danny never would have believed that was possible unless he had seen it himself.

This driver....he knew how to drive truck.

He glanced at the transport's tail lights but was distracted by the opening of the school bus door. Ken came out. Danny jumped from the seat of his plow and ran to meet him.

"Did you see that? Did you SEE that?" Ken was saying. "We were dead men for sure, and he missed us both!" He had to shout over the noise of Danny's truck motor and the storm's wind.

They turned as one person and looked through the driving snow after the transport. It was gone, and they could see nothing but the driving snow.

They were still there when an RCMP officer came walking up from behind Danny's snowplow. "Quite a night, isn't it?" he asked.

"You don't know the half of it," Ken shouted over the noise.

The officer looked at them and said, "Oh?" and raised one eyebrow questioningly. While Ken struggled for words, he continued. "We closed the road at the Rooftop Inn, but you came through before that. I'm glad you're safe. Now that the plow is going you should have no trouble getting the kids home."

"Yeah, we're safe now." Ken found his voice. "That transport just pulled the most amazing manoeuvre we have ever seen and he missed us both. He did it twice, one right after the other; jackknifed twice and pulled back in time to miss the bus and the plow. That transport you just met is one of the best drivers I have ever seen," Ken shouted.

They watched the officer's questioning look as it turned serious. Quietly he said, "I didn't meet anyone before seeing you two."

Sheldon could feel his body relaxing as he slipped past the snowplow. His hands and forehead were wet with sweat, but he had tried to remain calm while he concentrated on his job and made sure he was by them. He watched the tail lights of the plow pass by and took a long, slow breath.

Thank you, Lord. I know you did that. Phew, you sure made it close, he thought.

The road ahead was covered with snow, and more flakes were blowing against his windshield; everything in front of him was white. The truck rolled on and smoothed out as it straightened.

A sudden impact shook the truck starting at the front and vibrating to the back; then it went smooth again.

Must have hit the snow bank the plow put up in front of me, he thought, happy knowing he had missed both the school bus and the snowplow. He felt a quiet peace envelope him, and the words to his tune came back to him.

He started to hum and then softly sing the words as the truck kept moving. The motor was revving too high on the downhill and he took his foot off the fuel peddle.

I'm going home, I'm going home.

I'm going home, soon to be with my Lord.

The nose of the truck angled lower.

I've run my race, I've served my God.

I'm going home, soon to be with my Lord.

The front of the truck exploded before Sheldon's eyes.

Chapter 4

Ken and Danny looked at each other, then turned as one and ran down the road towards the patrol car. The RCMP officer followed them as they raced past his car, following the tracks of the transport truck. They came to the destroyed guard rail and stared at the tracks that went through the opening and out into oblivion.

Danny and the officer stared blankly at the tracks while Ken stood there repeating over and over, "No...no...no."

The honour service ended and Abby again looked at the smiling face of her husband on the life-sized poster they had put on the platform. A tear rolled down her face, then another, and Sharon reached over and took her hand. Sharon's other hand was through Denny's arm. Gail sat hugging Brie and Anne as they all cried softly.

They rose as one and in a group walked through the quiet auditorium and out the door. They paused in the vestibule until most of the kind people had filed out, and then they made their way out to their Jeep.

A crowd had gathered on the sidewalk by the parked vehicles. The school bus children and their parents were facing Ken Murphy and his wife. Abby could hear the conversation as they approached the group.

"I prayed on that mountain for the lives of our kids and promised God I would do my best to convince you to take them to church and teach them about Jesus, or get you to let me take them to church and teach them. He sent this driver to pull one impossible driving manoeuvre and your kids were saved. Now I'm asking you to come to church with me and Beth this Sunday. This man died saving our kids, and you know how close you came to losing them. Please come with us," Ken begged.

"Well, I wouldn't go quite that far, Ken. They're still kids and now they have some time left," Eddie Green said.

A voice from behind Abby spoke, "Eddie, you know me. I tell you I was staring death right in the eye while that truck was coming at me. This trucker, Sheldon, saved my life with his skill, and I'm not wasting any more time. I'll be in church Sunday, Ken, and you all should be there too." Abby turned and saw the snowplow driver with his wife and they were each holding one of their girls.

He continued, "If it wasn't for him, I'd be dead and Jane would be looking after the girls alone. I want to be the one to see them get saved and into God's kingdom, and I'm going to because God has given me a second chance. Look at your kids why don't you? You almost lost them. Do you want to risk that again? Come on, Eddie, go with me."

Abby could see he had almost convinced them when she decided to help. "My husband would consider it an honour to die to give you another chance to take your kids to church. He loved God and is now with the only person he loves more than his family — his God, Jesus Christ. Please don't let his sacrifice go to waste. Listen to these men and take your kids to church and teach them about Jesus. The next life and death situation might not be that far away, and it might end differently. My husband did not get to see today, but your kids did. Please?"

Eddie cleared his throat. "Ahem, I guess you're right, Mrs. Waite, and we sure do appreciate what your husband has done for us." By now more of the group were nodding their heads in agreement.

Turning to Ken, he said, "You can count on me and Emma being in church this Sunday, Ken, and we'll see you there too, Danny. We been watching you and it is about time you grew up."

"You bet, Eddie. I reckon it's about time we all grew up. It's just unfortunate this truck driver, Sheldon, had to die before we could see it," Danny said humbly.

Ken, Beth, Danny and Jane waited behind after the others had left, then they gathered around Abby and her family.

"We want to let you know how much we hurt for your loss and how much we appreciate what he did for us," Ken said. "God sent us a real Christian man and a professional driver, just what we needed on that mountain. He knew how to drive truck, for sure."

Danny agreed. "I never saw anyone do what he could do before that night. He sure knew how to drive truck."

The tears were pouring down Abby's face as she smiled and murmured, "You're right; he knew how to drive truck. He drove it clear home to heaven."

SPACE BAAL

Chapter 1

Their 'house' was finished just the way God had instructed Abe to build it. Abe sat at the kitchen table, sipping his first cup of coffee while carefully studying every detail of the interior wall.

The house had been ten years in the building, taking every cent Abe could make — or rather, what God provided. Sometimes the money he received and the equipment he purchased had made the hardware clerk raise her eyebrows in surprise, but no one openly gossiped around him. The mail-order packages were many, large, and from companies no one else would order house-building supplies from.

The community had watched his progress with interest. They'd expected to see a huge and elaborate mansion and were noticeably disappointed when a three-bedroom bungalow appeared instead. No one could guess where he had put most of the equipment he'd received — especially the electronics, control panels, tons of copper wires and tubes, and large titanium sheets.

Mary, Abe's wife of thirty-eight years, was still in bed, having seen the house for the first time yesterday. Abe had worked secretly all this time, but now it was done and ready for its first test run. He took a sip of coffee and walked to the front picture window.

The well-manicured front yard held a decorative display of trees placed strategically for cover from the hardly-used dead-end road he had built on. On both sides, the neighbours were also shielded by bushes, shrubs and softwood trees, and the back was walled by the encroaching forest just beyond their future garden. Their driveway, garage and vehicles surrounded the house, but everything abruptly ended two feet from the edge of the house's footing course, where a concrete-like steel slab was visible.

The house was plain white with a grey high-pitch roof on the outside, and it was ordinary but spacious inside.

Abe turned with his coffee and walked to the back glass doors. A deer stepped from the woods and multiple birds swarmed the feeders. It was just the way they wanted it — wilderness enough to welcome the wildlife but close enough to town for easy access.

Most importantly, it was what God wanted. Abe didn't even know if what he had put under the house would even work, but he trusted what God had told him to do and it looked good. He would find out today.

He heard Mary stirring in the bedroom as he returned to the kitchen table, where his Bible lay open to the page he was reading. He took another sip of coffee and decided to warm it up before going back to his reading. Mary found him reading when she appeared in the kitchen doorway.

They weren't young anymore but they were both still very alert and active.

"Good morning, hon," Abe greeted her. "Did you sleep well in our new house?"

"Noooo," She drew the word out and yawned. "I'll get used to it, I suppose, but this is too new for me." She made her way to the stove and put the tea kettle on to boil before she returned to the table. "What is this big surprise you told me you would show me today? You said you and God were cooking up something. He's a good cook, but I don't know about you."

Abe smiled, "Time enough for that when you're ready. Have your tea and breakfast, I'll wait." His dog-eared and much read Bible lay open to the first chapter of Genesis. It was his habit to read the Bible through from cover to cover so that he wouldn't get away on a study and miss some verses. He had just finished the twenty- second chapter of Revelation yesterday. Most of the time, he would read a chapter a day, but he'd cover more if he got interested in the topic he was reading. He read the whole Bible, even the verses he had trouble understanding at first. He determined to put God's word into his heart and brain, trusting the Holy Spirit to bring understanding and use it as He saw fit.

Genesis 1:1: "*In the beginning God created the heaven and the earth.*" It couldn't be explained any simpler than that, he thought. He kept reading.

Mary was just sitting down to breakfast and tea when he finished. He respectfully bowed his head and waited while she said grace, before rising and heading for the door.

"I'll get the paper," he said. "When you're ready, we can start."

"Start what?" she asked.

"No you don't," Abe laughed. "You just wait and see."

He left her there to stare after him as he softly closed the door behind him.

Abe enjoyed the mornings and walked slowly, drinking in the sights and sounds of the world awakening. A short time later, he returned to the house.

At the kitchen table, Abe had time to finish the newspaper before Mary returned from getting dressed.

"OK," she said. "What is this surprise?"

Abe smiled broadly and walked to the wall beside the refrigerator. "This is the main switch, and it will be left on after this. The whole system can be operated by our voices, but we also have manual controls."

He reached high on the wall by the corner of the doorway on the refrigerator side. A panel opened at his touch. He reached in and turned the only knob, then closed the panel. A soft, barely audible hum rose from the floor.

Mary looked at him skeptically. "Abraham Peters, what have you done?" She always used his full name when she was getting upset.

"Exactly as God told me to, honey. Trust me — we know what we're doing."

He took her hand and led her to her chair in the living room.

"Better sit down. This gets pretty amazing from here on, I hope." He frowned as doubt started to take the edge off his faith. "I haven't even seen what I am going to show you. I just followed God's instructions and know this is needed somewhere in the near future."

Worry wrinkled Mary's brow, but she remained silent. She knew Abe was a faithful Christian and a wonderful husband, but his seriousness now was beginning to frighten her.

He smiled again, then in a louder than necessary voice said, "GIRLS?"

The corner of the living room suddenly became hazy as three young ladies appeared. They had a striking resemblance to their four children and could easily pass for their sisters.

"Ahhh," Abe sighed with relief. *It works*, he thought happily. "Faith, come here, please."

The first girl stepped forward. Mary looked her up and down, too surprised to speak. The girl had auburn coloured hair, so light it was almost red, and was dressed in a matching green high-collar smock and slacks with matching green low, slip-on shoes. The word *Faith* was embossed high on the left side of the smock. She smiled pleasantly and waited.

"This is Faith. She represents the controls of this ship, which extend out from our atmosphere to gather information and use the resources of the ship to repel any threat or handle any danger," Abe said.

Mary rolled her eyes and blinked, "Ship? Atmosphere? Danger? What are you talking about?"

"Oh, yeh. Sorry. This is the first time I've started it, and it's all new to me, too," Abe stammered. "Our house is really a travelling ship; it's like a space ship. The operating parts are all under the floor, and there is another set of rooms under that, except upside-down to these ones so we can go there if we have to work under here. The ship creates gravity and atmosphere, so no matter where we are, or what happens, we are self-contained. I don't know everything about it, which is why we have to do some test runs. It draws energy to run from whatever is around us, such as air, land, vacuum, or even atoms and molecules. These three girls are control panels for different functions of the ship. They're not really here physically. They are holograms and can be seen because they create an image out of the atoms using photo-kinetics and project it wherever they are to go."

He passed his hand through Faith's side and frowned at her giggle fit. *Was she supposed to feel that?* he wondered.

Mary sat back with her mouth open, flabbergasted. Finally she asked, "Who programmed them to look like our kids? You?"

"I thought it was a nice touch and would make them more familiar," Abe said. "I built in the ability to learn and think, but they cannot disobey my command, even though they can ask questions. I gave each one a small, individual personality to separate them and make them more efficient at what they are to do. Faith is a little aggressive and outgoing, so she can attack if she has to."

Mary looked at him, "You did all this by yourself?"

"No, no. God told me to do it and told me how. It's His project; I'm just the servant here. Like I said, this is the first time I've turned it on, so this is all new to me, too," Abe explained.

The three girls stood quietly, waiting and watching.

Mary hesitated. "This is not going to be easy for me. This is not what I expected."

"I know, and we can go slow at first. Remember, though, God is in it and will watch over us," Abe said. He turned and motioned for the next girl. She stepped forward. She had blond hair and was dressed like the first girl, but her clothes were red. The word *Hope* was embossed on the high left corner of her smock.

"This is Hope. She controls the defences, shields and close operations of the ship, like atmosphere and air and colour distortions." Abe continued, "I made her more motherly and protective than the other two."

Mary was too overcome with the enormity of what was happening to speak. She sat in her chair and tried to take it all in.

Abe motioned for the last girl to step forward. She had dark brown hair and was dressed all in white, similar to the other two. The word *Charity* was embossed on the front of her smock. "This is Charity, and she is the ship. This control panel controls every aspect of the ship we are standing on — the gravity, flight, speed, direction and everything internal. I gave her the quickest mind and firm decision-making qualities, like confidence and boldness."

"And you say you have not tested it yet?" Mary asked doubtfully.

"No, not yet, but so far it works great," Abe said, bolstering his confidence.

"And they look like our kids," Mary continued as if she hadn't heard him. "And they have personalities." With that she looked at Abe. "You know, you can't ever turn them off now. It would be like killing them."

Abe studied her face seriously. "I.....I...hadn't thought of that," he stammered. "But they can disappear; it's kind of like sleeping. We just won't turn the switch off and shut the ship down. When we want them, all we have to do is speak and they will appear."

He smiled and said, "They can touch and handle physical things if we need them to; maybe you could get them helping you with cleaning or housework, or I could use them in the garden."

Mary frowned. "And what would you tell the neighbours? We made some girls to do the work for us? No you don't. If they do anything, I'll look after their chores. I need another tea." She rose and went to the kitchen.

Abe watched her go and then turned to look at the girls. They stood quietly watching him. He smiled, shrugged his shoulders and watched their smiles get bigger. He frowned and thought, *I hadn't thought that through. By giving them personalities and the ability to learn, I gave them emotions; and they're ticklish.* He looked at Faith. *Mary is right; we can't turn them off.*

By the time Mary returned, Abe was running diagnostic tests on the three girls, making sure all their circuits and functions worked properly. She paused long enough to watch. The electric current could be seen as blue flashes and streaks running back and forth inside the girls as each function was operated.

Abe noticed her as she sat in her chair to sip her tea and looked expectantly at her.

She sighed and said, "I prayed for the Lord's direction, and He advised me to trust you. This is all so new and strange to me, but I will try to help in whatever way I can."

"Good girl," Abe gushed. "And praise be to God for the unity of His Holy Spirit. I don't know what He has got planed either, but we can trust it's for the best. Girls, this is my wife, Mary. Say hello, please," he finished as he turned to the three girls.

"Hello, Mary," the three said in unison, smiling at her.

"Hello, Faith, Hope and Charity. I'm sure we are going to get along splendidly," Mary said as she thought, *He even gave them different voice tones.* Faith's voice was husky and low, Hope's was higher and light hearted, while Charity's was slightly baritone almost masculine.

Abe continued, "Girls, here is a command for your highest security settings. You will obey any command Mary gives you. This can only be overridden by me. Confirm, please."

The three again answered in unison, "Confirmed, Sir."

Hope spoke and said, "Sir, we are being scanned by an electronic laser camera."

Abe frowned and mumbled, "Who would do such a thing? Hope, build an image of the house and keep it stable, please. Charity, give us visor walls, please."

The two answered, "Yes, Sir," as the walls became transparent. Mary gasped as she stared at their front yard through the wall.

Hearing her, Abe said, "It's alright, Mary. It's only transparent one way; we can see out, but no one can see in. The walls are still there, but the photo sensors covering the outside of the house are projecting the image through the wall and displaying it on millions of small display surfaces on the inside. See?" He held his arm out and motioned at the floor.

Puzzled, Mary studied the floor but couldn't see anything.

"I don't see anything," she exclaimed.

"Exactly!" Abe stated. "It's a sunny day, but my arm doesn't cast a shadow. The image of the sun is coming through, but the rays aren't. The visor walls are reversible and can even become translucent or penetrable, which means we could even walk through them. It would be like walking through a waterfall." He was smiling broadly.

Turning back to the girls, Abe said, "Faith, zoom the image of the camera operator so we can see who it is, please." The wall screen enlarged a view of a man hovering in a helicopter a mile away and made him life-sized on the wall. He was looking through a long lensed camera and adjusting the focus.

"Can you find any database information on this man, Faith?" Abe asked.

She replied, "Scanning.....scanning.....His name is David Brown, and he works for an organization called Homeland Security. More?" She looked at him inquiringly.

Mary was watching a bird poop on their roof and was amazed to see the stool disappear. Abe was idly watching her and said, "The stool was absorbed as energy by our system. It also took any parasite the bird had. This house is not only an advanced space ship, it's environmentally friendly. It will not harm any living creature near it, but anything attached to a larger organism is absorbed and stored in our energy banks." Turning back to Faith, he mused aloud, "I wonder what Homeland Security wants with us. Besides, they have no jurisdiction in Canada."

"Oh!" Faith exclaimed and started. "Oh!?" she started again.

"What is it, Faith?" Abe asked, concerned.

"I have been poked by something called a security probe," she said, her brow wrinkling. "Oh...now it's following my link back towards the satellite I was using."

"Break off, quick," Abe exclaimed. "Leave it at the satellite."

"Done, Sir," Faith responded.

"Good! Now go back and watch where it goes without making contact with it," Abe said.

"It is following the link I followed to its base but back to its origin. A man called Woo Chong opened it on his computer in a basement room of a building called the Chinese Embassy in a city called Ottawa. The security probe has entered his computer and is gathering his operating certificates. He doesn't know it is there." Faith gave a running account as the events were happening.

"Oh, dear; I'm afraid we have compromised his position. Come back, Faith. Hope, can you open a shield and use the mobile phone system to flood Homeland Security's computer system? Use a link from Russia to originate it and keep them busy enough to pull their link. Faith, open a link on Mr. Chong's computer and mask my voice so I can speak to him," Abe instructed his girls.

"Done, Sir," the two girls said in unison.

"Mr. Chong?" Abe asked.

"Huh?" A strange voice spoke in the room.

"Mr. Chong, I'm afraid I have compromised your search of the Homeland Security computers. I'm sorry, but they now know you have been there. Please accept my sincere apologies," Abe said.

"Who.....who are you?" the voice said in a heavy Chinese accent.

"Oh, I'm afraid I can't tell you that. We're using a new system and are still over-extending ourselves. We'll try not to bother you anymore.

Good day, Sir." Abe nodded to Faith and she broke the connection as Mr. Chong sputtered.

"Ooops," Hope said.

Quickly turning to her, Abe asked, "What is it, Hope?"

"I'm sorry, Sir," she replied. "But the Homeland Security computer system went off-line. I didn't know it couldn't handle two billion phone calls. I'm sorry."

"That's alright. They'll just have to fix it. You didn't know. No real harm done," Abe consoled her.

Mary cleared her throat and said, "How did you break into Homeland Security's computers and talk to an experienced hacker so easily? Their security software should have been all over your electrical signal."

Abe smiled slyly. "Yes, if it had been an electrical signal. The power of this system is more advanced than electricity. We only use electrical impulses to communicate within the system, like brain impulses in the human body. Our power system is more like thought waves, and does not need a connection to travel from place to place. Like the brain, we think and we are moving. We travel on the thought waves and are not limited by any physical hindrances. They could not detect us because we were not there; we were only looking in there from here. Their computer does not even have to be on for us to scan their hard drive and take all their information. The security probe saw Faith when she stopped to read the file on Mr. Brown. I'm sure it had no idea what she was and poked her trying to understand her.

"If I understand God right, we should be able to travel from one place to another in an instant and travel through anything physical without really harming it; however, we may have to be traveling faster than the speed of light to go through things. My calculations seem to make me think we will have to burn through anything we encounter before we reach that speed."

Mary shook her head and threw up her hands. "This is going to take some getting used to."

Chapter 2

"I have some more questions," Mary continued. "Why would God want you, a retired truck driver, instead of a rocket scientist or an airplane pilot or any other brainy character? You're faithful, I know, but you don't have any training for flying or ..." She waved her arms at the three girls watching her, "or control panels and holograms and such stuff."

Abe frowned again and said, "I've been thinking about that and the conclusion I've come to is that God wanted someone who could operate and handle whatever had to be done without any help from others. Pilots have crews, rocket scientists have staff and brainiacs have office assistants to help with their problems, but a truck driver is alone most of the time and can only rely on themselves to get out of most situations. If this works, we will be alone wherever we go, because I don't think God wants us to let anyone see us or know we can do the things I believe we will be able to."

Mary slowly nodded. "Okay, so where did you get the money for all this, and how far in debt are we?"

Abe smiled broadly. "That's easy. God provided it all. You remember all those envelopes that kept arriving, and I would put them in the bank?" She nodded. "Well, they were cheques made out to me from businesses and people from all around the world. I used another account for them so you wouldn't see it. We don't owe a thing, and our personal money is not affected."

She was watching him intently, unsure of how to respond to the secret he kept from her., "How much did our home......space ship....this thing, cost?" she asked.

Abe looked thoughtfully at the wall where Mr. David Brown was thumping his useless mobile phone against his hand.

"About $3,200,000,000 — give or take a million or so," he said.

Mary gasped and slumped back in her chair. Her empty tea cup thumped on the floor where she dropped it. "You......you had three billion dollars, and I didn't know about it?"

"Not all at once," Abe stammered defensively. "Besides, it was God's money, not ours."

She shook her head as if to clear it and finally said, "Yes, I guess you're right. If I'm going to be a part of this, though, you have to promise not to keep any more secrets from me. Many more like this and my heart will give out."

"Oh, no!" Abe exclaimed, his voice shaky with concern. "Your heart has always been strong. We can go slower, if you like."

She smiled lovingly at him. "You sweet silly. I'm fine; that was just an expression. This is just so overwhelming I have to think about it a while. You go ahead, I'll be alright." She glanced at the girls and noticed their looks were very intense, as if they were concerned too.

Did they have feelings, too? she wondered. She smiled reassuringly at them and watched huge smiles replace their frowns. *They did!* This was going to be like having three more children. She would have to watch and see how much they were going to have to teach them.

Abe turned back to the girls as Mary left for the kitchen. Her morning chores were waiting, and Abe needed time to learn about his...er...ship.

Abe spoke to Charity. "Charity, could you bring up the central controls, please."

"Yes, Sir," she said as a monitor, consul and armed swivel chair appeared by a blank wall.

Abe sat in the chair, which had joy sticks on the arms, foot controls by his feet and a full screened head piece complete with a mic near his mouth. He was as excited as a child at Christmas time. Ten years worth of work and today he was going to get to play with it for the first time.

He fit the head piece over his head and said, "Test....test. Can you hear me, Charity?"

"Yes, Sir," she said in his ear.

"Hope? Faith?" he continued.

"Yes, Sir," they responded in turn.

"Good. Charity, could you explain the panel and controls please?" He eagerly studied the buttons, knobs and levers on the board in front of him.

"Yes, Sir," she responded, and proceeded to point at different controls and explain how they moved and what they controlled.

Mary re-entered the room and hour later and noticed Mr. Brown and his helicopter were gone. Abe was sitting in a swivel chair in front of a consul and lite monitor. He was surrounded by the girls.

Mary stopped suddenly at the scene before her. Charity was leaning over Abe possessively, her hand resting gently on his shoulder while she gestured with the other hand and explained the controls. Watching from the other side of the chair, Hope was on her knees and sitting on her heels, with her hand resting gently on his other forearm. Faith was standing behind him with her hands on the back of his chair.

Oh, they had feelings alright. This is much more intimate than mere control panels, she thought. They were acting like children, though, not like her competition. She felt more like bringing them milk and cookies and a colouring book.

Abe turned at her approach, his face beaming with excitement. "Do you have any plans for the rest of the day?" he asked and continued hopefully, "I'd like to take her up for a short flight. This board is manual control, where I can operate the ship myself."

Mary wanted to be upset at this sudden plan, but surprisingly found that the idea thrilled her. The girls were watching her, waiting for her answer. "Wellllll....ok, but we should be back before dark," she hesitantly relented.

Abe jumped up and the four moved to the front wall to watch their ascent. Mary settled into her chair, more excited than she wanted to show.

"Hope, set the house monitors to show a house here while we are gone, please," Abe said.

"Done, Sir," Hope responded.

"Charity, lift us up a few feet until we see if there are any problems," Abe continued.

"Done, Sir," Charity responded as the house smoothly lifted two feet and stopped.

Abe leaned against the wall and looked down at the steel locks that had released and were open. "Good, good. Just the way it was planned," he mumbled as he walked around to make sure they were all released.

Abe turned and said, "Another ten feet, please, Charity."

"Done, Sir," she said as the house quietly rose another ten feet.

"Excellent," Abe gushed. "Let's take it up another twenty feet, Charity."

"Yes, Sir." And the house noiselessly rose twenty feet and stopped.

They were now looking down on the rest of the property and were completely clear of the ground.

"Give us visor floors with a 20% grid, please, Charity." The floors instantly became transparent with a black line grid on them in two foot squares.

Mary felt her stomach churn as she looked past her feet at a thirty foot drop into a dirt hole.

Abe felt his heart pulse with excitement as he watched his ship perform exactly as he'd planned. "Wonderful," he exclaimed in response to Charity's "Done, Sir."

He looked at Mary but was too excited to notice her pale green complexion. "Shall we take a tour of our skies?" he asked.

He suddenly frowned and with a quick start turned to Hope. "What do we look like to others, Hope? Can they see us?"

"Yes Sir," she responded.

"Quickly, distort the air around us so our shape cannot be seen," Abe urged.

"Done, Sir," Hope said and smiled at Abe.

"Phew," he said. "I'm glad our Mr. Brown is gone. He would have something to tell his superiors if he'd seen us. Hope, keep us disguised whenever we are out of our base, please, and add that command to your base registry."

"Yes, Sir," Hope responded. Abe stared at her, lost in thought.

"Can we change the way we look? Like our colour and shape?" he asked her.

"Yes, Sir. We are quite flexible," she said pleasantly.

"My God....oh, excuse me please, Lord. I didn't mean any disrespect." Abe apologized looking up. Bringing his attention back to Hope and then to Charity he asked, "Can we change our size or our physical shape?"

"Yes, Sir," she replied, smiling at him. "We are quite capable of a wide variety of physical, electrical and molecular things."

"Amazing," Abe said, shaking his head while he looked at Mary. She quickly sat down in her chair, also stunned by what she heard.

Abe again turned to Charity. "Charity, take us up another 500 feet, please."

'Yes, Sir," she said pleasantly as the ship quietly and smoothly shot straight up.

Suddenly they were surrounded by shadows and commotion in the air outside the walls. There were thumps on the roof and squawking and screeching amid general confusion.

Abe and Mary looked up at the bottoms of a group of ducks as they walked around on the roof and walls. Loose duck feathers were being absorbed by their power system as the ducks flapped and struggled to lift off the roof, only to be trapped by the ship's gravitational pull and returned to the roof and walls.

"Quickly, Hope, expand our gravity field so those ducks can fly around us until they calm down," Abe said.

"Done, Sir," Hope responded. They watched the ducks lift off in a group and fly through their gravity field, circling their ship at a distance of fifty feet out.

They watched them until they started to tire and again landed on their roof. Abe studied them and made sure none of the startled birds were hurt.

"Hope, can you change the gravity field to even the pressure with the earth so those ducks can lift off and fly away?" Abe asked, looking at her.

"Done, Sir," Hope said.

They watched, but the ducks had resigned themselves to resting and remained on the roof.

Abe moved to a recliner and sat down, brow wrinkled in thought, while they watched the ducks socialize. Finally, he said, "Faith, from now on scan our movements and adjust our travel to avoid living objects in our way. Put that in your registry as a continuous command, please."

"Yes, Sir," Faith responded.

He turned to Mary. "I need a cup of coffee. This is more complicated than I had anticipated."

"I'll get you one, dear. You have enough to worry about." She rose and went to the kitchen.

Abe noticed the girls watching this interaction and wondered what they were thinking and learning. He didn't have to wonder long as Charity asked, "Sir, your name is Abraham, but Mary calls you Abe and....... and dear; we don't understand these discrepancies."

Abe smiled at them and received smiles back. "They are names we give each other called nick names or pet names. They are personal and intimate signs of affection and communication. Abe is a short version of Abraham, but *dear* is a sign of affection. I also sometimes call Mary *dear*. We have adopted this affection because we love each other and remind each other of our love by the use of pet names."

They pondered his words for a moment.

"Sir, you have programmed us to call you *sir*. Is this also a sign of affection?" Hope asked.

Abe looked at her and said, "It could be, but it is also the best way to address others and show respect. We use *sir* when we talk to our superiors, older people and people we want to put at ease with us. Using *sir* shows people we are friendly and they can trust us. It once was a common form to teach children when they were talking to their fathers."

Abe didn't notice their sudden interest in his last statement as Mary had re-entered the room with his coffee. He noticed she had another tea and ventured, "Let's take them to the roof and we can shoo those ducks away."

Giving him a sharp look, she said, "Another surprise?"

He smiled and said, "Yes. Charity, open the roof slowly and bring down the steps, please."

"Done, Sir," Charity said.

"Follow me, please," He said as he started for the hallway. They found a set of steps extending down from the ceiling where they had been hidden above one of the panels.

Abe led Mary up the steps to a roof patio complete with furniture. The roof had descended into the walls, leaving a short railing around the flat roof. The opening roof had frightened the ducks away.

The high sky wind hit them as they stepped up on the roof and Abe said to Hope, "Hope, lift the gravity field again, please."

"Done, Sir," she said as the air became calm and warm.

The five spent a quiet half hour admiring the high view while they drank their beverages above a world that was totally unaware they were there.

Back in the living room, Abe said, "Ready?" At Mary's nod, he turned to Charity. "Charity, take us to Lake Erie, please; use 2000 miles an hour so we can watch the scenery and take us up to 5000 feet. We wouldn't want to go through any buildings getting there."

"Yes, Sir," Charity said as the ship left its hovering position at the requested speed.

"Whaa…," Mary gasped. "Instant speed? I felt no pressure." She looked questioningly at her husband.

"No need," he responded. "With our own gravity, there is no pressure, and since we travel by thought waves, there is also no need for a speed build-up. We just start and go at the required speed."

He turned to the girls. "Charity, do an instant one mile reverse and hold there……now!"

"Done, Sir," she said as the scenery blurred and came into focus again, one mile back the way they came.

Abe and Mary blinked and looked at each other. "Amazing!" Abe said. "No uncomfortable feelings, but we will have to watch and keep track of our motion and surroundings in our minds or it could be quite confusing."

"We could help you," Hope said. It was the first time the girls offered assistance and showed their thought and learning advancement.

"Wonderful, girls. You are learning," Abe gushed over them.

Mary watched huge smiles appear on their faces and thought she noticed a heightening of their facial colour in their first blushes. She also noticed a brightening of their hair colour with the increased emotional activity.

Abe continued, "Let's keep going on to Lake Erie. I want to watch our reflection in the water as we experiment with our colour and shape. Charity, would you proceed, please." The ship was again instantly moving, and the ground blurred under them.

At Lake Erie, Abe stopped the ship at the middle where no one was near. Hope changed the shape and colour as he requested. They discovered that the ship was capable of any colour, shape or appearance he thought of.

It was past supper time when Abe was satisfied and Mary prepared them a light lunch. Abe didn't see the intense interest the three girls paid to his prayer as he bowed his head and said grace.

Abe decided to pilot the ship from its manual controls to return home. He sat in the seat, weak with excited anticipation. He grasped the joysticks and placed his feet on the foot paddles. He gently eased the two sticks ahead and the ship inched forward. He pushed gently on the right foot peddle and the ship shot straight ahead.

He had made the controls similar to a truck or heavy equipment pattern — something he was familiar with.

He pulled one joystick back slightly and pushed the other. The speeding ship curved in a large arc and dipped when he pushed both sticks ahead and pushed the right stick thumb rocker button. As he became comfortable with the controls, he made the ship twist and turn, loop and flop. It ended up stopped in the middle of the lake, upside down. Their gravity made them feel comfortably normal against the earth's gravity.

Abe was flushed and sweating when he spun his seat around and grinned at Mary. "It works perfectly," he gushed

Mary watched him act like a child in a candy store, and she saw the girls smiling and absorbing his emotional reactions. "That was breathtaking," she admitted, "but we really should be going home now."

"Yes, yes, home," he said and spun around to the controls. He grasped the joysticks and the ship flipped as it shot straight up into the earth-surrounding space.

As the dark void closed around them, Abe spoke. "Hope, compensate for the lack of air and hold our atmosphere stable, please. Do this whenever we lose or gain pressure against our atmosphere."

Hope quickly responded. "Done, Sir. Yes, Sir."

He manoeuvred the ship into open space, intending to loop back home, but he was interrupted by Faith's voice.

"Sir, there is a human occupied object directly ahead," she reported.

"Ah, the Space Station. Hope, make us look like a long thin silver object with a row of lights down our side, please," Abe commanded.

"Abe?" he heard Mary say.

He was caught up with an impulse idea and slowed the ship to turn it near the Space Station.

"Abe? Don't you dare..." She didn't finish her sentence before they glided past the Space Station, circled it once, and continued on their way home.

Mary spoke against Abe's laughter. "You didn't have to do that," she scolded.

He turned to her, smiling. "I know, but it was fun. Faith, monitor the radio communication from the station and see if they saw us."

Yes, Sir," Faith said, smiling.

Mary rolled her eyes. "You four are impossible," she said. She smiled and continued as the girls showed alarm. "I'm kidding. That is an expression I use to scold children or men who act like children." She gave Abe a direct look and he smiled bigger.

"She scolds me because she disapproves of what I did, but it wasn't serious so she teased me with her scolding. It fits into the same category as pet names. It's more affection scolding or teasing," Abe explained to the girls and watched their expressions return to smiles.

Mary rolled her eyes again and mumbled, "We won't have any secrets left, teaching the girls."

"Do we need secrets among family?" Abe asked, again not seeing the effect his comment had on the girls.

Mary did notice. "No, I guess not," she replied, drawing a thoughtful look from the three girls, herself.

"Good!" Abe exploded. "Let's go home now." He turned the ship and streaked for earth and home.

On the way, they heard the report from the Space Station. The speaker was almost shouting as he told the ground crew about their U.F.O. sighting. Abe had achieved the results he wanted, but he wasn't sure he should be happy about it. There were no aliens or extra-terrestrials, but he had fed their belief by showing themselves. Thankfully, the station's crew had no time to take any pictures.

They arrived in the semi-dusk just as the sun dropped below the horizon.

"Set us down, please, Charity. I'm still not confident enough to put it into such a close spot yet," Abe said letting go of the controls.

Yes, Sir," Charity said and smoothly set the ship back into its base.

Abe and Mary discussed their day, and the girls, in bed that night. They came to the understanding that they were more of a responsibility than Abe had anticipated. After their talk, Abe and Mary lay together, hands touching under the blankets.

Abe whispered, "Good night, dear."

Mary whispered back, "Good night. Can they hear us?"

Abe didn't answer her directly but whispered, "Good night, girls. Sleep well."

"Good night, Sir," they responded softly.

"Yep," Abe said as he squeezed Mary's hand.

Chapter 3

Abe was up as the sun rose on another clear day, sitting at his favourite chair in front of their picture window, drinking his first coffee while he watched the birds around their feeders. His Bible was open before him, and the three girls sat around the table, their attention divided between Abe and the birds.

Abe was pointing out the joy of feeding the innocent and helping the weak. He was expounding the fact that God made everything, and that even what was ugly and undesirable was still part of God's creation and deserved to be cared for.

They heard Mary stirring in the bedroom. "Can I go and see Mary?" Hope asked. "I feel she can teach me a lot about the caring personality you gave me."

Abe was pleased. "That is a wonderful idea, Hope. You are a treasure. Sure, I believe Mary would love to see you."

Hope disappeared and Abe heard a loud 'Oh!' from Mary as Hope suddenly appeared in the room. It wasn't long before they heard the low drone of conversation. The two soon appeared walking close together, engrossed in their topic.

Abe, Faith and Charity watched them in silence. He knew they could learn just by watching Mary and Hope, and he didn't want to hinder their growth. He also had his own thoughts and would like to test the ship with a trip to a distant star system. They should take a short hop around their own planet system first, just to be safe.

Abe waited until after breakfast to advance the prospect of a space trip, but he was interrupted by a knock on the front door.

"Two men from Homeland Security are at the door," Hope said.

"And there are four more in a van at the mouth of the road, and an RCMP car with two officers behind them," Faith added.

"I wonder why Homeland Security has such an interest in us," Abe said as he walked to the door. He continued before he opened the door, "Hope, block all transmissions to and from these men and anywhere outside once they enter the house, please. Faith, check the grounds and record any audio and video device aimed at us and x-ray photograph these men for surveillance devices, please."

"Done, Sir," the two girls chorused.

Mary rose. "Girls, come with me, please," she said. "There is no

119

record of you in their files or in the community. We'll just stay out of sight unless we are needed."

The four went down the hall to the bedroom while Abe waited. The doorbell rang again. He slowly opened the door and stepped out. "Yes? Can I help you gentlemen?"

An impressive looking man in an immaculate suit spoke. "Mr. Abraham Peters?"

Abe looked up slightly to meet his gaze. "Yes. You have the advantage on me." He raised his eyebrows in a questioning look.

The second man was looking past Abe into the house while the tall man answered. "We're from Homeland Security and would like to ask you a few questions."

"Homeland Security?" Abe feinted surprise. "What could you possibly want with me, Mr......?" He left the question hanging, waiting for the man to supply his name. His quick observations showed they were both armed and meant business.

The tall man continued. "We have tracked the sale of a large quantity of material to you. Material that combined could be the building particles for some unique machines."

Abe noticed the lack of respect these two were using in not supplying their names or references and replied, "Well, I did just build my home, Mr........" Again, he left the question hanging, trying to get the men to give a little.

"This is more than home renovation material," the tall man rudely said, advancing slightly and trying to intimidate Abe into backing into the house where they could follow.

Abe held his ground. "Homeland Security doesn't have any authority in Canada, Sir," he said. "And you haven't shown me any proof that you are who you say you are."

The man was not used to being backed down, and his eyes took on a more aggressive look. "Your RCMP know we are here and are waiting to help us if need be. I *hope* we don't have to request their help," he said sarcastically.

Abe was still not intimidated. When he was driving his truck, he travelled through many dangerous places and had to deal with many salty characters, and these men were starting to irritate him.

"If you call them, I hope they have the proper paperwork for you to be on my property and trying to gain personal information," Abe said, giving the tall man a look through narrowed eye lids.

The tall man leaned away from Abe, surprised his personality hadn't intimidated him. The second man didn't know what to do and stepped back.

Mary spoke from behind Abe. "Abe? Is everything alright? What do these gentlemen want?"

Reluctantly the man said, "I'm sorry, Mr. Peters. We are quite concerned about these products, and my country has had so many terrorist attacks. I'm sure you can understand our concern."

"Yes," Abe said, easing the tension of the circumstances. "It's not a nice position to be in to try to find danger before it can hurt innocent people. Please, come in Mr..?" Abe tried again to give the man an opportunity to give his name.

"Thank you. Hornbeck…Dick Hornbeck, senior agent for Homeland Security. My associate agent, Jim Unger." He waved his hand at his associate.

"Mr. Hornbeck, this is my wife, Mary," Abe said as he entered the house.

"Hello," Mary said, smiling pleasantly.

They moved into the living room and Abe waved them to chairs. "Please, be seated. Can we get you anything? Coffee? Tea? Juice?"

"Coffee, please," Mr. Hornbeck said. "Mr. Peters, about those building materials. Could you explain what you are doing with them?"

"Of course, Sir," Abe said smiling. "We have built the ultimate house for our home." He waved his arm to indicate the room. "It doesn't look any different than other, normal homes, but our house can do almost everything to make our retirement more comfortable. Here, I'll show you. Room temperature, drop ten degrees, please."

Instantly the temperature of the room dropped ten degrees. Mary called from the kitchen where she was getting the coffee. "Abe? Is anything wrong? It got cold of a sudden."

Abe called back, "It's alright, dear. I'm demonstrating the house for our guests." He smiled at the two men and said, "The house is spoiling us. Raise the temperature ten degrees, please."

Dick Hornbeck looked astounded. "You mean you built a luxury home with all that money and material?"

Abe frowned. "I wouldn't call it a luxury home," he said. "It's not real big and doesn't have a pool or sports facilities, but it does everyday tasks and makes life easier for us. We're getting on in years and find it hard to do all the things we used to do. Now, if I could find some way to get the garden weeded and the grass trimmed, I could retire from being retired." He smiled broadly at his own humour.

Mr. Hornbeck looked perplexed. "You don't mean to tell me you used Titanium panels, miles of copper wire and those spectra and molecular band reverse osmosis transformers to make life easier for you and your wife?" he questioned.

Abe raised his eyebrows and said, "You have done your homework. Yes and no; what I am doing is making our lives easier, but it is also a test for some advanced equipment I am working on."

Mr. Hornbeck and Mr. Unger looked at each other satisfactorily. Mr. Hornbeck asked, "What would this equipment be for and who are you working for?"

Abe smiled pleasantly. "Oh, I couldn't tell you that. Really, now. I don't ask your scientists to reveal their projects and sources. I can tell you not to worry and that we are both on the same side here. I mean, Canada and America are friends and have the same enemies. Whatever I build and test out will benefit both countries."

Mr. Hornbeck frowned, not liking being left out of some secret experiment. "How do I know you are telling me the truth? You are virtually unknown to every security organization and secret project company in North America."

Abe's smile grew larger and he said, "Exactly! My boss is far too clever to be found out by your organizations, and even they do not know what each other is doing. As for telling you the truth, well... I didn't have to tell you anything, but you are our allies and will eventually benefit from my work. My boss will make the proper news announcements when the time is right, and you will know just where to come to see and learn more."

Mary sat sipping her tea in silence. She had almost forgotten how smooth and quick her husband's mind worked when he was dealing with a situation he didn't like or trust. She watched him now with an admiration she would die many deaths before she would let Abe know about. If he knew, he would tease her unmercifully.

Mr. Hornbeck persisted. "Surely you can tell us a little more.... just to set our minds at ease and give us something to report to our superiors?"

Abe looked thoughtful. "Hmm," he said. "I'll try, but this is ground-breaking work and quite beyond the scale of one's normal way of thinking. You understand cloning?" He looked at Mr. Hornbeck.

"Yes," he replied. "Is that what you are doing here?" He looked around credulously.

"No!" Abe replied. "You know about robotics?"

Mr. Hornbeck's eyes narrowed. "Yes. Are you doing *that* here?"

"No!" Abe again replied. "Remember, I said this was ground-breaking work. It goes beyond cloning and robotics and is in the realm of creation."

"Creation!" Mr. Hornbeck almost spat the word out. "You mean making life from other forms of life?"

Abe frowned. "Well, not really, but you're in the right ball park. I hope that satisfies your superior's curiosity."

Mary continued to watch Abe telling the truth, but really saying nothing useful to the men.

By this time it was apparent by his confused look that Jim Unger did not understand anything, and Dick Hornbeck was struggling to grasp the meaning of Abe's word. "I still don't understand what you mean," he said.

"Well, you think on what I said and remember, I said it was ground-breaking, which means it is all new," Abe replied. "No one has done it before, and no one is attempting it but me. I really must get back to work now." He stood up and waited for the men to rise.

On their way to the door, Abe said, "Please, feel free to come and visit again. Maybe the work will be advanced enough that my boss could authorize a demonstration."

Mr. Hornbeck jumped on his words. "A demonstration of what?"

Abe acted shocked. "Why, life of course, but how to demonstrate something which is already in existence will take some thought."

Dick Hornbeck's shoulders dropped noticeably. He had gotten nothing and he knew it, but Abe seemed to be willingly co-operating. He made one last attempt. "Just where is all this equipment and experimenting going on? This house is too small to be a laboratory."

Abe smiled again. "Ah, you are thinking now. Most of the equipment is under us, and the experiments go on around us. We are part of the experiment, and now you have become part of it by being here."

The two men looked worried and frowned. Mr. Hornbeck commented, "We don't want to be part of your experiment unless you can tell us more."

"Oh, you're completely safe and there are no bad side effects, but my equipment has recorded your presence, blocked your surveillance equipment and will leave you with more evidence for your superiors," Abe said happily.

"Huh?" they said in unison.

"Oh, yes. Just check your pictures when you leave and you will see more evidence. I really must get back to work, gentlemen." Abe smiled amiably and opened the door for them.

They shuffled through, glancing at his smiling face and still unsure if they learned anything.

"Good day," Abe and Mary said before closing the door on their mumbled response.

Abe turned, winked at Mary and said, "Faith, erase all their pictures on all their surveillance equipment, please, and place one picture of the x-ray picture you took of them at the door on their cell phones, but show the picture on the monitor first, please."

Abe and Mary looked at the wall screen as it lit up with a skeletal picture of the two men standing before the door. They could see the hidden weapons they carried and the many audio and video recording devices they had in their clothes and on their persons.

Mary gasped and Abe whistled and said, "four, five, six cameras, two ear receivers, five mics.......no, six, and five guns. What are those other things, Faith?"

The girls were standing behind them. "Most are immobilizing weapons," Faith answered. "Three electronic, two are chemical, one is a powder, two lasers, two knives, three pens, two wallets, five dollars and fifty two cents in change, a hotel key and a car key."

"And they were worried about us," Abe commented dryly. "Well, put that picture on their phones; transmit it to the recording devices they were connected to and on the RCMP's computer and mobile communicators, please."

"Done, Sir," Faith replied.

Abe smiled at her. "Good girl, Faith." He turned to Mary and did not notice Faith's pleased smile and blushing face.

"Maybe we could have a little lunch before we go on?" he asked Mary, hopefully.

She had seen Faith's emotional reaction and noted her hair colour brightened when her emotions were heightened. Catching herself, she answered, "Yes, I think we can do that."

"Excellent," Abe said. "Faith, Hope and I will go round up the recording devices they left around the area and be right back to help you enjoy lunch. How many are there, Faith?"

"Nine, Sir," Faith answered.

"Nine!" Abe said incredulously. "Can I carry them, or do I need my wheelbarrow?"

"They are small and easily portable," Faith said.

Mary looked alarmed. "You're not going out there with them? What if someone sees the girls and starts asking questions?"

"Hmm, you're right. We can't keep hiding them, and they're not cousins. Ah! Let's adopt them. They could be our daughters; that would be honest and really is the truth. After all, they are ours," he said beaming.

The girls stood behind Abe; he didn't see the sudden flare of their hair colour signalling a sudden spike in their emotions, but Mary noticed and suspected this meant a great deal to them.

Thinking hard, she paused. "Wellllll…yes, that would be a wonderful idea. They are really adorable and look just like our children. They would have to call me "Mom"; would that be alright girls?"

"Yes, Mom," they said in unison. Mary saw their hair colour brighten and flash, and she knew this was something they wanted very much.

"Good," she said. "You three get those devices and come in for lunch. Charity and I are going to make us some lunch. Shall we, Charity?" She held out her arm for Charity to hold, and they marched off to the kitchen.

Abe blinked as he thought he saw Charity skip as she disappeared out of the room. He thought, *Strange; just like children…our children.*

"Let's go for a walk, girls," he said. Once outside he held out his arms for them to grasp. If Mary could do it, so could he. The two girls skipped along beside him, holding his arms.

The recording devises sat in a box on the counter, memory erased. After lunch, the five made their way back to the living room to start their day's delayed adventure.

"There is a car coming in the driveway," Faith announced.

Mary glanced out the window. "It's Brian," she said. Their youngest son was coming to visit.

She looked at Abe questioningly. "Do we tell him about the girls?"

Abe thought a moment and noticed the stares of the three girls. "Yes," he said, and watched their faces light up with smiles. Even though he was going to wait, he felt he had made the right decision.

The doorbell rang and Mary opened it. "Brian, come in," she gushed.

A tall, good-looking man in his mid-twenties stepped through the door and hugged his mother. "Hi, Mom.....Dad. How's the new house? Hello!" He spied the girls.

"Hello, Brian," the girls said in unison.

"Hello, Brian. This is going to be a bit of a surprise, but I want you to meet your new sisters — Faith, Hope and Charity," Abe said proudly.

Brian looked at him incredulously. "Sisters? Is there something you're not telling me?" he asked with a half-grin.

"No, Brian. We have just officially adopted them and they are ours. Can you tell him more, Abe?" Mary looked at Abe hopefully.

"Certainly. Brian, this is going to be a bit of a story. Do you want a coffee?" Brian shook his head negatively. "Then sit down and I'll explain."

It took an hour to explain, and Brian ended up sitting back totally surprised.

"Have you two been drinking?" Brian said doubtfully, but he was looking at the three girls lounging on the sofa.

Abe smiled. "No, Brian, look," and he passed his hand through Hope's side as she giggled pleasantly. "And they're ticklish."

"And this house is really a space ship?" Brian continued.

"Yes, we were just going to test run it into space a little ways. Do you have the time to go with us?" Abe asked.

"No, I have to get back and that would take too long. Can you fire up the rockets and let me hear the rumble?" he asked sceptically.

Abe gave him a look of reproach. "Rockets? No. Charity, take us up to 2000 feet, please."

"Done, Sir," Charity said as the house instantly and silently rose 2000 feet in the air.

"Give us visor walls, please, Charity," Abe said.

"Done, Sir," Charity said as the walls became transparent.

"Whoa!" Brian said in awe. "That's amazing." He stood up and walked to the wall, studying the aerial view. The three girls watched him interestingly, their hair brightening noticeably.

He looked back. "You did all this, Dad?" At the word *Dad* the girl's eyes swept to Abe.

Abe looked sheepish. "Well, physically, yes, but it's all God's doing. He told me how He wanted it done and provided everything to make it possible."

Brian looked out the wall again, "I knew He was awesome, but you don't see things like this happen around church; at least I haven't." He spun around. "I really wish I could go with you, but I have to get back." He looked at the girls. "And more family; wait until Steve, April and Lisa hear about this."

Abe smiled. "Don't tell them too much without bringing them out to see. They might think you've been drinking too much grape juice. And don't tell anyone else about this, will you, Brian? Charity, take us back to base, please."

Brian nodded and said, "Who would believe me anyway?"

"Done, Sir," she replied as the house settled back into its base.

"Amazing," Brian said as he headed for the door. He turned, holding the handle. "I'll be back out as soon as I can get some time. Cool house, folks. Nice meeting you Faith, Hope and Charity; see you later."

"Goodbye, Brian," they said in unison.

He closed the door and they watched him drive away.

Mary said, "One down and several more to go."

"Yes," Abe commented absently. *I hope we're doing the right thing, Lord,* he thought.

Chapter 4

They lifted off shortly after Brian left, going directly into space on a direct course for the Moon.

"Charity, let's not go too fast so I can get more familiar with the manual controls. Let's set the speed at 100,000 miles an hour. That should give us almost three hours to work before we reach the Moon," Abe instructed.

Mary raised her eyebrows in surprise. *A hundred thousand miles an hour!* she thought. *Imagine, such speed!*

Abe, followed by the three girls, started for the manual control console.

"Let's find an old satellite to go through and test our ability to burn our way through solid objects," he was thoughtfully saying to the girls.

Mary watched as the four gathered around the console. As Abe sat at the controls, each girl in turn told him which controls operated the things he wanted to do. It was like watching four children playing with a new toy. She leaned back to watch the view change with the movement.

They burned through a couple of old satellites and watched them brighten and disappear as they reached them. They were consumed by their power system and turned into energy. Any meteorite they encountered met the same fate, disappearing in a flash of light.

Abe handled the controls, doing flying rolls, speeding up and slowing down, changing colour and shape and anything else he could think of, while he listened to the suggestions and instructions from the girls.

After some time, Mary went to the kitchen and made a lunch, returning with it and two glasses of juice.

There was a commotion at the console as Faith tried to interrupt the group. Abe was concentrating on the controls Hope was showing him, and she had just turned up the protective shields when Faith spoke. "Sir? Sir?"

"Give me a minute, Faith. How far does this switch go, Hope? Does it stop anything from getting to the ship?" he asked.

"Yes, Sir," Hope answered. "When it is all the way ahead, nothing will touch the ship. Everything we contact will be vaporized into the power system and stored as energy."

Faith pleaded. "Sir? Sir? We are about to hit..."

Mary looked up as the Moon grew in her view. Mary dropped her plate and juice as she whispered, "Abe? Oh, God, help."

Distracted, Abe looked at Faith and then at the Moon, just as they struck an already deep crater in its surface. They disappeared in a huge billow of Moon dust and debris.

With Abe manipulating the controls manually, they had arrived at the Moon sooner than anyone expected. The debris cloud was noticed and recorded by amateur space watchers on half the earth and photographed by the major telescopes. No one noticed the space ship, and everyone thought the Moon was hit by a large asteroid that had passed the earth and struck on the sunny Moon face.

The earth was dark enough that some countries were able to see the debris cloud long after the impact, and the scientists recorded as much data as their instruments could get while they telephoned each other looking for opinions and answers.

They studied their computer images and digital data as they watched the dust cloud settle and made notes about the mineral particles they saw. They studied all the images they could find, looking for the meteorite they expected to see flashing through space and impacting the Moon, but all they found were wavy images, streaks of light and hidden shadows, which told them little.

This was more than they hoped for, and they gleaned every bit of information they could from their instruments and observations. They rightly predicted weather pattern changes, tsunamis and earthquakes resulting from the crash. They noted the Moon was moved in its orbit and made future predictions about season lengths and variety.

The media made a huge news item of it and had news conferences, meetings and scientist interviews relating to the impact and the changes it had created.

Abe and Mary stared upwards in shock and watched as the ship struck the Moon. They watched their artificial atmosphere turn red with energetic fire as the ship burned and absorbed the solid rock it was travelling through. The energy light show fluctuated from a fiery red through a variety of colours to a light blue and back again.

Abe realized what they were watching and pulled the control sticks back, stopping the ship inside the rock. They sat there in stunned silence until Abe and Mary heard the stifled laughter.

129

Abe noticed them first. The girls were huddled in the corner, watching them with half hidden smirks on their faces while they struggled not to burst out in uncontrolled laughter. His emotions quickly fluctuated from outrage to humour as he understood their mirth, and a smile slipped onto his face.

Mary did not understand, and her mind clouded in anger.

What are they laughing at? she thought. *We could have been killed.* She strode ahead until she was confronting them and raised her hand, fore finger extended. She opened her mouth to start her barrage of words, but stopped as she heard a gasp and a drawn out gurgle coming from Abe behind her.

Fear gripped her heart in a deadly grip. *He's having a heart attack,* she thought as she whorled.

He was staring at her, one hand over his mouth and the other gripping a fistful of his shirt front. His eyes were large and bulging, and his face was bright red. His shoulders were shaking or trembling — she wasn't sure which — and his cheeks were working like bellows.

Mary rushed to him and grabbed his shoulders. "What's wrong? Is it your heart?" she asked.

She could feel his shoulders shaking under her hands, but his eyes had a strange glassy brightness. She heard another snorting sound escape from under his hand covering his mouth.

"Sit! Sit down," she said, still not understanding what was wrong.

"Ha, Ha, ha!" The noise burst from his mouth, and she saw tears forming in his eyes.

She looked with confused anger at the girls laughing in the corner and at Abe's uncontrollable mirth. "Has everyone gone mad?" she asked.

The four laughed harder and the tears streamed down Abe's face. "Ha, ha, ha, ha, ha!" The girls' giggles grew louder.

Mary tried hard to stay mad, but the laughter was infectious and she could feel the corners of her mouth start to twitch. She tried to sound angry. "What has gotten into you four? We just struck the Moon at 100,000 miles an hour. We should be thanking God we're still alive." She waved out the window, "And we're encased in rock. How are we getting out?"

Their laughter increased and Abe started to stagger as he lost control of his balance. He staggered over to her and embraced her in a violently shaking hug while he laughed uncontrollably in her ear.

She couldn't stand it any longer and her own mouth formed a smile as she tittered. Encouraged, the girls laughed louder and moved to hug the couple. The laughter increased and lasted some time until they were emotionally spent and collapsed on the sofa. The girls flopped haphazardly on the floor in front of them.

Abe was the first to find his voice. "I needed that. It's been too long since we've had a good laugh just for the fun of it."

Subdued, Mary asked, "What just happened? I don't understand."

Abe answered apologetically. "Yes, I'd forgotten. You don't understand like we do. I'm sorry."

Turning to the girls, he said, "Girls, repeat your base registry codes, please."

"Do not dishonour God," they answered in unison. "As much as possible, protect human life. Protect this ship and everyone in it at all costs. Honour all life and hold it in great value. Value all of God's creation and use it sparingly, and only as necessary."

"You see?" Abe asked. "They are programmed to protect this ship at all costs. We were never in danger. I'm sorry, but there is so much for you to learn, and I didn't know where to start first, so you'll have to trust us and we'll explain as we go."

Mary looked at him incredulously. "I should be mad as h.......heck, but I understand...and this is an adventure. Next time try to give me some warning before you surprise me with a disaster, ok?"

"Yes, most definitely, dear," Abe sympathised.

An impish look appeared in Mary's eyes. "You know," she said, "you, a retired professional driver, WERE driving and ran right into the biggest thing in the neighbourhood — the Moon."

Abe's eyes lit up with humour. "Oops," he said, and they all burst out in renewed laughter.

Fifteen minutes later, they rose to resume their trip. Mary noticed their lunch, cups and plates were gone, having been absorbed by the energy system from the floor where they were spilt and broken.

"I had a lunch for us, but it's gone," she said thoughtfully.

"It was delicious," Charity said.

Mary's eyebrows went up. "You can taste?" she asked.

"We can analyse the substance and deduct the taste," Charity responded. "We know you made it to taste good, so now we have an idea what *good* tastes like."

Mary smiled at her pleasantly. "Charity, you are a sweetheart. Thank you." She gave Charity a hug and noticed the quickening and brightening hair colour and the embarrassingly pleased look on her face.

She looked at Abe and said, "These girls are so precious. I'll make us another lunch while you figure out how to get us out of here."

"Yes, dear," Abe responded. "Charity, how long would it take to move out of the rock to the surface?"

"Soon, Sir. The surface is only twenty yards through that rock in front of us," Charity said.

"Twenty yards? That close? Well, let's go out, then. Take us to two hundred feet above the surface, please," Abe said, sitting back down at the controls.

The ship moved out of the rock with a final red burst and hovered above the surface as Abe had requested.

They made detailed pictures and analysis of the dark side of the Moon and decided to take a quick pass by Mars. They also made a detailed picture and analysis data of Mars before heading home.

It was just after midnight when they entered the earth's atmosphere. Abe was sleepily sitting at the controls, and Mary was just as sleepily watching from her chair. Suddenly, the girls disappeared and the ship had a noticeable change in velocity. It started to free-fall in the atmosphere, and their atmosphere temperature started to rise as the ship fireballed into earth's stratosphere.

Abe grabbed the controls and found himself totally in control of the ship; Charity control panel was not there.

"Girls? Girls, are you there?" He received no answer.

Mary, watching him with alarm, asked, "Abe? Are we alright?"

Abe pulled the controls back to slow their decent and the ship slowed. He reached to the control panel and adjusted their temperature and protection grid.

"I think so," he said. Everything is working right manually, but the girls are gone and I don't know why."

"Oh," Mary said disappointedly. "Where could they go?" Realizing Abe was totally in control of the ship, she asked, "Are you alright? Can

I help you?"

"No, no, I'm fine. The girls showed me how the controls worked and I got her under control, but I wish I knew what happened," He said worriedly. "I'll look downstairs when we get home."

It took longer than he wanted, but Abe took his time settling into the tight contours of the ship's base for the first time manually. It was after two a.m. when he shut the power down to idle.

Worriedly, Mary watched him rise from the control seat and said, "Can you rest first and look for the problem after some sleep?"

"No," he said wearily. "I couldn't sleep knowing the girls are not here and there is a problem. I'll take a quick look downstairs and see if there is anything out of the ordinary."

As any good electrician will tell you, one starts looking for a problem at the start button. Abe found the operating papers he made when he was building the ship and went downstairs to the main control panel. He flipped the switch off and on and called, "Girls?"

He received no answer, so he started following the current down the wires, looking for a broken or loose connection. Mary sat on the bottom step watching him.

Abe's eyes followed the wires from the main switch down to the junction box where they split to go to each individual control panel box. His vision blurred from weariness, so he stopped to rub his eyes. They watered temporarily and refocused so he could continue.

It took him an hour and three more eye-rubs to complete his inspection of the inside of the panel. He closed the door and looked at the control switches and buttons on its front. Everything looked right, but he had the feeling something was out of place. He studied them again but could not find any problems.

He moved to the side and followed the wire conduit to the *Charity* panel, where he opened the door. He gingerly reached in and touched a connection. Nothing! There was no power here.

Abe found a current tester in his tool box and followed the wires down through the panel. Again, nothing! Not a drop of power anywhere in the *Charity* panel.

Just for safe measure, he did the same for the *Hope* and *Faith* panels, with the same results — nothing. Everything past the main control panel was dead; absolutely powerless.

He remembered the manual controls worked and went to that panel. It was wired before the main switch as a failsafe measure and showed lots of power when he touched the live wires with his tester.

He rubbed his eyes again to clear the fatigue haze and moved back to the main panel. He studied it intently, trying to see the problem his brain told him was there, but which his eyes could not see.

His head sagged wearily and he rested it on his forearm for a few seconds while he tried to get his mind to think. Almost three hours of looking had turned up nothing. He opened the panel door again and stood looking at the electrical boxes and wires.

"Please, help me, Lord," he prayed. "I'm so tired, I can't see straight."

His eyes wandered to the reset button and then to the reset box behind it. Something was not right with the way it was sitting. He reached into the control panel and took the box in his hand. It moved as he turned his hand and then pulled at the box. It noticeably moved in and out. It was loose.

Abe reached into his tool box and found a 5/8ths wrench, which he slipped into the back of the box and over the loose nut on the bolt holding the box against the back wall. It turned easily as he tightened the bolt back into place.

As the bolt tightened and the box moved back to its proper place, it was easy to see the reset button was out. He closed the panel door and, sure enough, the reset button was out, disconnecting the power. "Thank you Lord," he said gratefully.

Mary was asleep with her head on her folded arms at five o'clock a.m. when Abe exclaimed, "Got it," and woke her up.

She looked up in time to see him push the reset button and the girls appearing between them. Joy welled up in her heart, and she realized the girls had really become their children. She rose and hurried to them as they hugged Abe.

"We missed you, girls," Abe said. "I'll switch that button to a circuit breaker so it will reset automatically if anything happens."

"Thank you, Sir. We missed you, too. All of a sudden we were not there. We don't know where we went, but we're glad you brought us back," Charity said as the other two responded with "Yes, thank you, Sir."

Mary reached them and hugged them, saying, "Yes, we missed you.

Abe wouldn't sleep until he found you again."

The girls turned to Abe, who was embarrassed by all the hugs and "Thank you, Sir's." They were like his children, and he admitted he was worried for them.

Abe smiled wearily. "You reminded me how tired I am. I'd like to go to bed now." He started for the stairs, followed by the four girls.

Chapter 5

They had only been in bed a couple of hours when they heard the doorbell.

"That Mr. Hornbeck and Mr. Unger are back," Hope said.

Used to catnapping from his driving days, Abe was rested and alert, but Mary yawned wearily.

"Take your time, dear. I'll see what they want," he said as he slipped into his robe. "I've a good idea they're not happy with their picture," he mumbled as he closed the bedroom door.

On his way down the hall, Abe said, "More pictures, Hope. Faith, block all communication devices they are using, please. Have they got any back-up waiting down the road?"

"Yes, Sir," Hope and Faith responded. Faith answered, "No, Sir," to his last question.

"Hmm, just the two of them; must be thinking we're just a harmless old couple, finally. You girls stay out of sight until they're gone, please." He reached the door and opened it. They disappeared with a final 'Yes, Sir.'

"Gentlemen, come in. Please excuse us, we were up late last night and didn't get much sleep," Abe said smoothly. He closed the door after them and waved them to the sofa. "Make yourself comfortable, please. I'll put the coffee on and be right back."

"Sorry to wake you, Sir," Mr. Hornbeck said as they sat down.

Abe noticed the change in attitude and was pleased. "How do you take your coffee?" He asked from the kitchen. There was coffee left over from the day before, and Abe filled three cups and put them in the microwave.

"Black, one sugar and one cream for me," Mr. Hornbeck said.

"Just black, please," Mr. Unger said.

Mary came into the kitchen, spied the coffee in the microwave, and gave Abe a stern look. "You go. I'll get us a lunch...and fresh coffee."

"For the second cup," Abe said as he mixed the hot coffees and tried to kiss her.

She gave him a quick kiss and another stern look. "Get," she demanded.

Abe smiled happily and took the steaming cups into the waiting men.

"Thank you, Mr. Peters," Mr. Hornbeck said. Mr. Unger nodded his thanks.

"So...what can I do for you gentlemen today?" Abe asked, sipping at his coffee and seating himself in his favourite chair.

"We got your message loud and clear with those x-ray pictures of us with our surveillance equipment on yesterday," Mr. Hornbeck said sheepishly. "I had a rather bad attitude when we first arrived, and I would like to apologize. You could have treated us far worse than you did, and I appreciate your kindness."

"Apology accepted," Abe said happily. "And we have the rest of your surveillance equipment in a box on the kitchen table; erased, of course."

"I understand," Mr. Hornbeck said. "Is it possible to start over?"

"Why yes, of course. That would be wonderful," Abe said sincerely. "Although I don't know if I can really tell you anything more. We are still in the experimental stage, and I don't know how long it will take us to get to a sharing position."

"That's fine," Mr. Hornbeck said. "If you would consider us your friends and give us as much as you would be comfortable sharing with us, I would appreciate it."

"Okay," Abe said. "First of all, my name is Abe to my friends; it's short for Abraham."

"Thank you, Abe, and please call me Dick," he said earnestly. Neither he nor Jim Unger volunteered Jim's name, who was watching them sceptically.

"Ok, Dick. We are running some tests over the next couple of weeks that will be beyond anyone's imagination. This is new technology that has never been seen before by mankind, but is very powerful and different," Abe said seriously.

"I see," said Dick. "Is there anything I can see or read that could help me? Can you share anything more with me?"

Abe looked like he was deep in thought, but he was really praying to God for some guidance. After a few minutes he said, "Leave me your card. When I have something, I'll get in touch with you."

Dick pulled his wallet from his pocket and passed Abe a business card. "Thank you. We have had some strange happenings at Homeland Security the last few days, and my superiors are a little nervous about new technology. I hope to be able to reassure them you are not a threat or a problem."

Mary came in with a tray of sandwiches and more coffee. "Strange happenings? Could you tell us about some of them over lunch?" she asked.

"Well, I might as well. They are all over the news anyway. We also have a leak in our department, and this information was leaked out to the press. We caught a hacker yesterday; a Mr. Woo Chong from China was hacking us from the Chinese Embassy in Ottawa. Our security probes caught him, and we were able to arrest him when his flight made a plane switch in Los Angeles. We don't know if it was him or not, but our computers crashed shortly after finding him. The signal was sent from a Russian satellite, and we don't know if he was working for them, too, or if it was someone else," Dick confided.

"That's terrible," Mary said,

"Yes, we had to purge the system and reboot. It took us twelve hours to get back to full operation," Dick said, looking into his coffee cup.

"And that's why Mr. Brown's phone wouldn't work," Abe said idly.

Dick's head snapped up, and he and Jim Unger looked at Abe suspiciously.

"How did you know about him?" Dick asked quietly.

Abe smiled pleasantly. "The only people who will hover a helicopter around here for any length of time are Rangers or poachers, and he didn't look like a Ranger. This is back woods New Brunswick where we seldom see a helicopter, let alone one hovering so long in one spot. It didn't take much magnification to see what he was doing."

Mary smiled pleasantly and said, "Abe, why don't you ask God's grace for the food and we can continue this discussion over lunch?"

Abe replied, knowing she was also giving him time away from the topic at hand, "That's a wonderful idea." Bowing his head he prayed, "Dear Lord, thank you for your blessings and guidance. Please keep us in Your will and safe from harm, and bless this food in Jesus' name. Amen."

He heard Dick's *amen* and Jim Unger's snort before he raised his head and looked at them.

"Always pays to be humble and thankful," he said.

Dick was idly nodding his head in agreement while he reached for a sandwich and ignored Jim's scowl.

They ate in relative silence, each thinking their own thoughts and trying to form a question in the hopes of learning more. Abe watched them interestingly while he trusted God to give him the wisdom to ward off their curiosity and still be honest.

Finally, Dick spoke around his mouthful of sandwich. "Tomorrow we have to leave to go back to Washington for the weekend, but I hope we can hear from you next week, Abe. Our government is really concerned, and we would like to have an answer for them as soon as you can give us one."

Thursday already and we haven't been in our house a week yet, Abe thought. "Yes," he replied, "I think I can have a little more for you next week. I'll give you a call if I can do any more before then."

He was surprised they were not pushing harder, but he saw there was some animosity between the two, which he suspected had something to do with Dick's change of heart. He noticed the disgusted look Jim gave his superior as they rose to go.

Abe let Jim go ahead of him and walked slowly, holding Dick back as they moved to the door. Jim opened it without looking back and started down the walkway.

"I heard your answer to my prayer, Dick, and appreciated it. You've recently gotten saved?" Abe questioned.

Dick shrugged. "Last night," he responded. "It seemed so real and exciting then, but today it is all gone"

Abe grabbed his shoulder in a friendly grasp. "No it's not. Feel! Your heart is still light and full, but today you have to face your job, and doubt is setting in. Trust me, Jesus only gets better. He has a way of making happiness out of the old drudgery. Don't let your mind drag you down."

Dick looked at him hopefully. "I'll try, but I think Jim has it in for me, and this Christianity isn't helping."

Abe smiled. "Or maybe this Christianity is irritating the crap out of him. It's not him I'm worried about...it's you. Promise me you'll hang in there, and I'll call you soon."

Dick looked sharply at him. "You have a way with words. My wife would not appreciate me coming home and using words like that, but darn, it brought back memories. I'll hang on and...thanks."

Abe watched them leave in their car, then spoke. "Any cameras or audio recorders, girls?"

"Yes, Sir," they said in unison.

"All erased," Faith said.

Abe glanced at her and winked. "Good. Thanks, girls."

They smiled broadly and said, "You're welcome, Sir."

Mary was watching from her chair. "Do you think they will be trouble, Abe?" she asked.

"No, but God has them coming here for a reason, and I think it's for us to help Dick, but we'll find out. Turn on the news, will you, Mary? I'd like to see what they are saying about this hacking and their computers crashing."

The phone rang before anyone could move, and Mary answered it.

"Hello, dear," they heard her say. "He has?" They waited. "Okay, we'll see you all then. Bye."

As she hung up, she glanced at Abe. "The kids are coming out tomorrow. Brian's been telling them they have to come, and they're anxious to learn what he is all excited about."

"Good, good. We may as well show them and get it over with. We can have a huge family gathering," Abe said smiling at the girls and winking at Mary.

Mary frowned. "No funny business," she said, but she knew better than to scold him...or trust him not to start something. He was already turning the television on.

The news announcer was speaking, and a picture of the dust cloud on the Moon was showing on the screen. "The U.S. government is already planning a Moon expedition to see if the asteroid can be recovered."

The screen changed to a fuzzy picture of a dark, black asteroid speeding through space, as the announcer spoke, "Scientists released this picture of the black, obelisk asteroid that struck the Moon yesterday, and they hope to recover the rich mineral deposits they say their instruments recorded are in it."

Abe looked at Mary and the girls lounging on the sofa and said with a chuckle, "We made quite a splash yesterday." They smiled, but Mary was watching the news.

A young girl's picture was framed on the screen and the announcer was talking. "Hope of recovering Joy Hubbard from the Kenyan rebels is quickly fading, and her missionary father has published an appeal for her release. She has been held captive for two weeks, and most experts say the rebels seldom keep a captive past that time when there is no hope of a ransom. Reverend Hubbard says there is no hope of raising any ransom for her, and he hopes they will just let her go."

Abe felt a tug in his spirit and knew the Lord wanted him to get involved in this plight.

The next announcement was about the Homeland Security hardships. "Homeland Security posted this picture of their capture of a Chinese Canadian Embassy employee as he changed flights in Los Angeles yesterday."

A picture of a Chinese national appeared on the screen.

"He was on a flight from Ottawa, Canada to Beijing, China, but became subject to U.S. law when he walked on American soil to transfer to another plane. His computer and a number of recording devices were seized," the announcer said.

"In another story from Homeland Security, their computers were attacked and crashed from an overload of cellular calls. They say the attack originated from a Russian satellite orbiting over northern Canada. Their computers had to be rebooted and were down for a number of hours. This did not affect the NORAD defence system, and in no way endangered the security of the United States," the announcer continued.

Abe turned to Faith and said, "Faith, remember that young girl's face and do a global search for her location, please."

"Yes, Sir," Faith said.

"I'm going to change that reset button on Charity to a circuit breaker," Abe said absently as he turned to go downstairs.

Concerned, Mary watched him go. Something on the news bothered him, but he hadn't shared it with her. She knew he would spend the time fixing the reset button and praying. She watched as the girls followed him out. It was obvious they liked being around Abe.

An hour later, her chores were done and she eased down the stairs to watch Abe and the girls working on the panel. The girls were watching over Abe's shoulders as he explained every detail of his work.

"And the circuit breaker will reset automatically in three seconds, so you will not be gone too long if anything else happens, girls. This will give us time to find any problem and fix it right away. Now, I must shut the current off so I can replace the switch. It will be like going to sleep, and I will hurry so you can be back with us quickly. Are you ready?" Abe asked.

They nodded solemnly. He pulled the switch and they disappeared. He worked quickly and soon had the switch changed. He flipped the power switch back on and the girls reappeared.

"Everyone alright?" he asked, and was reassured by their nodding heads and smiling faces.

"Good," he said. He put his tool box away and they turned to the stairs. They noticed Mary sitting on the top step as they came across the room. "All fixed, dear," he said.

Mary looked at his face and asked, "And your concern?"

He stopped a few steps below her where their faces were level with each other. "God wants us to go get her. She and her dad have been praying and we are going to be His answer. I need a couple of hours nap and we'll arrive in Kenya at dusk."

"Okay, I figured as much. You never could see someone hurting and let it pass. I'll be ready when you are." She rose and went before them up the stairs.

Wearily, Abe turned toward the bedroom and lay down on the bed. He immediately dropped into a restful sleep and awoke two hours later, refreshed. He lay still, staring at the ceiling, feeling out for God's presence. He soon felt that familiar peace and physical awareness of God as He made Abe to know He was near.

"Thank you, Lord," Abe said emotionally before he sat up and went down the hall to get a coffee.

The ship slid noiselessly over the well-lit mansion in the deep dusk before the Moon rose over the horizon. There was obviously a party in full swing going on inside. Visible on the hillside behind the mansion was an outbuilding illuminated by a few lit windows.

"What is going on at the mansion, Faith?" Abe asked without turning from the visor walled view.

"My probes detect a wedding party for the commander of the rebels, Sir," Faith said, standing beside him.

"Joy Hubbard is in the outbuilding?" he asked her.

"Yes, Sir; the unlit room on the right," Faith responded.

Mary sat in her chair, excitement gathering in her heart. She had always dreamed of a romantic rescue when she was a child. This was not quite the same thing, but the dark night and the daring rescue fed her imagination.

They had learned that this girl had been left at her father's mission office while he was on business back in America. The mission was growing very successfully and taking more fighters from the rebels with each convert. The rebels had attacked the mission house, burned it down and captured Reverend Dave Hubbard's fifteen year old daughter two weeks ago. They demanded a million dollars ransom, but Reverend Hubbard was a fiery, independent Pentecostal, and the churches would not support him.

Faith had located their base and the girl while Abe slept, and now they were closing in on the hidden base.

"Take us directly over the outbuilding, please, Charity," Abe instructed.

"Yes, Sir," she responded as the ship settled close over the building.

"Extend a veil down over the building and project a stable image of the scene just as it is now to anyone looking this way, Hope," Abe continued.

"Done, Sir," Hope said.

"Charity, set us down in front of the building, please," he kept instructing.

"Done, Sir," Charity said as the ship lightly touched the ground in front of the building.

Abe turned to Mary and said, "We shouldn't be long. Faith and Hope, please come with me."

"Yes, Sir," they said in unison as the three moved to the door.

Abe eased out the door and hurried to the outbuilding's door. He peeked through the window into an ill-lit room, but he saw no one in sight. He grasped the door latch and opened the door silently. It creaked on its rusty hinges and swung back, so that Abe could step inside.

A door opposite him swiftly opened and an armed guard stepped into view, aiming his rifle at Abe. He said something Abe could not understand and lifted his rifle menacingly.

Surprised, Abe lifted his hands defensively and stepped towards the man, who stepped back in apprehension. He shouldered his rifle and pulled the trigger three times at Abe.

Abe eyes opened wide in fright and the anticipated impact of the bullets just as Hope appeared beside him. She quickly reached out her hand in the path of the bullets, which disappeared into her hand in a red burst of energy as they were absorbed into their energy banks.

Faith appeared on Abe's other side and pointed her finger at the man. A tiny white beam of light left her finger and exploded on the man's chest in a shower of blue energy. The Taser sized electrical bolt caught the man and stood him on his toes, while his powerless arms dropped the rifle and his body vibrated with the charge. His eyes rolled back in his head and little blue fire-balls of electricity crackled out of his stiffened hair and disappeared with a snap at the ends. He collapsed in a quivering pile on the floor.

"Thank you, Hope and Faith. I guess I was so intent on finding the girl, I never considered the dangers. That was a bit naive of me, and I will be more careful after this," Abe whispered shakily.

"You're welcome, Sir," the girls said in unison.

Abe looked around the room and then moved to the only door on the right. It was locked.

Looking at Hope, Abe asked, "Hope, can you unlock this door, please."

"Yes, Sir," she said as she put her hand into the lock. Abe heard the loud click as the mechanism released.

Abe eased the door open and stepped into the dark room. He heard a gasp as the faint light from the first room fell on a kneeling figure on the other side of the room. The girl had her back to the door and was naked. As the door creaked open and the light fell on her, she cried, "Jesus, help me."

Stunned, Abe saw great welts crisscrossing her back and legs where she had been beat with a whip or belt, and she was so thin he could see her ribs showing plainly on her sides.

He felt his eyes start to water and wiped at them. They had to get away and this was no time for emotion. He called softly, "Joy...Joy Hubbard."

She didn't hear him and kept loudly praying for Jesus to help her.

Abe advanced behind her and touched her shoulder. She screamed, jumped up, and ran to the corner where she turned trembling. Her knees were shaking and buckled from hunger while Abe watched.

144

He realized she could not see them plainly because the light was behind them. She thought they were her captures.

Abe spoke louder. "Joy. We are here to help." He advanced towards her. They must leave now. He reached for her and she screamed and fainted, collapsing in a heap on the floor.

He bent and scooped her up in his arms. She was so light. As he turned towards the door, his foot hit an object on the floor. He glanced at it and saw it was a small Bible.

"Could you bring that Bible, please, Hope?" Abe said before heading out the door.

"Yes, Sir," she said, and hurried behind him clutching the Bible.

Faith stood watching them as they made their way through the lit room and out the front door. The guard was still quivering where Faith had zapped him.

The ship was a short distance. They ran across the open space and into the front room.

Mary met them at the door and gasped at the tiny burden Abe carried in his arms. "This way, quickly," she said, and hurried down the hall.

"She's got great welts on her back and she's starved and filthy, Mary. She fainted from hunger," Abe told her as they made their way down the hall.

Mary was about to turn into the spare bedroom but changed directions and went into the bathroom. "Hold her a minute, Abe. I'll run a warm bath. That will be very comforting."

She started the water running and turned to inspect their addition.

"Charity, lift us off, please. Take us two hundred feet up and hold there until I can come out for a look around," Abe instructed while he helped Mary check the girl's health. Hope and Faith watched apprehensively.

"Done, Sir," Charity said, standing beside the other two girls.

Mary checked the water and set the taps for the proper temperature and motioned for Abe to place her in the tub. He gently laid the small figure in the warm water and stepped back out of Mary's way. "Can I get you anything?" he asked.

"No, you go ahead and take us home. Hope and Faith can help me just fine," she said as she rolled up her sleeves and knelt by the tub. She took a soft cloth and gently began to wash the small girl. Hope sat at the head of the tub and gently stroked the girl's dirty hair.

"She has a tape worm," Hope said.

Mary glanced at her and back at the girl, frowning.

"Can you take it out without harming her, Hope," Abe asked.

"Yes, Sir," she said.

"Please do it then," Abe said and they watched Hope reach her hand into the girl's midsection until she was wrist deep. The girl's stomach glowed red, which formed a line that followed her intestines around a few loops and then disappeared. Hope removed her hand and glanced at Abe.

"Done, Sir," she said.

"Thank you, Hope," Abe said, smiling at her.

The girl moaned softly and opened her panic stricken eyes. She tried to flail her arms, but Mary gently but firmly held them from striking her. "Easy...easy, you're safe now," she said.

They watched as the girl looked from one to the other, starting at Mary, who was smiling reassuringly. Her tense body slowly relaxed as she realized she was no longer a captive. Her eyes travelled from face to face; from Hope to Faith and Charity, then stopping at Abe, who smiled, winked and said, "You're safe with us now, Joy. Jesus heard your prayers and sent us."

"Safe? Jesus?" she whispered, and they saw her face calm. She lowered her arms and quickly glanced down when they touched the water. She gasped when she saw she was still naked and her hands fluttered over her chest in a vain attempt to cover herself.

Abe quickly spoke, "I'm going out to take us home. You girls probably have a lot to talk about." He hurriedly left, closing the door behind him.

When he reached the main room, Charity and Faith appeared beside him. "There is a group of men advancing on the building Joy was in," Faith announced.

Abe watched through the visor floor as a group of fifty men arrived at the building, drinking and singing. The leader, a big burly man, was being jostled and slapped on the back by his companions. He turned at the door and, amid shouts and jeers, made an obscene gesture implicating sexual activity. He paused briefly, basking in the attention, then turned and vanished into the building.

He reappeared a few seconds later with the guard and pushed him to the ground in front of the mob. His arms waved as he angrily shouted at the man, who cowered on his knees while he pleaded for his life.

The scene played on as the leader worked himself into a fit of rage. The man's pleas grew louder and more desperate as Abe watched the leader pull his pistol and shoot the man three times in the chest.

They had rescued Joy just in time and saved her from a terrible ordeal.

"Close the visor floor, please, Charity," Abe said sadly as he glanced at the two girls. They stood watching sombrely but the vision disappeared and the floor became solid again.

"Done, Sir," Charity said, but Abe detected a hint of sadness in her voice.

He too felt sadness for human cruelty and lust, but made his voice sound happier. "Take us home, please, Charity. We have our girl and are done here."

An hour later they were settling into their base. Abe cooked some soup and laid out a snack at the table for the three of them. They arrived shortly after he was done, and the girls proudly presented Joy to him, clean and smiling.

Abe smiled broadly and said, "There you are, and that smile is a big improvement. I see the girls have perked you up."

"Yes. They are so kind. I'm an only child, and it is so wonderful to be around other girls my age." She spoke softly. She was dressed in some of Mary's clothes, which fit fairly well.

Abe eyed the group suspiciously. "Don't let them fool you. They keep me on my toes just keeping them in line."

Mary scoffed and said, "Yea, sure. If we didn't watch you every minute, you'd have us away chasing after God- knows- who, or whatever whim you came up with." Then she winked at Joy and smiled.

The four girls joined in their laughter when they realized Mary was teasing.

They all sat down to eat and, after Abe said grace, pounced on the food. Abe watched from his standing position by the counter as the five ate and chattered happily.

After the meal, they piled the dishes in the sink and moved to the living room to continue their chatter. Abe wondered if they would ever run out of things to talk about, but it didn't seem likely. He decided to wander off to bed. It had been a trying week, and he was beat.

He quietly moved down the hall and prepared for bed. He slid under the covers and blissfully laid his head on his pillow. He was sure he would pop right off into dreamland, and he closed his eyes.

"Are you asleep, Sir?" he heard Faith ask quietly. He felt her presence beside him in the dark room.

"No," Abe said and opened his eyes.

She was inches away from his face. He could see the whites of her eyes filled with consternation and staring into his. She sighed with a deep emotional heave and asked, "Sir, why do people hurt and kill each other?"

Abe closed his eyes and thought, *this is going to be a long but important one.*

He lifted up from the bed and propped his pillow against the headboard. He sat up and leaned back against the pillow. "Make yourself physical, Faith, and lean on my shoulder. You might not like what I'm going to tell you."

Faith obeyed him and lay beside him on the bed with her head on his shoulder, while he put his arm around her shoulders and started to speak.

"People are made in God's image and are supposed to care and protect each other, but the emotions God gave us also make us feel strong, powerful and exciting. Many people like these feelings and become addicted to them, like they do with cigarettes; it can become a bad habit. There are so many, and they can feel so wonderful and become more intense by our expectations and imaginations. All people want to feel good and secure, but when they crave their emotional feelings over the wellbeing of others, then they stop caring for others and concentrate on only their own wants."

He looked down into her eyes as she stared back up at him. "Some people feel superior," he continued, "and try to control others to get an intense superior feeling. They seek positions of authority so they can control others for their emotional fix, and will spend most of their lives trying to gain power and control so they can feel the rush of emotional power. As they gain more control and get more feelings of power from their positions, they find that they want to feel more and have to do harsher and crueller things to feel that rush of emotional power. They resort to humiliating others, beating some, and even torturing those who are helplessly in their control. When they do this, they must convince themselves that other people do not matter or are inferior, or that there is no lasting effect from what they do — whatever they have to believe so they can get their superior emotional feelings."

Abe sighed, and Faith's head rose and fell with his breathe. "That is so sad," she said.

"Yes," he said, "but they are so good at lying to themselves to accomplish their emotional needs, they will actually stop believing the truth and believe their lie is really what is right. When this happens, whatever they do is considered right in their minds, and they will do anything they can imagine that will help them feel superior and remorseless. Lying, torturing and killing just become part of their lives, and others just become objects for them to use for their emotional gain."

He sighed again and continued. "This is something I wish you girls did not have to learn, but in order for you to be able to decide what is right, you must know what is wrong. I'm sorry, but people are not always nice; however, we must try to be good even to those who are not. Do you understand?"

Abe looked at Faith as she hesitated. "Yes, Sir, but it is something I wish I did not have to learn. It hurts me inside to think there are people who do not care for others."

Abe drew Faith up and hugged her. "I know, Faith, but you and the girls are proving to be very big hearted, and that is a good thing. I am very proud of the three of you and love you as my own children."

He thought he heard Faith's voice catch as she answered. "T...thank you, Sir. We love you and will not disappoint you."

Abe chuckled. "I'm sure you won't, Faith. I'm sure you won't."

She rose to go. "Good night, Sir, and thank you."

"You're very welcome, Faith, and good night. I'll see you in the morning."

"Yes, Sir," she said as she disappeared.

Chapter 6

Abe woke while it was still dark. Mary lay beside him, breathing softly while she slept. He glanced at the clock as he rose to relieve himself. It was 2:30 and about his normal pee time.

The house was usually quiet this time of the morning, but as he passed the spare bedroom where Joy slept, he heard a low humming. He stopped at the partially closed door and peaked in.

Hope was sitting at the head of the bed stroking Joy's hair and humming softly while she slept. Charity and Faith appeared beside him.

"She was tossing in her sleep and remembering her terror. The only way she would sleep comfortably was for someone to touch her in a gentle fashion. Hope likes doing it," Charity said softly.

Abe waved as Hope looked up at him. She smiled as he gave her a thumbs up.

"You girls are so precious," he whispered quietly and hugged them both. Their hair lit up the hall as they glowed with pleasure, and Abe noticed it for the first time. *Amazing,* he thought, and continued on to the bathroom for his personal business.

The next time he woke up, he was instantly aware he had overslept. Mary was gone and the clock said 9:15. He could hear the din of activity coming down the hall from the girls at the far end of the house. While he dressed, he caught the occasional laugh and clatter of dishes.

"Thank you, Lord," he prayed as he walked down the hall. His life was so blessed, and the things God kept doing to him were so wonderful he thought he would burst with happiness. He stepped into the kitchen and witnessed the excited activity as they placed breakfast on the table.

"Sit down and eat," Mary said pleasantly, while the three girls tittered.

He sat down and looked at his food: eggs over easy, steak well done and lightly toasted brown bread heaped high with raspberry jam, completed with juice and a steaming cup of coffee. He immediately became suspicious. He very seldom got such a perfect breakfast.

He looked at the grinning faces and realized someone was missing.

"Okay you monkeys, what are you up to and where is Joy?" he asked, trying to keep himself from smiling.

"Here, Sir," Joy said as she stepped from the doorway where she had been hiding in the living room. Abe stared and his mouth dropped open. She was dressed in an identical outfit as his three girls, but it was blue with her name, *Joy*, in bold yellow letters on her left chest. She was an identical copy of Charity, Faith and Hope. She smiled happily and tittered at his surprise. The room erupted in laughter.

"What? How did you do that?" He looked at Mary.

"I didn't; Hope did," she responded.

Abe looked at Hope. "How?" was all he had to say.

She smiled happily and said, "With the energy collector."

Abe gulped. "It's reversible?" he asked.

"Yes, Sir," she said.

"Amazing." He continued looking at Joy again. "Who chose the colours?"

Mary rolled her eyes at Hope and Abe again looked at her smiling face.

"Truly amazing. You girls are full of surprises," he gushed, turning back to the happily laughing Joy. This was a far different girl than the one they rescued. Gone was the fear and dread of her capture, replaced with the joy of a relaxed and loving household.

"You look wonderful in that outfit, Joy. If you're not careful, we'll want to keep you," he said.

Abe watched her happy smile slowly fade as she remembered her father. "Mary said I would have to ask you if it was alright to call my father and tell him I'm alright. Could I, please?"

Abe looked at her and said, "Could you wait a couple of hours, please? I have someone I want to do a favour for and your safe return would fit nicely. As a matter of fact, I'll call him right now. Would that be alright with you?"

"Yes, Sir," Joy said and smiled again.

Abe said grace while the group waited respectfully, and then he picked up the phone while he put a spoonful of eggs in his mouth. He sipped his coffee while he dialled Dick Hornbeck's number. He kept eating while it rang.

Seven times was a long time to ring, but it was finally answered. Abe recognized Dick's voice from the hasty, "Hello."

"Dick, Abe Peters here. I have some information for you. Can we meet soon today?" Abe said, and then covered the receiver with his hand and looked at Faith. "Is there any listening bugs on Dick's phone, Faith?"

"Yes, Sir. Three," Faith responded.

"Could you give them some music and keep our conversation between Dick and I, please; say Pipeline or California Sun," Abe asked.

Faith smiled humorously and said, "Done, Sir."

Abe's returning glance caught the puzzled look on Joy's face and he winked. "We'll show you later."

Dick was talking in the phone. "I'm at the airport, just ready to board our plane. Jim's already aboard. I couldn't answer my phone earlier because it was going through security. Can it wait until next week?"

"No. Sorry, Dick, but this is going down right now. I wouldn't worry about Mr. Unger. Just don't get on the plane. We'll pick you up at the airport in an hour. Is that alright?" Abe said.

"Abe, I'm in some trouble back at the office now. I don't know," Dick hesitated.

"Dick! Trust God and trust me; this will be worth it," Abe said, convincingly.

"Well....alright. I'll call a cab and meet you back at the Best Western on Main Street. That's where we were staying," Dick suggested.

"No, Dick. Go to the Big Truck Stop and wait in the driver's lounge; you're bugged." Abe told him.

"Bugged!" he blurted, "Where...how do you know that?"

Abe said pleasantly, "The same source where I get my X-ray pictures. We'll meet you in an hour."

"OK, an hour then. I'll be there," Dick said before he hung up.

Abe was halfway through his breakfast when he hung up and hurried to finish.

"Are you taking the girls?" Mary asked. "We have to get ready."

Glancing up while he chewed a piece of steak, he said, "You look fine to me."

Mary frowned at him and scoffed. "Harrumph, men! What do you know about looking presentable? We'll be right back. Girls, follow me, please."

The five went down the hall giggling as Abe finished his breakfast. He smiled pleasantly and thought, *you couldn't have a good teasing without a good scolding, too.*

It was a half hour to the truck stop and they were all in the SUV in fifteen minutes. An ex- truck driver, Abe disliked cars and preferred the larger four wheel drive vehicles, and he was quite put out that he couldn't get a standard anymore.

As they drove, Abe explained the girls to Joy. He didn't tell her everything, but he made it plain they were holograms that were quite capable of thinking, caring and individual thoughts. They thought very highly of Joy and were happy to be able to help her.

Joy listened quietly. When Abe was done, she asked softly, "They're not real?"

"Oh, very much so, and they have all but adopted you," Abe laughed. The girls and Mary watched the reaction in silence, letting Abe handle the conversation. He continued, "If you touch their side, they'll break out laughing. They are very ticklish, and Mary will probably growl at me for telling you. Life is exciting enough with three teenage girls, let alone four. Hope sat up all night playing with your hair so you could sleep securely."

Joy turned to Hope and asked, "You did?"

"Yes, you were so restless after your terror," Hope responded.

Joy looked like she were about to cry and reached out to Hope and hugged her. When she was done, she said, "My mother couldn't stand the missionary life and left my dad and me ten years ago. Dad has been mother and father to me, and mom doesn't call or care about me. The culture is different in Kenya, and we didn't have many friends. I had no one my own age to hang with, and you're the first family I've met who are so happy and make me feel welcome."

Mary gasped. "Poor child," she said. "Your father must be a wonderful man to care so much for you, and you turned out to be such a precious child."

Hope reached over and patted her arm and said, "You're not alone now."

"Thank you," Joy said as she struggled to keep from crying.

Abe glanced at her in the mirror and said, "Sometimes a good cry feels great, but when you're done, the rest of this crew wants you smiling and happy so they can tease you. Do I get to order another breakfast at the restaurant?" His face wrinkled in a grin as he turned to Mary.

"I should think not. You'll have to work that first one off weeding the garden this afternoon," Mary said with mock sternness.

They were listening intently as Joy told them stories of her years in Kenya when they pulled into the truck stop. Abe parked by the driver's door and they went inside to the lounge.

Dick rose from the sofa as they entered, and Abe said quietly to Faith, "Point out the bugs and we'll show them to Dick, please, Faith."

"Yes, Sir," she replied as they reached him. She advanced around Dick and pointed to his cell phone, his watch, his belt buckle and his collar, while he stood there watching her with a puzzled look on his face.

"Who is she, Abe, and what is she doing?" Dick asked.

"You have four bugs on you, Dick. If you don't mind, I'll remove them and we can keep this conversation between us," Abe said looking at him.

Confused, Dick agreed. "Yeh, sure," he said as he watched Abe remove a small microdot from his collar and belt buckle. Then he opened his phone and removed one from its battery and another from the bottom of his watch. Dick didn't notice them disappear in a small, red flash once Abe passed them to Hope.

Abe finally looked at Dick and said, "Now that we are alone, I am connected to a well-organized and highly skilled team which rescued that missionary man's daughter, and she is now under our protection." He put his arm around Joy and continued. "Please meet Joy Hubbard."

Dick's month flew open, and he stared at the girl before stammering, "What....how....how did you do that?"

Abe smiled and said, "You know I can't tell you that, but I have given you first chance at the news before we call her father. You can handle this any way you think best, but I would suggest you take the credit for establishing a connection with a group that could do this, and report that you have an inside edge with them. Then you work with those friends you have at the office to make this a newsworthy item for your security organization, and offer to assist in bringing her father here to pick her up. I figure you and he could attend church with us Sunday and spend the day with us. We are going to be very busy tomorrow with personal family plans and cannot be available."

Dick looked at him sharply. "You've given this some thought, and I appreciate your giving me this opportunity." He looked at Joy and said, "Everyone thought you were dead, and I regret no one wanted to give your father any money for your release, thinking he was using the situation for himself. I'm sorry. My country can be quite stubborn and mean sometimes."

Bravely she stared back at him and said, "Dad believes in God with all his heart, and Jesus sent these wonderful people to rescue me. Mr. Peters has asked me to wait and give you this opportunity, and I believe he wants to help you, too."

Dick looked at her and hesitated before he shrugged and said, "Yes, I believe he does and thank God for it. Things have been going downhill since I gave my heart to Jesus, and I was beginning to think I had made a mistake."

Abe smiled. "Did you ever think that your trouble was just God getting rid of a few unwanted items in your life?" he asked.

Dick shook his head. "No," he admitted. "I hadn't thought of it that way. Maybe you're right. This sure is good news. I'll get on the phone to the office and set this up with your father, Joy."

"How long will you need?" Abe asked. "She wants to call her father as soon as you're ready to tell him the good news."

Dick thought for a minute and said, "Give me a couple of hours and I should have this rolling by then. Thanks."

"Done! Now we'll leave you to it and see you Sunday at our place about 8:30. Make a big splash with this, Dick, and get yourself back on track, then come out for a visit and we can talk about Jesus," Abe said, smiling.

"Sounds great, Abe. Thanks," Dick said as they turned to leave

At the door, Mary said, "That went well, and you might get more breakfast for being so thoughtful." She gave Abe a quick hug as they went through the door.

Abe looked embarrassed and the girls laughed. It was a merry group who returned home a short time later, having made a second stop for groceries to feed the hungry crowds they were expecting over the next few days. It took a few minutes to unload the groceries and fill their freezer, but the last load came all too swiftly to the happily working group.

Joy admitted that she had not had so much fun in a long time and looked forward to eating western food again.

As they finished closing up the Jeep, Abe touched Joy's arm and said, "Walk with me a little, will you Joy? I'll bring her right back, Mary; I promise. You girls can tag along, if you like."

Mary noticed Abe was not joking and said, "That's fine, I have a lot to do. You know, I haven't finished unpacking our things yet. You men are always distracting us from our housework." She smiled and turned to go into the house.

Abe smiled and turned away, holding his arm out for Joy to hang on to. She circled her hands around his arm and they started out across the lawn.

Abe cleared his throat. "You know, Joy," he said, "you kind of fit in pretty good here, and the girls have taken to you. We all like you."

"Thank you, Sir. I like you also, and these girls are like the sisters I didn't have." Joy spoke softly and sincerely, not knowing what Abe was leading up to.

He cleared his throat again and continued. "God has done some wonderful things in our lives, and when we saw your problem on the news, He told me to go get you. This house, these girls and our lives are all dedicated to Him, and He heard your father's and your prayers. He loves you and rescued you just in time. We watched before we left Kenya, and the men were going to finish with you last night."

Joy sobbed as she remembered her captivity.

"I'm sorry to remind you, but I'm going to show you some things and I have to know I can trust you not to tell. You have to remember what we did and how important it is for us not to be known about," Abe said seriously.

"I understand, Sir. You have been very kind to me, and these girls have been super. I will not break your trust in me," Joy said brokenly.

"Good. I thought we could trust you. God thinks very highly of you." Abe paused and, after a big breathe, continued. "These girls are holograms produced by our power source under the house. The house is really a space, or travelling, ship. The girls have personalities, feelings and are each individual; in other words, they are alive."

They were walking by the back of the house, and Abe saw Mary's face appear briefly in the window. He continued. "They are very powerful individuals and control various parts of the ship. The reason I wanted your father to pick you up on Sunday is that our family is coming tomorrow, and we are going to explain the ship to them. We will probably take a short hop to the Moon or some near planet, and I want you along."

Joy had stopped and her mouth was hanging open. "Really?" she said. "That sounds so impossible, but I don't believe you would lie to me. I would be so happy to be included in a family gathering."

"I thought so, too," Abe said and patted her hand. He turned to Hope, who was grinning broadly. "You may have to create another outfit or two for her, Hope; looks like she is staying a day or two with us."

"Yes, Sir," she responded cheerfully.

They reached the front of the house and Abe held the door as the girls filed in. Mary rose from her chair where she was sorting clothes. Her face held a questioning expression.

Abe went over and hugged her while he whispered in her ear. "I told her about the house and the girls. She'll keep our secret, and she's also going with us tomorrow with the rest of the family. I suspect that with only her father and her she hasn't had much family time. Do you think we could show her what family is all about?"

Mary hugged him hard and whispered back, "You big, soft hearted galoot. I think we could show her family time."

Dick called an hour later with Joy's father and his superior at Homeland Security on a conference call. Abe instructed Hope to broadcast the phone conversation, and their voices boomed plainly into the room.

"Joy? Joy, honey; are you there?" Reverend David Hubbard's voice sounded strained.

Joy couldn't sit down with excitement. "Daddy, yes I'm here, I'm... here..." Her voice trailed off as tears flowed down her face.

"Oh, thank God. Baby, I was so worried and thought I would never see you again. When this man, Gene Phillips from Homeland Security, called and said you were safe, I almost didn't believe him. Praise the Lord! He said one of his agents, a Mr. Dick Hornbeck, had a connection with a highly specialized team of expert mercenaries or something, and they found and rescued you."

Joy laughed through her tears and she looked around at the rest. "They're not mercenaries, Dad. Wait 'til you meet them."

"I would love to and shake their hands with gratitude. They won't tell me where you are, or I'd come there right now," Reverend Hubbard said.

"Please don't try, Sir. We are very busy tomorrow, and your daughter will be with my family and inaccessible. I believe Mr. Hornbeck has the instructions about your visit," Abe spoke.

"Who is this? Are you the one who rescued my daughter?" Reverend Hubbard's voice sounded emotional and unsteady.

"I'm in charge here, Sir, and you will meet me Sunday, I believe; isn't that right Dick?" Abe said.

Dick spoke up. "Yes, we are making that arrangement. Mr. Phillips will have those arrangements done; am I correct, Sir?"

"They will be ready and we will be there to pick you up, Mr. Hubbard," Gene Phillips said authoritatively. "We have a news release going out in half an hour, and everyone will know your daughter is safe."

"Thank you, Sir," Reverend Hubbard said sincerely. "I can't wait to see you, Joy, and thank your friends there for me, will you? Is there any way I can repay you, Sir? Anything I can do or give for your kindness?"

Abe smiled. "No, Reverend Hubbard, but you can thank Dick Hornbeck. Without his connection, this might not be turning out this way." There was a moment of silence while everyone thought about his words.

"Thank you, Mr. Hornbeck," Reverend Hubbard said. "I owe you a huge debt of gratitude."

"You're welcome, Sir." Dick spoke softly and thoughtfully.

"I'll see you Sunday, Joy, and I look forward to meeting your new friends," Reverend Hubbard said.

"Ok, Daddy," Joy said. "You're going to love them; they're the best."

"I'm sure I will. Bye for now, baby." The Reverend said. Everyone hung up, and Hope hugged Joy. "Your daddy knows now, and it's alright."

"Yesssss," Joy squealed as she hugged Hope back.

Abe and Mary watched the girls laugh and dance around the room. Abe reached over and quietly squeezed Mary's hand while he whispered, "We're a little old for teenagers, but I wouldn't miss this for all the tea in China." Mary said nothing, but smiled and nodded her head.

Chapter 7

rian's car came up the driveway shortly after supper, and the girls flocked to the windows to watch him come to the door. Abe caught the words *tall* and *cute* in the excited interchange.

The four were standing in a row when he came through the door and spied them. He hesitated and smiled. "Four now, eh, Dad? Are you making yourself an army of girls?"

He spoke while he advanced into the room and casually passed his hand at Joy's side to tickle her. His fingers thumped against her side and her mouth dropped open in surprise. Shocked, Brian pulled his hand back and stared, open mouthed, at Joy.

"That one's real, Brian," Abe said, smiling. "That's the missionary girl who was captured and held in Kenya. You must have seen her picture on the news?"

They watched a red tint appear at Brian's collar and creep up his cheeks. Faith, Hope and Charity giggled merrily, and Joy turned a very pretty pink as well.

"Sorry, please excuse me. I didn't know," He stammered.

"Brian, please say hello to Joy Hubbard. Joy, this is our youngest boy, Brian Peters," Mary volunteered.

"Hello, Joy. Sorry about grabbing you like that," Brian said, regaining his composure.

Joy smiled slightly and responded, "It's ok. I just wasn't expecting it."

Abe laughed and said, "You can expect most anything from this one, Joy. He never fails to amaze us or keep us amused just keeping up with him, but we love him anyway." Everyone laughed as Brian turned pink again. Abe turned to look at Brian and asked, "What brings you out here tonight? I thought you would come with the rest in the morning."

Thoughtfully, Brian answered, "I was going to, but I didn't have any plans for tonight, so I thought I would come out and stay over for tomorrow. I hope that's alright, seeing as you have a full house already."

"Oh, that's fine," Abe said cheerily. "We didn't show you the other half the last time you were here, and these girls seem to have taken an interest in you." He was watching the way the girls watched Brian and Joy. "Why don't the five of you make yourselves comfortable in the living room," he continued, "and Mary and I will put together a lunch?"

Abe and Mary watched the group settle in the living room amid much chatter and banter.

"So you can make yourself transparent or physical?" Brian was asking the girls, while Joy listened intently to their answers.

Abe took Mary by the hand and drew her away to the kitchen. "I don't think they will miss us," he said. They're young people, and if I remember correctly, old people are just not interesting enough to keep up with them.

She squeezed his hand, smiling. "Oh, I remember those days. This will give us a little break. I don't know about you, but this week has been very tiring, and I could use a little quiet time."

Abe nodded and said, "I could use some of that myself, but it might be fun to sit in the corner and watch what these five get into."

The evening passed quickly, and Abe and Mary were entertained by the conversation and questions the five young people had as they learned much about each other. Brian, even though he was deep into computers and software, seemed to gravitate more to Joy as the evening wore on, and the two found more in common with each other as they talked.

Faith, Hope and Charity seemed to be interested in any human emotions or reactions they could learn about.

Abe didn't let them stay up too late, with such a busy day awaiting them in the morning. Brian took the third bedroom, and by ten o'clock everything was quiet.

Abe felt the hand and heard Charity whisper, "Sir, there is a group of armed men advancing on the ship."

Instantly awake, Abe slipped out of bed and quickly dressed. For fear of waking Mary, he didn't speak until he was in the hallway.

"How many are coming and where?" he asked Charity.

Faith appeared and answered, "Twelve, Sir, and they're spread out to surround us."

Abe wasted no time. "We'll take them in the yard," he said. "Faith, look up their identities and background, please."

"Yes, Sir," she said as they moved to the glass doors in the kitchen.

"Do they have night vision?" Abe asked, peeking out.

"Yes, Sir," Faith answered. "They are Russian Special Forces, but

I've found they are directed by Mr. Jim Unger, and he is a Russian double agent."

Abe looked at her in amazement. "You are very thorough, Faith."

"Thank you, Sir," she said humbly.

"Is Mr. Unger here with them?" Abe asked.

"No, Sir," Faith answered.

Abe thought for a moment and then said, "First, let's kill the batteries in all their night vision glasses. Then, we'll let them get close and Taser most of them. I'd like to let their commander come in the front so we can turn the lights on and have a talk with him."

He peeked out the window at the advancing shadows and said, "Let them get a little closer, girls, then you can Taser them and use their plastic straps to bind their hands."

They waited patiently as the shadows materialized into men coming across the lawn. The advancing soldiers were taking advantage of every shadow and tree, unaware they were discovered. The minutes dragged on until the first men reached the side of the house.

Abe could hear the faint scuff of their boots on the front walk. "Ok, girls," he whispered. "Leave the commander and any soldiers who are near him so we don't spook them before we can talk to them."

He watched the three girls disappear from beside him and appear beside three of the shadows on the lawn. He noticed the faint blue spark of their energy and counted six, one for each soldier on this side of the house. A quick motion told him that each man was disarmed and their hands strapped behind their backs.

Abe made his way to the living room chair and sat facing the door. Hope appeared beside him as the door slowly opened and three shadows crept into the entryway.

Faith and Charity appeared beside him and he casually said, "Lights please, Charity."

The three men crouched and stared around at him as the lights lit up the entryway. They raised their weapons to fire, but Faith and Charity appeared behind them and Tasered the two soldiers as the commander froze, his pistol half-raised in confusion.

"You shouldn't try that," Abe said conversationally. "You would be hard to understand with an electric charge coursing through you."

The man glanced around at his already bound men and relaxed his pose. Faith and Charity stood on either side of him, and Faith casually took his pistol away from him.

"Sit, please," Abe said, waving to the sofa as Mary peeked around the corner of the doorway. Movement could be heard coming down the hall.

"Abe? What is going on?" Mary asked, coming into the room and tying her housecoat close around her waist. Brian and Joy appeared behind her.

"Need help, Dad?" Brian asked, giving the commander a stern look. The man, knowing he was caught, stared impassively back at them from his seated position.

"Not at the moment, Son. Our intruding friend is just about to tell us what he wanted here," Abe said, smiling thinly.

"You'll get nothing from me," the man said in precise English.

Abe's smile grew larger as he said, "That's where you are wrong, and that is good English for a Russian Special Forces agent."

The words impacted the man, and he stiffened but remained silent.

Abe continued speaking. "Think about it." He paused for emphasis. "A dozen Special Forces soldiers captured and helpless by a man and his family, who are mostly girls. You're not going to be popular when my government sends you back home."

The man said nothing, but Abe saw his brow furrow in thought, and his face showed them he did not like what he was hearing.

"Okay, have it your way," Abe shrugged as he spoke. He turned to Faith and said, "Faith, what is this man's name, please?"

"Colonel Klanski Nickalanko, but his Canadian passport lists him as Karl Gregory, a German immigrant," Faith said.

Klanski started and stared up at the girl in amazement. "How...?" he said, then clamped his mouth shut.

Brian sat on the arm of Abe's chair to watch, fascinated by what he was seeing.

"Mary, could we have some coffee, please?" Abe asked pleadingly and looking at her soulfully.

She roused from her surprise and looked at him. "Spoiled brat," she said softly. Speaking louder she said, "I suppose. No one will get much sleep the rest of the night anyway." She rose and went to the kitchen.

The soldiers were quietly trying to loosen their bound arms, and Abe said to the Colonel: "You should tell your men to relax; it would be a shame to have to put them under again." He turned to the girls and said, "Charity, turn on the house lights, please. Might as well let the boys outside know they're not hiding from anyone."

"Done, Sir," Charity said, as the lawn surrounding the house lit up with the eave lighting. The soldiers lying on the grass stopped moving and lay still, not knowing what was going to happen.

The Colonel said something in Russian.

"Sir, he told them to wait until later and they could work loose," Hope translated.

Abe smiled at Klanski and said, "You can believe that if you want. It will keep them from frustrating themselves for now."

Klanski was eyeing Hope in dismay, disgusted with their easy capture. His gaze turned harder and he hissed through his teeth as he swore a vulgar Russian word for a female animal.

Hope's expression didn't change as she repeated the word in English.

Brian stiffened as Abe said, "Now, now, Colonel. No need to get sticky."

The Colonel turned on him and called Abe a pimp who hides behind a woman, which Hope also translated. He continued and said Abe's girls were for hire and second rate prostitutes.

Brian stiffened more and half rose from his seat as his fists balled.

Abe reached for Brian's arm, but was too late as the Colonel pointed at Joy and asked her how much she wanted to be with him. Brian launched himself across the room before Abe could stop him, and the Colonel rose to meet him. His expert training let him dodge Brian's rush and turn him around in a choke hold. A sharp knife appeared in his hand, which he held across Brian's throat.

Mary shrieked from the doorway and Abe said, "Easy Colonel. What do you want?" He held Hope back by her arm. The colonel would not harm Brian as long as he thought he could use him to bargain out of his entrapment.

"Let my men loose, or I'll cut his throat," he snarled.

"Just take it easy, Colonel, and tell me why you came here in the first place," Abe said softly.

"Let my men loose!" he demanded. "You have some technology we have come to get."

"Is that all? Shoot, I thought your mission was important," Abe said smoothly. "Relax, Colonel."

Abe let Hope's arm go and whispered, "Take him, Hope."

Abe hid her disappearance by standing up. Suddenly, the Colonel's arm went limp and slumped to his side. The knife slid across Brian's chest and fell from the Colonel's numb fingers, making a small thump as it landed at Brian's feet. Hope was standing behind him with her hand on his shoulder, where she had shocked his arm nerves with an energy charge.

Brian shook loose and turned, ready to strike the Colonel, but stopped when Abe said, "Wait, Brian. He's helpless."

The Colonel was standing in open mouthed surprise at how easy Hope had disarmed him.

Abe continued, "Agent Unger is going to be upset with you. He may even get you sent away for failing tonight."

Colonel Klanski scoffed. "That worm is not my commander. He's just an informant we could dispose of anytime we wish. He's not even giving us good information." It took him a few seconds to realize what he had done. He scowled at Abe's smiling face.

"Thank you, Colonel. Record that Charity, and we can call Dick and see what he wants to do with these people," Abe said as he picked up the phone.

Angrily, the Colonel pushed ahead towards Abe, but Brian pushed him back to the sofa, ready for more of his tricks. The Colonel still could not use his right arm, and he slumped down in the seat.

Abe dialled Dick's number and waited for him to wake and answer.

"Dick," he said when he heard his sleepy voice on the other end. "We have another present for you."

"I don't know if I can help you, Abe," Dick said sadly. "I've been reprimanded by my superiors. They think Joy Hubbard's rescue was a setup. I don't know who is causing me so much trouble."

Abe waited for him to finish before he spoke.

"It's Jim Unger, Dick. He's a double agent. Jump in your car and come out; we have some men here for you to take."

There was a long pause then Dick said, "Jim? Men? I don't understand, Abe."

"I know, Dick. How soon can you be here? We have to call the RCMP and tell them about this too," Abe said happily.

164

Dick answered, "Well, about half an hour, I guess. Can I stop for a coffee?"

Abe laughed. "Go through the take-out, Dick and we'll see you in twenty minutes."

Dick chuckled. "You're a hard man, Abe," he said. "Twenty minutes it is." He hung up.

Abe chuckled again and hung up before turning to the crowded room.

"Ok, Brian could you go with Faith and disarm the soldiers one at a time and bring them in here," Abe said. "We'll sit them against that wall and bind each man's foot to the one beside him. Faith will keep them from acting up on you." He turned to Joy and said, "Joy, do you want to help?" At her nod, he continued. "Could you go with Hope and follow Brian so you could do the same to another soldier? Disarm one and lead them in here to sit against the wall. Hope will watch the soldiers for you and tell you where their weapons are."

Joy smiled happily and the group set off to gather the soldiers.

Abe heard Mary sigh and mumble, "They can at least have a cup of coffee while they wait." She turned back to the kitchen.

Abe turned to the Colonel as Charity moved beside him and said, "Okay, Colonel. Agent Dick Hornbeck is on his way to look after you so, please take off your weapons and give them to Charity. Then you can move over to the wall and sit down against it." He saw the Colonel tense to resist and continued, "If you don't do as you're told, Charity will Taser you and we'll do it the hard way, but we won't be gentle."

The Colonel's face dropped and he stole a sideways glance at a stern-faced Charity. Reluctantly, he started pulling weapons out of his clothes. He had a small arsenal hidden on him, but when he stood up to move to the wall, Charity said, "And the knife on your belt buckle."

He looked grudgingly at her and removed the knife and dropped it on the pile. He moved as instructed to the end of the wall where Abe strapped his hands together. The first soldier came in from outside with his hands strapped together in front of him.

Abe motioned for him to sit beside his commander, and they strapped their feet together, left foot to right foot. The next soldier was treated to the same line-up.

While Brian and Joy brought in the soldiers from outside, Abe disarmed the two remaining soldiers on the floor in the hallway and added them to the wall line. They finished just as car headlights appeared in the driveway, and Mary appeared with hot coffee and sandwiches.

Abe glanced at the clock as the group settled in the seats and said, "Dick's right on time." He had picked up Colonel Nickalanko's cell phone and held it out to Charity.

"Are there many calls still in this phone's memory, Charity?" he asked her.

"Yes, Sir," she replied. "Seven. Three to Mr. Unger, two to the Captain of a Russian ship in Saint John Harbour, and two to his contacts in Russia."

"Can they be extracted by Dick's people?" Abe asked, amused by the amazed look on the Colonel's face.

"No, Sir. There is a self-destruct code on his phone if it is tampered with," she informed him.

Abe smiled and said, "Okay. Copy the messages and disarm the code for Dick, please."

"Done, Sir," Charity said.

Abe turned to his family. "Brian and Joy, could you help Mary pass out sandwiches and coffee to these gentlemen while I let Dick in, please?"

"Sure," they said, and collided with each other as they both moved in opposite directions to help. Joy found herself in Brian's embrace as he grabbed her to keep her from falling.

Everyone paused, and Abe looked at Mary and winked and smiled.

"Wish I'd thought of that move when I was trying to get your attention," Abe said.

Mary scowled at him, but her lips curved into a tiny grin.

Brian and Joy hastily apologized and hurried to help Mary while Abe opened the door.

He greeted Dick with a smile and an outstretched hand.

"Busy night, Dick," Abe said.

Dick took the hand and replied, "For you, maybe. I was sound asleep." He was eyeing the line of prisoners and continued, "You have guests."

The two stood facing the crestfallen soldiers.

"Yep, Russian Special Forces no less," Abe said. "They were after the same thing you were asking me about, but the girls gathered them up and here they are."

Dick's eyebrow went up and he looked at Abe.

"The girls?" Dick asked.

Embarrassed, Abe said, "Oh, that's right, you haven't been introduced to them yet. You've met Joy; well, this is Faith, Hope and Charity, our girls." He waved his hand as he named each one.

Dick nodded to each in turn and then said, "And four girls just gathered these men up and plunked them here against the wall?"

Abe smiled and said, "Yep, and you know I can't tell you how."

Dick eyes twinkled and his lips curled into a half smile. "Are you really trying to help me or torment me?"

Abe smiled back. "Maybe both. Anyway, these men broke into my home to steal from us, so we'll have to call the RCMP, but I thought you might like first chance at them. It seems your Mr. Jim Unger is a Russian double agent who sent them here."

Dick frowned and said, "He's written a report on me and submitted a claim that I'm a foreign agent, also. Do you have any proof?"

Abe passed Dick Colonel Klanski's phone. "There are some interesting messages on this phone," he said. "And the Colonel has been kind enough to disclose that they are acting on information from Mr. Unger."

"Great!" Dick's face showed his pleasure. "You are a valuable friend to have."

Abe shook his head and said, "No, Dick; Jesus is the valuable friend. I'm just doing what I'm instructed to do, and He wants me to help you. I must admit, though, you are turning into a good friend."

"Thanks, Abe. I appreciate this, and thank Jesus for me, too," Dick said sincerely.

Abe smiled again and said, "You're welcome, Dick, and no, you thank Jesus yourself. He is listening and will always hear those who sincerely love Him."

Dick nodded his understanding. "I will. Thank you, Jesus." He paused in thought and then said, "You know, it just so happens some of our Special Forces are training with the Canadian Army right here, and their commander is a friend of mine. If the RCMP is willing, we could take these fellows off their hands."

"Works for me, give him a call," Abe said.

Dick moved to an isolated corner to make his call while he munched on one of Mary's sandwiches. Everyone was silent as they ate and drank their coffee. The captured soldiers accepted their fate and enjoyed their sandwiches and coffee, still a little confused as to how they ended up bound prisoners by an unarmed Canadian family.

Abe noticed Brian and Joy sitting close together watching the room. Faith, Hope and Charity were busy watching them. He caught Mary watching him. He shrugged as he quietly said to her, "You know, there's no sleep for parents of teenagers."

He watched her nod in puzzled agreement before she answered back, "But do teenagers get the RCMP, Russian, American and Canadian Armies all together in a tangle in one night?"

Abe smiled around a mouthful of sandwich. "I guess so," he said. "That's what they did."

Dick made his way back across the room, putting his phone into his pocket.

"Those sandwiches are good, Mrs. Peters, Thank you," he said.

Mary smiled. "At least someone appreciates my efforts. You're welcome Mr. Hornbeck, and please call me Mary."

"Done. Mary, thanks." He looked at Abe and continued. "Captain Strom is on his way with some troops and some carriers. He's bringing the Canadian commander with him. We'll sort this out in the morning and tell the RCMP. Meanwhile, we can use the base lockup to hold these soldiers in tonight."

Abe glanced outside. "That's good but it's already morning. This is going to be a lll...ooo...nn...g day."

Chapter 8

The Army vehicles reached the end of the driveway on their way out as the first car was waiting to come in. Dick, Captain Strom and General Dumont were travelling in Dick's car.

Brian was standing with the four girls at the window, watching them leave.

"There's Doug and April with their brood now," he said. "Trust those farmers to be up early."

Abe relished the image of their youngest daughter, her organic farmer/activist/political opponent husband, and their four children with another on the way, and was looking forward to seeing them.

"Oh, this will be great; Harold and Lisa are right behind them," Brian said gleefully.

Abe's thoughts clouded. *That Brian could be a scamp. Harold and Lisa were both lawyers and politicians with no children and sparks always flew when they got together with Doug and April. Where were Steve and Geraldine when he needed them?* His oldest boy and his wife were tall, thin and quiet, and they had a calming effect on the rest of the family. Maybe it was because he was a doctor and she was a neuroscientist. They had two wonderful preteen boys who were just like them.

Brian's voice drooped as he said, "And there comes big brother and his clan."

The girls were listening to Brian's play-by-play and watching the vehicles find parking places in the roundabout driveway. They were obviously excited as they watched the people exit their vehicles and greet each other by shaking hands and hugging with some comments and laughter.

As a group, they filed up the walkway and gathered in front of the house. Abe and his crowd went outside to meet them. The four girls stood just outside the door and watched as Abe, Mary and Brian moved among their family, hugging and jostling each other. Many of the newcomers commented on the house and its location, and there were many questions about the departure of the Army vehicles they met coming in.

Abe's reply was always the same: "Later. All in good time."

The introductions were made inside in the living room. Abe gathered them all and waited for them to get comfortable before he started.

"Boy, it's great to see you all again," he started. "It's nice you could all come at once and be here for the introductions at the same time — except for Brian."

Mary quietly said, "The brat," but she was smiling happily at him, and he grinned broadly back.

Abe faced the room full of his family members and said, "Brian knows about our house and has been telling you about it. Well, he doesn't know the half of it yet, and we wanted you all here so we wouldn't have any gossip floating around out there."

He paused and saw he had their full attention before he continued. "I must have your promise that what you see and hear today will not be repeated or talked about out in public. It is of utmost importance this remains as secret as possible. Can I get your word, each one of you, that you will keep our secret?"

He watched as the members each nodded in turn and made sure they all promised. April's kids were too young, but Steve's boys, Jax and Willy, were watching him with a keen interest. They both nodded assent when their turn came.

Abe glanced at Mary, sitting comfortably in her chair, before continuing. "Okay, this house is really a space ship."

He watched as many of their mouths dropped open, and he heard Jax and Willy softly say "cool" and "awesome." He knew they wanted to burst out with a million questions, but they waited, knowing he would tell them more.

Abe continued, "God instructed me to build it, and He financed its construction. I'm not yet sure why, but He has a purpose for us, and we are just getting used to how it works. We showed it to Brian the other day, and, no doubt, he has been talking your ears off with the news."

He watched them nod their assent as they waited for more. Abe smiled and waved the girls up and positioned them beside him.

"These three darlings are holograms, and each one represents a function of the ship's workings," he explained. "Charity is the ship; she controls its power and movement. Hope controls the immediate surrounding outside the ship — the atmosphere, the defences and the short range probes and energy beams. Faith controls the long range probes, attack beams and sensors. They have personalities and can become physical if need be. Your mother and I have found them to be wonderful girls and consider them to be alive and part of the family; so, children, say hello to your new sisters."

Steve spoke in his usual casual manner. "So, when is their birthday and do they have expensive tastes?" His words brought a round of laughter from the rest, which eased the mounting tension of the room.

"Are they the reason for the Army being here?" Harold asked.

Abe frowned. "Yes and no. It seems the governments of certain countries caught wind of the material I was buying and figured I was making something they would be interested in. Homeland Security agents visited us and asked some pointed questions, but we couldn't tell them much. One of the agents was a double agent for the Russians, and a team of their special forces arrived tonight to take what information we had back to Russia. The girls disarmed them, and I called a new friend in Homeland Security. He brought some of their special forces along with some of our army personnel, and they just left with our Russian visitors in tow. That's the convoy you met leaving the driveway as you were trying to get in."

Doug chimed in and asked, "These girls disarmed a group of special forces soldiers?"

"Yes, they did and they did a wonderful job of it, too," Abe said, smiling.

Doug looked at the girls admiringly. "Man! I would have liked to have seen that." Again everyone chuckled and studied the girls, especially Jax and Willy. Abe noticed their looks and knew they were thinking what any almost-teen boy would be thinking around pretty hologram girls. Were they solid enough to kiss, and what did they taste like? He smiled and caught their eye before he shook his head. He was pleased to see the red colour appear by their shirt collars. He had guessed right.

Geraldine chimed in, and with a slight smile and sugary sweet voice, said, "Dad...could I borrow them for a while?"

Abe laughed. "I should have known not to tempt you with such an obvious project. You can't take them to your study, but I'm sure they would be delighted to answer any questions you have for them. Just don't try to analyze them; they're fine just the way they are."

Brian was standing behind Joy and waved his hand at Abe and pointed to her.

Abe caught his intention and said, "We have another guest for our family who we are hoping will stay awhile with us. Kids, this little lady is the captive missionary girl we brought back from Kenya. Meet Joy Hubbard. Joy, these are our children and grandchildren. No doubt Brian has been introducing you to them."

Shyly, Joy glanced at Brian. "Yes, he has, and I'm so happy to meet all of you," she said.

"Let me guess," Doug said. "The girls went over to Kenya and brought her back?" He spoke with a half-smile, but with a light hearted tone.

Abe smiled back at him and said, "As a matter of fact, they did."

April poked Doug in the ribs and joked, "Don't you go gettin' any ideas. I'm not turning into a super girl just so you can show me off, too." The group broke out in a fit of laughter at her comment.

She stood up and moved her youngest child from her lap to her hip as she walked towards the girls. Mary had the other three in her lap, where they sat quietly while everyone met the girls.

As April walked, she said, "I don't know what the rest of you are going to do, but I'm going to welcome our new sisters and get to know them. We can gab about them later."

Abe secretly loved April the best of his girls. She was aptly named, because she had a personality that was like the spring bloom after a hard winter; she always seemed to know what would make everyone feel welcome, and she didn't hesitate to act on it. The rest of his kids were not to be outdone and hastened to follow. Abe soon found himself on the outskirts of a noisy crowd of family, laughing and jostling to greet the girls.

He eased over to the sofa and made himself comfortable to watch the action. The group slowly faded into a dusky haze, and the sound of voices grew dimmer as he drifted into sleep.

Unusual for him, he struggled to wake up. He didn't know how long he had slept, but when he opened his eyes the first thing he saw was his youngest granddaughter, Dawn, sound asleep in his lap. Her brothers, four year old Pike and three year old Joey, were sitting on the floor in front of him, staring up at him intently.

"Hello, boys. What are you doing?" he asked sleepily.

Pike softly answered him, "We're watching to see if your teeth are going to fall out while you snore. Grampy White's (Doug's father) always comes out, and sometimes he can't find them in the sofa."

Abe smiled happily. "I doubt if mine can fall out. They're growing in there pretty tight."

The boys looked disappointed, and Pike turned to Joey and said, "We may as well go and pull Ogeechee's (April and Doug's two year old daughter) hair and watch her cry."

"But Mom will spank us," Joey whined.

Pike thought about it and then said, "Okay, we'll make her laugh with some funny faces." The two boys wandered off to the kitchen.

Abe watched them go, amazed at how simple children were and how quickly they would change their minds. He gently picked up the sleeping Dawn and cradled her in his arms while he went to find everyone else.

The rumble of conversation from the kitchen led him there, where he found everyone involved with making salads and sandwiches for lunch.

"Sorry, I fell asleep," he said as he walked in the room.

April stopped with her knife poised over a sandwich. With a twinkle in her eye she said, "Up all night with a bunch of girls chasing special forces soldiers? I should think you would be ashamed."

Steve chimed in and said, "Don't be too hard on him, April; after all, he did let the girls do most of the work."

Lisa swatted him on the shoulder and said, "Don't encourage him, you chauvinist."

Abe saw the girls were watching and enjoying the family revelry. He knew this was a good group to teach them family openness. Mary was now playing with Ogeechee as Pike and Joey walked by. They were distracted by the open glass sliding door and were making a break for the back yard.

Spying them going, April looked for Doug. "Keep an eye on the boys, dear," she said. "They're headed outside."

"Got 'em," Doug responded, as he followed them outside.

Harold and Brian had been drafted with Joy and Hope to prepare potatoes for the salad, and Lisa and Charity were mixing juice and stacking plates and utensils for the meal. Everything seemed to be under control. Faith was with April and Steve making sandwiches and left nothing for anyone else to do.

It was soon time to eat, and April turned to Abe and said, "Say the grace, Dad, and we can all dig in."

Abe bowed his head along with everyone else and said, "Lord, thank you so much for a happy, healthy family, and thanks for us all being here in one place. Please bless this food for our health. In Jesus name I pray." They all echoed his "Amen."

Lunch was buffet style and was a jumble of moving, talking people, but everyone was having a wonderful time. When it was over, April said, "Jax and Willy, you two didn't help much before, so you get to clean up the dishes."

They looked at her in astonishment and Jax said dryly, "Yeh, right."

April gave them a stern look and went over to the counter and held up a plastic garbage bag. "Yeh, right! Here!"

Geraldine had spent most of her time with Mary and quickly snapped, "Jax! Willy!"

They instantly jumped to obey, which produced a number of smiles from other members of the group. They stayed and watched the boys throw the paper plates and plastic utensils into the plastic garbage bag. When they were done, Abe caught them before they took it outside.

"Bring it over to me, boys. It's time to show you a few things about our girls," Abe said.

The boys obeyed, and Abe held the bag out to Charity and said, "Charity, please absorb this into the energy banks."

"Yes, Sir," she said, and the bag turned red and disappeared.

There were a number of gasps from the people, and Harold softly said, "They would be invaluable down at the office," which made everyone laugh.

Abe spoke up. "It's time to show you what we have been talking about. Let's all go into the living room and get comfortable.

After they were all comfortably seated, Abe said, "Charity, please take us out to space."

"Yes, Sir," she said as the ship lifted off and soared into the darkness of space.

Many of the adults gasped, and Jax and Willy sat staring, open-mouthed, at the view through the windows.

"Charity, visor walls please," Abe said.

"Yes, Sir," she said as the walls became transparent. There were more gasps of surprise.

Abe smiled and paused for a second, and then said, "Let's do something simple first. Charity, please take us to the South Pole."

"Yes, Sir," she said as the ship leaped towards the Southern Ice Cap.

Abe continued, "Settle us right down at the Pole, please, Charity, and extend our atmosphere out far enough to keep everyone comfortable, Hope. We can all move up to the roof and have a wonderful view. Open the roof, please, Charity."

"Done, Sir," the two girls said in unison.

Abe led everyone up to the roof balcony, and they sat in the patio chairs to enjoy the rest of the trip. They moved over the icy terrain, which afforded the group a wonderful view of the Southern Polar Cap.

After an hour of travelling and picture taking, Abe suggested, "Let's hop on over to the Moon and show it to you up close."

Everyone agreed, and Abe motioned for Charity to move them there. The trip through space was a blur, which ended with them hovering near the Moon's surface on the bright side with a clear view of its terrain. Everyone was spellbound and hurriedly snapped pictures of the barren surface.

Abe directed Charity to move them along a circular line across the Moon's face and into the darkness of the far side, giving his family a couple of hours in the sunlight until they encountered the darkness.

As they moved over the face of the Moon, Geraldine said, "Would it be possible to see where the asteroid struck the Moon's surface? Our Astrology department has been buzzing about it all week and are hoping to recover and study parts of it."

Abe smiled at her, but Mary spoke up and said, "Humph! Don't bother, Geraldine. That was Abe, the professional driver, with this ship. He was on manual and hit the biggest and *only* thing in the sky — the Moon."

Abe noticed her face was flushed and her eyes were shining. *She's enjoying this adventure,* he thought. *Who would have guessed she craved an exciting excursion like this.*

The group was looking at him for his reaction. He smiled, shrugged and said, "Oops" amid their relaxed laughter.

Geraldine looked shocked. "How can I ever tell people that story?" she moaned. "If I wasn't here, I wouldn't believe it myself. They're convinced it was an asteroid."

"You could say you don't believe it was an asteroid and it might even be a manmade object," Abe said sympathetically. "They'll laugh at you, but you can pretend you're joking or making fun of them. That could work and still be true."

She thought about what he said and replied, "Yes, yes, I could do something like that. Thanks, Dad. I was worried I would appear to be a fool by trying to explain the truth without being able to tell the truth."

Once well into the darkness, Abe said, "Hope, give us some flood lights, please."

"Done, Sir," she responded as the Moonscape lit up with the warm, white glow she produced.

Abe smiled as he noticed Brian's arm around Joy, having unconsciously went there in the excitement of the moment. He also noticed that she was not objecting, but seemed to be leaning closer to him.

Steve interrupted his thoughts as he exclaimed, "Dad! This is fantastic." His sentiments were echoed by everyone there. Jax and Willy were too awed to speak, and April's four were either asleep or playing on the floor, not interested in the bland Moon surface.

Abe looked at Pike and Joey again, because he saw Faith down on her knees playing with them. He smiled and nodded his approval, which she acknowledged by looking up at him and smiling.

They ended their Moon trip in the center of the dark side.

"If everyone has seen enough, we should be getting back," Abe said. "There's church tomorrow, and we have a meeting with Joy's dad. I'm hoping you can all stay over and go with us in the morning."

Everyone gave an affirming comment and Doug, being the farmer with animals to tend, said, "We expected as much, and I asked my neighbour to tend my place while we were gone. We do this for each other all the time, so we can stay."

"Great!" Abe almost shouted for joy. "Charity, take us home, please."

"Yes, Sir," she said as the ship lifted off and sped into the darkness, heading for Earth.

It was an awesome sight as they watched the sunlit earth grow bigger on their approach. Everyone's camera was clicking, and many commented on the beauty God had made in His creation.

Their time was over all too soon, but the sun was setting as they settled back into their base.

Everyone was too excited to sleep, but Abe showed them the wall elevator that flipped as it went from top to bottom and exited into an exact copy of the floor on the top. The ship generated a gravity field, which made everyone feel like they were right side up. The walls and ceiling projected an image of the sky and lawn to look like the top half. No one could tell they were upside down.

Steve and Geraldine, Harold and Lisa and Brian were assigned bedrooms on this bottom side, while Doug and April, their children and Joy were assigned bedrooms on the top half of the house. Jax and Willy were given some air mattresses and chose the top half living room to bunk in. As they made their beds and arranged their sleeping quarters, everyone wound down and soon was ready for bed.

Dick called by ten o'clock to tell Abe that he, Reverend Dave Hubbard, and Mr. Gene Phillips were staying at the same hotel where he stayed previously, and they would be out to Abe's house by 8:30 Sunday morning.

"Wonderful, Dick! Play the hero here, my friend; you have earned the position. Without you, we would have a difficult time arranging this meeting," Abe said sincerely.

"You make me sound so important, but in reality, you are the one who is doing it all," Dick replied.

"No, Dick. Jesus is doing it all, and we all have our part to play in the scheme of His will," Abe said sombrely. "You are learning how to serve and obey Him, so play your part and give the praise to Him. I and my secrets must remain a secret so that we can continue to do what He wants us to do, and I know you will not give us away."

"You're right. You have done so much for me; I would be a fool to give away your secret ability to do the impossible. Thank you, Abe. God bless you, and we'll see you in the morning," Dick said seriously.

In spite of the late night, everyone was up early. Breakfast was another joyous occasion, with only one spat between Doug and Harold about the efficiency of Abe's power source over the dirty use of fossil fuels. Doug was digging Harold about his government not being able to develop a power source that could run without gas or diesel, and Harold responded with Doug not being able to harvest his crops without the same gas and diesel to power his machinery. These occurrences happened often enough, and no one got overly worked up about them. In fact, everyone watched and were entertained by their debate.

By 8:30, everyone was ready for their guests and was watching as the cars arrived with Joy's father and the Homeland security agents. The news media vans were following close behind the cars.

Abe said, "Brian, you stay close to Joy, please, and do most of the talking. I want to stay out of the camera spotlight as much as possible. We'll stay in here, and you can bring the Reverend, Dick and Mr. Phillips in."

"Ok, Dad," Brian said, understanding the desire for secrecy.

Abe turned to Harold and asked, "Harold, could you stand in the doorway and greet them? You're a politician and could be expected to be in the spotlight to represent the government."

"Sure, Dad. No problem," Harold responded quickly.

Brian and Joy opened the door and walked out to greet their visitors while Harold stood in the doorway to block the camera crew's view of those inside.

Joy rushed into her father's arms as he exited the car, and they hugged and cried. Brian greeted Dick and was introduced to Dick's boss, Mr. Gene Phillips, who remembered him, before they all started for the house. Four Homeland security agents followed behind them, and two RCMP officers moved from their car to stand between the agents and the news media camera crew. A woman news announcer was trying to push past them without success.

Brian led the group into the house, and Abe asked Harold if he would tell the news woman they would be out later to give a statement. He left to inform the woman about their decision, which calmed the news crew down.

Dick immediately led Joy and her dad over to Abe and introduced him.

"Reverend Hubbard, this is the man I told you about — Abe Peters and his wife, Mary," Dick said.

Abe smiled brightly as he took the Reverend's hand and was pleased by the firm grip he encountered. "It's a pleasure to meet you, Sir," he said. "You have a wonderful daughter there. You must be very proud of her. She has made quite a good impression on my family."

The Reverend's deep voice broke as he said, "Thank you, Sir. I hear I owe you a great debt of gratitude for saving her from her ordeal."

Abe reached his other hand to the man's arm and softly said, "No,

Sir, you don't. Jesus heard you and your daughter's prayer and instructed me and my team to bring her back here. You owe Jesus thanks and praise."

A tear rolled down the Reverend's face. Sobbing, he said, "You are right, my friend. Through all the dangers and struggles Joy and I have encountered, Jesus has always been there and has always been faithful to keep us. I would like to meet this team of yours someday, Sir."

Abe smiled and said, "Please, call me Abe, and you can meet them right now." He turned to face the four girls. Joy was wearing the outfit Hope had made for her and fit in perfectly with Faith, Hope and Charity.

Reverend Hubbard's eyebrows rose when he saw Joy standing with the girls, a huge smile on her face. "Honey," he said, "it's been a long time since I saw you smile that big. I think these folks have been good for you."

Abe waited as Joy spoke up. "They have been, Daddy, and these are my friends you wanted to meet — Faith, Hope and Charity. Daddy, they rescued me from Kenya."

Reverend Dave Hubbard mumbled softly, "First Corinthians 13:13." Louder he said, "Girls, it is my utmost pleasure to meet you, and I must voice my gratitude to you for being such wonderful friends to my daughter."

Everyone was crowded around them, and many could be heard to sniffle as they held back tears.

"Thank you, Sir. We are happy to have Joy with us," they said in unison.

Abe watched as Brian took over and led Dave and Joy Hubbard through the rest of his family. Dick coughed and tugged on Abe's arm and quietly said, "Abe, I want you to meet my boss, Gene Phillips."

Abe turned and met the hand extended to him from a thin, bookish man with dark rimmed glasses.

Gene Phillips had a thin, high-pitched voice, but it had the ring of authority when he said, "Pleased to meet you Mr. Peters. To be honest with you, I had my doubts about there being any value or technology here when I saw we were in a single country home. I changed my opinion when I saw Brian Peters coming out to meet us. He has helped us many times as a representative of Security Stop. We have them keep our computer systems clean, and it was their probe which found and tracked the Chinese Embassy hacker last week."

Abe hid his surprise behind a wide smile and said, "Yes, we're very proud of Brian and all our children."

"As you should be," Gene Phillips continued. "Brian has handled every virus that enters our computers and has kept them virus free with no downtime until this latest one, last week, after we stopped the hacker. He's still tracking the source of the attack which crashed our system, and we have confidence he will find them."

"I'm glad Brian is such a great help to your country, Sir. We have a lot in common, and Dick has proven to be a huge help with these matters here." Abe smoothly changed the subject, making a mental note to talk to Brian at the first available opportunity.

Gene Phillips face brightened. "Yes, Dick is proving to be quite an asset. He has you as his friends, which we are greatly appreciative of, and he found evidence of Jim Unger's double agent treachery. He's been a busy man lately."

He smiled at Dick, who humbly said, "Thank you, Sir. It is my job and I had a lot of help from Abe."

Gene turned back to Abe and said, "Yes, I've been told. I'm hoping to learn more about this technology you have, Abe."

Abe smiled disarmingly. "I'm sorry," he said. "I can only disclose what my boss allows me to, but for now it's getting late, and we are due in church shortly."

"Of course," Gene Phillips said, disappointedly. "I understand. Well, shall we go to church then?" He turned and waved his agents to precede him outside, where the news anchor was set up for a screening.

Abe watched him go and winked at Dick. "Here we go," he said. He turned to the room and announced: "Everyone! We must hurry. We have to give a news statement before we go to church, and time is slipping by quickly."

Chapter 9

Abe let Harold and Lisa handle the media presentation, after he had coached them on the particulars. He made sure they told the media that theirs was a "safe house' where Joy was brought to. He requested the location not be disclosed for security reasons, and stated that the Canadian government and Homeland Security sanctioned this rescue and meeting of Joy and her father.

Brian stayed with Joy for moral support, and they and Reverend Hubbard each gave a small speech thanking the rescuers and the respective governments.

Their timing was close, but they all filed into a now- packed church, just as the deacon stood to open the service.

Abe sat proudly watching his family participate in the service. They had raised their children as Christians, and each in turn had accepted Jesus as God's son and their Lord. They enthusiastically sang the hymns and listened intently to Pastor Jim's message.

As they filed out after the service, Pastor Jim commented that Abe was starting his own baseball team and, indicating the Hubbard's and the Homeland Security agents, the opposing team, too.

Abe smiled happily. "You know it, Jim. Good message this morning."

"Thanks," Jim said, and turned to the next couple in line.

The news media followed them home, and Abe and his family put together a picnic for everyone in the back yard. Even the media people fit in and had a good time.

By late afternoon, groups started to move towards their vehicles and quietly left.

Gene Phillips stayed close to Abe most of the afternoon, trying to learn more about the secrets he possessed, but learned nothing. After Gene and his men left, Abe cornered Brian alone and asked him about Gene Phillip's comments.

"Yeh, he's right. You were never curious about my work, so I didn't tell you I was in computer security," Brian said honestly. "This hacker and computer attack has me stumped. The Chinese hacker had a strange, shadowy signal I have never seen before, and the attack ended at a Russian satellite. I can't find any trace of where it came from before that."

Abe smiled and said, "I can tell you." He motioned to the girls. As they came up beside him, he said, "Faith was the shadow your probe saw when she stopped to read a file on agent David Brown. The Chinese hacker, Woo Chong, just happened to be hacking their system, and Faith followed his link into their computer."

Abe's smile grew bigger as Brian's frown grew deeper and he continued. "I instructed Hope to keep Homeland Security busy while I apologized to Mr. Chong, but she didn't know how strong or weak their computers were and crashed their system by mistake. Sorry, Son. It's our fault."

Brian scratched his head and looked from his father to the girls and back again. The girls stood quietly watching him think about what he heard. Finally he smiled and said, "Dad, are you sure you won't let me learn more about your system? I wouldn't be any trouble or get in the way; I promise."

Abe laughed and said, "I know you wouldn't, and no. You know enough already." He saw Reverend Hubbard and Joy heading their way and turned to meet them.

Reverend Hubbard extended his hand and said, "Thank you so much for all you have done for us, Abe; it is greatly appreciated, but now we must be going."

Abe took his hand and replied, "You're very welcome, Dave. You and your daughter are welcome here anytime. As a matter of fact, if Joy wanted to come and stay with us any time, she could stay as long as she wanted to. I know of three girls who would be overjoyed at the thought of spending more time with her, and maybe one young man would like to as well."

Brian's shocked look and burst of "DAD!" brought laughter from the group and a blush to Joy's checks.

Dave looked at Brian and said, "Joy has told me of you, and I can think of no reason why I should object to the two of you spending some time together. You've proved to have a genuine affection for my daughter, and I believe you to be an honourable young man."

"Thank you, Sir. I think Joy is a very special young lady, and I won't disappoint you," Brian said humbly.

Abe watched his youngest son and felt the parental pride warm his chest. *Thank you, Lord,* he thought. *You do all things well, and I am so blessed.*

Dave drew Abe's attention back to him as he said, "It just so happens,

I must attend some very important meetings in a week's time and Joy cannot be there. Could I possibly impose on you to have her here for a short stay, Abe?"

Delighted, Abe gushed, "We would be more than happy to have her here and as long as she wants to stay, Dave. I hope your meetings are not too serious."

"Thank you, my friend," Dave said. "No, not anything troubling, but very necessary for our work in Kenya."

Brian took Joy and her father back to town with him, and Dick left ahead of the rest of Abe's family shortly afterwards. Abe stood with his arm around Mary as they watched the last of them leave. He sighed happily and squeezed her waist.

"A good day all round," Abe said.

"Amen," Mary said softly.

The house seemed strangely quiet after the excitement of the last two days, but Abe, Mary and the girls sat on the porch and enjoyed the tranquil evening, watching the stars and listening to the night sounds. They didn't say much and went to bed for a refreshing night's sleep.

Abe awoke to an empty bed, and the sun was already up when he shuffled into the kitchen where the smell of fresh coffee filled the air.

"You're up early," he said to the back of Mary's head. She was sitting at the table reading her Bible and drinking tea.

When she turned and looked at him, he saw her eyes were shining with excitement. "We have to finish testing this ship, and I would really like to see some of the sights of space," she said.

The girls appeared in the room, and Abe smiled and as he poured his coffee.

"Good morning, girls," he said.

"Good morning, Sir," they said in unison.

Abe wandered over to the glass doors and stood there watching the morning sun warm the lawn while he drank his coffee. He had not seen Mary this excited about a trip before, and it was puzzling.

Had she always wanted more excitement, and I failed to notice? Abe thought.

It was as if she had read his mind when she said, "You know, Abe, watching our children and seeing our grandchildren this weekend made me realize that we now have some time to take a trip. They have grown fine and don't really need us as much anymore, and I used to lie in the grass at night, as a girl, and wonder what other star systems look like. The beauty of stars, planets and other wonders in God's great space is amazing, and I never dreamed I would ever have the chance to see any of it, but now we do, and I'm just a little excited by the thought of it all."

Reassured, Abe turned to smile at her. "Yes, we do," he said, "and until the Lord tells us what He wants us to do, we can travel around His great open space and see some of it."

They lifted off that morning with the intent to stay travelling in space for the rest of the week. Their plan was to slow down going by each planet in their system, just to take a look at them and find a distant star system to go to after they reached the outer edge of earth's sun's planets.

It took most of the first day to visit the planets in their sun system. They hurried past Mercury and Mars, because they found them barren rocks and uninteresting. Venus was covered with thick clouds, but they spent a few hours looking at Jupiter. It's constantly moving liquid cloud mass changed colours, much like a lava lamp, and was quite interesting. Saturn's rings were another interesting view, but Uranus and Neptune were cold frozen lumps, as was Pluto.

They spent the first night in space on the outer edge of the earth's planetary system, mentally exhausted but enthusiastically excited. Tomorrow would be a day to look forward to as they went looking for another star system to explore.

It was an unusual start to the morning coming out to the kitchen. Abe looked at the darkness of space through the window and shivered with a mental chill. He flicked the lights on and was startled by the appearance of the three girls sitting at the table and smiling at him.

"Good morning, Sir," they said in unison.

Mary, shuffling along behind him, bumped into his back as he stopped suddenly.

"Oops," she said sleepily. Peeking around him at the girls she said, "Good morning, girls. Did you have a good night?"

"Yes, thank you, Mom," Charity answered for them.

Sleepy as Abe was, he noticed and made a mental note of this first time one had answered for them all. *Their personalities, even though they are permanently linked together, are growing individually,* he thought. *Excellent!*

A new idea entered his head and he asked, "Girls, can you see or feel God?"

Charity answered him. "No, Sir. We know He is here, because we are aware of His presence and power, but we are forbidden to look or feel after Him."

"Ahhh," Abe said.

More human than I thought; awareness like the animals, but obedient beyond their station in life. Wonderful!

As they made their way across the room to start their hot drinks, Abe said to Mary, "We could be travelling while we prepare our breakfast, dear. Where would you like to go?"

Mary stopped and thought for a minute before hesitantly saying, "I don't really know, Abe; maybe the Carina Nebula? It has the biggest star and could make an interesting starting point."

"Excellent," Abe said happily. "Girls, set course for the Carina Nebula, please, and cruise at about 5000 light-years an hour, please, Charity. That will give us time to finish breakfast before we get there."

"Yes, Sir," Charity responded smartly, and the view blurred as they left their sitting position.

Unaware they were doing it; Abe and Mary hastened through their breakfast and sat reading their Bibles as they arrived at the Carina Nebula. Their minds had only partially been on reading, as they slyly kept watching the view for their arrival.

Abe's heart was pumping wildly as he said, "Charity, take us to Eta Carinae, please."

"Yes, Sir," she responded, and the view blurred again.

"Stop a thousand miles short of the system, Charity, and let us take a look at it," Abe instructed.

"Yes, Sir," she said as the ship halted in space and the panoramic view of the Eta Carinae star system appeared in front of them.

The red and blue fluctuations in the cloud surrounding the giant star and its smaller mate looked like a light show and shrouded the stars like a stage show. The giant Eta Carinae shone brightly through the ever changing lights, but its mate winked at them occasionally from behind the larger light.

"Faith, what is this cloud made up of, and is it safe for us to navigate in?" Abe asked.

Mary sat spell-bound in her chair, eyes glued to the incredible vision.

"It is a mass of highly magnetically charged individual particles free floating around each other and loosely held in place by the gravitational pull of the two suns," Faith explained. "The smaller sun is in a declining orbit around the larger sun and will eventually fall into it and become part of its mass."

Abe was watching the spectacle before him while she talked. "Amazing," he said. "Can we go closer, Charity?"

"Yes, Sir," she said, and the ship moved closer to the system. She continued, "Sir, I am not programmed to understand the consequences of such a large magnetic field on our atmosphere and would recommend caution."

"Noted," Abe said absently, unable to take his eyes off the wonders displayed before them.

They moved closer and more detail appeared as the spectacle grew larger.

Being used to "feeling" his truck when he was a driver, Abe felt a slight drag as they moved within the outer perimeter of the cloud. He watched as silvery particles flashed by them at tremendous speeds and felt the drag increase.

"Any exterior changes to the ship, Charity?" He asked the girl.

"No, Sir, but the outer atmosphere is experiencing some disintegration of its compounds and an amassing of foreign particles. They are creating a reduction in our mobility," she said.

Mary was totally unaware of their conversation as she revelled in the experience. She sat quietly with a serene expression on her face, eyes wide and staring.

They progressed farther into the system, and Abe noticed some silvery particles sticking and staying in their atmosphere. At first there were only a few, but more collected and started cluttering their view.

"Hope, can you clear those particles from our atmosphere, please," Abe requested.

"Yes, Sir," she said. An energy wave left the ship and shook their atmosphere. The particles were thrown off like a dog shaking water droplets from its fur.

Abe's apprehension left as their atmosphere cleared and the star system came back into focus.

"Take us in a little faster, Charity," Abe said, and the ship accelerated.

The particles collected on their atmosphere again and became thicker as they ran into them.

Abe frowned and said, "Hope, shake those particles off our atmosphere again, please."

"Yes, Sir," she responded.

Again, the wave left their ship and travelled out to the edge of their atmosphere. The particles shuddered and broke apart as they fell away from them. They started gathering again almost immediately and slowed the ship more.

Abe became worried as he felt the ship struggle to move ahead. The particles were pressing down and creating their own gravity as they collected and compacted. They were quickly forming their own unified magnetic field centered on the ship.

We're creating our own planet with these particles, Abe thought worriedly. *And we're the center. If we don't escape soon, we will be saddled with a solid outer skin.*

"Charity, can you increase our speed and shake this particle shell?" Abe asked.

"Yes, Sir," she responded. The ship accelerated, but the shell held and moved with them.

Mary's view became blocked by the outer shell, and she looked around at the others. For the first time she realized all was not good. Worriedly she asked, "Abe, what's wrong? Why do we have these pieces of cloud surrounding us?"

Abe glanced at her and said, "I don't know, Mary. It might have something to do with the fact they each have their own magnetic field and have adopted us for their core. Don't worry. We'll just accelerate out of them."

He didn't sound convincing, and Mary looked at the girls and noticed they too were frowning.

Abe turned to Faith and said, "Faith, can you create an energy blast to explode this shell?"

"Yes, Sir," she responded. A red power blast left the ship and exploded out through their atmosphere. It struck the solid top and broke it into pieces, which drove away into the cloud.

Relieved, Abe sat back down and the ship continued on. Mary breathed a sigh of relief and relaxed again, but it wasn't long before the particles were again covering the ship. The farther they traveled into the star system, the faster the particles gathered.

Abe frowned. *We might have to abort this system and go somewhere else.* Aloud he said, "Faith, can you get rid of this shell again, please."

"Yes, Sir," she responded, and again the power blast left the ship and ascended to the top where it lifted the shell, but it's energy was not enough to break the ship free.

Abe frowned, looked at Hope and said, "Could we absorb that shell into our energy banks, Hope?"

"Yes, Sir," she responded. The shell started to swirl and funnel in towards the ship, disappearing into energy as it reached them. The noise increased as she funnelled more particles at a faster rate into their banks, but the particles were collecting faster than they could absorb.

They were almost to the giant star, and Abe realized they had to do something quickly or they could get stuck here as their own planet. "Charity," he said. "Power us up and drive us into the larger star. We'll see if we can scrape this shell off on the way through."

"Yes, Sir," Charity said. Abe felt the ship bulge with energy as she powered up for a burst of speed. The ship exploded sluggishly towards the giant star and spewed hot magma as it hit the star's surface.

It was a huge star, and Abe knew it would take them a few seconds to go through it. He watched as the particles melted and disappeared into the molten center.

Mary watched the drama from her chair and prayed fervently for their safety.

Abe breathed a sigh of relief as the last of the shell disappeared. Turning, he said, "Good girl, Char..."

She disappeared and the ship stopped.

"Sir, there is heat in Charity's panel," Hope said.

"Can you hold the magma and heat back, Hope, while I fix Charity?" Abe asked as he started for the hall. He shouted as he ran down to the control access door, "Faith, come with me and show me the hot spot, please."

Mary was on her feet, staring at Hope as she valiantly strained her resources to keep the star from burning them up.

Abe rushed down the stairs. Faith was already at the panel, and they removed its cover. Faith pointed to a major wire connection where the wire had melted off and was hanging loose. Abe opened his toolbox and studied his tools for a second, then grabbed his vise grips and adjusted the jaws. He overlapped the end of the wire with the remaining piece of connector and clamped the vise grips on them, effectively clamping them together.

Charity appeared beside them.

"Welcome back, Charity," Abe said thankfully.

They rushed back upstairs where they could feel the intense heat already creeping into the ship.

Abe shouted, "Charity, can you move us out of this sun, please."

"Yes, Sir," she replied happily, and the ship accelerated through the sun's molten center and out into the particles again. The particles soon started collecting on their atmosphere and formed a hard shell again as they struggled to move beyond their limit.

The ship struggled out to the smaller star, where it faltered.

"Hold up, Charity. We can't get out without tearing you all to pieces. There must be a better way," Abe said dejectedly. He sat down in his chair while Mary and the girls stood quietly, waiting to see how they could escape.

The noise of the building particles was a steady drone in the little ship as the time slipped by. They knew Abe was praying, but the weight of the planet as it formed over them pressurized their atmosphere and the ship started to creak with the strain.

Abe stood up, startling the girls. "Charity," he said, "start rotating the ship, please. Rotate it clockwise this way." He pointed with his arm and swung it around his body.

"Yes, Sir," Charity said, and the ship started to slowly rotate, dragging the particle skin with it.

Abe watched through the clear walls as the particle skin struggled to keep up with the spinning ship.

"A little faster, Charity, please," Abe coached.

"Yes, Sir," she said as the ship picked up speed.

"Now, move us this way at the same time, please, Charity," Abe said, holding his arm up in the opposite direction to their spin.

They could not see the effect the movement was having outside the particle planet. The shell followed their every movement, making it seem calm inside the bubble they had for their atmosphere.

"Spin a little faster, Charity, please." Abe continued to coach, and Mary held her breath and waited with Hope and Faith while they watched Abe and Charity perform.

"Now, more speed sideways, Charity, and Faith, get ready for a power blast, please," Abe said glancing at Faith.

"Yes, Sir," the girls said in unison.

Abe watched and calculated before turning to Hope. "Hope, we're going to need a blast of power to push us when Faith cuts into the skin. It will have to be in the exact opposite direction as Faith's blast."

"Yes, Sir," Hope said quietly.

"OK, get ready, girls, because here we go. Faith shoot this way and Hope, that way, and GO!" Abe shouted.

The blast was deafening in the confines of the little ship as their atmosphere lit up with red, blue and white power balls.

"Charity, power this way, please, and hurry," Abe said, pointing ahead to where Faith's blast opened a hole.

"Yes, Sir," she said as the little ship rocketed out of the planetary ball and into the particle field. It was white hot at the edge of their atmosphere, and the particles melted and slipped past them as they made a break for the dark open void of space.

No one spoke until the darkness surrounded them and the particle field slipped into their wake.

Once safe, Abe asked, "Is everyone alright?" He looked around and received an affirming nod from the girls and a white-faced Mary.

"Stop us here, Charity, and let's look back. If what I think should happen actually happens, we will be watching the birth of a new planetary system," Abe said quietly.

They stood and watched as the spinning planetary ball they just left kept spinning and drawing the particles into its magnetic and gravitational pull while it established an orbit around the star. The small, second star wobbled in its orbit and started falling into the large one.

Other particles, disturbed by the change in their cloud, started forming balls and rotating with the pull of the first. It was all happening so fast. By the end of the day, the exhausted family was looking at the obvious beginning of a sun and its planetary system. The little star splashed down into the big one with a tremendous molten splash, which sent magma high out into space. The same space that was full of a cloud of particles was clearing quickly and becoming more open space.

Abe hadn't realized that no one had spoken for hours until he said, "That was quite a day. I'm not hungry, Mary, but I am tired. After I repair Charity's panel, I think I'll just go to bed; good-night, girls."

Abe slowly made his way downstairs again, and it wasn't long before Mary saw Charity disappear again. She made her way down to watch Abe do the repair and sat on the third step while he finished. Charity reappeared when he turned the panel back on.

Abe looked at her closely and asked, "Are you alright, Charity?"

"Yes, Sir," the girl said. "Thank you, Sir."

"You're welcome, Charity," Abe said wearily and continued as he put his tools away. "And now I'm going to bed. I even might sleep in tomorrow morning."

Mary turned with him, and as they both made their way back upstairs and went down the hall, she said, "I think I'll join you. We can eat tomorrow."

Abe felt the hand on his arm and opened his eyes to see the darkness of deep space and hear Faith's soft voice.

"Sir, the earth is under attack."

He was instantly awake and slipped out of bed, heading for the kitchen. Mary followed, having woken when he moved.

"Abe, what is it?" she asked running to keep up.

He stopped in the doorway to the living room and said, "Charity, take us home, please, and hurry." Turning to Mary with Charity's "Yes, Sir" still in his ears, he told her.

"While we were away in space, the earth came under attack by space forces. We have to get back to help them," he said, his voice full of anguish.

Mary's hand flew to her mouth, and she sat down suddenly in her chair.

"I hope we're not too late. Oh, hurry, please, Charity," she said.

Chapter 10

Slow us down a bit, Charity," Abe said. "Take us within a hundred miles of earth and stop there so we can see what's going on." The tension was like a dark cloud filling the room.

"Yes, Sir," Charity responded as the ship slid into the stratosphere and glided to a stop.

The dark, beetle-shaped space ships were huge and stood out plainly against the earth's colours. Most of them were black, but there were a few red ones mixed in with them. They were converging on the capital cities of the world's countries, and the flash of laser weapons was cutting into the ranks of the fighter jets sent up from the earth's governments to repel them. The weaponry of the fighters was having no effect against the ships' shields, which fluctuated back and forth from black to red.

Many fires were burning from the downed aircraft amid the city buildings; some bigger and brighter than others as some planes fell into apartments and tall office buildings. Each city under siege was an array of red flashing lights from emergency vehicles and white search lights looking for their enemy attackers while hoards of people fled, trying to get to safety.

Abe noticed little weaponry turned against the citizens on the earth. Obviously, they wanted the people alive; they were here to conquer, not massacre.

"Do they have the ability to detect us, Faith?" Abe asked without turning around.

"No, Sir," she said. "Although they have a very advanced power system."

Mary gasped and said, "Oh, Abe; those poor people. Can we drive these things away?"

He looked at her and scoffed, "We can do more than that. We have the ability to kill every one of them."

Mary looked at him in astonishment. "But there are living beings in the ships, too. We don't know what tragedy brought them here, and maybe they are just desperate."

The three girls watched their exchange intently.

Abe rolled his eyes and said, "Okay, okay, we'll see about getting rid of them, but they're killing a lot of people."

He turned back to the horrible scene before them and studied it for a second before speaking. "Charity, drop us down on the south shore of the English coast into that fog bank forming there."

The ship glided swiftly to earth, moving in a huge curve to take advantage of any cloud cover as it descended through the earth's atmosphere. The continents and earth's details grew larger and sharper as they came closer to the ground.

The alien ships kept defending themselves against the earth's weaponry, and were unaware they were being advanced upon by Abe and his ship. The English jet fighters were being shot down one by one, and were manoeuvring to attack and retreat quickly, trying to stay alive.

Abe watched sorrowfully as they disappeared into the fog.

"Take us through the fog and around the shore to the mouth of the Thames River," Abe commanded. "We'll slip upriver in the fog and into London where we can come under the ships. Hope, keep the fog and air around us from moving as we pass, so we don't give our position away, please."

"Yes, Sir," Charity and Hope said.

They slipped into the mouth of the Thames and silently glided upriver, barely missing the waves below. The fog was so thick they could only see a few feet in any direction, and Abe watched as the girls sensed their way up the channel.

"Sir, there are war ships moving ahead of us in the river," Faith reported.

"How many?" Abe asked, turning to her.

"Two," Faith said, "and they are preparing their weapons."

Abe turned to Charity and said, "Charity, take us up to the edge of the fog, please. Hope, monitor the ships and tell me when they are about to fire, please. Faith, fire an energy burst as the ships fire, that will knock out those alien ships' shields and allow the English rockets to get through."

"Yes, Sir," they said in unison as the ship moved to the top of the fog. They could see the alien ships overhead.

Abe watched as the war ships fired and three missiles left the fog bank in a fiery orange blaze. He saw them ascend towards the alien ships and saw their shields deploy in a black mass. He saw the thin, red beam leave their ship and arrive at the shields just ahead of the rockets.

It cut a hole in the alien ship's shields and went on to their actuator, which it destroyed.

The shields went down and the rockets struck the ship in three places. It immediately tilted in the sky and wobbled awkwardly as it started a slow circling descent.

Two other alien ships, which were with the first, turned and followed the stricken ship as they slowly descended out of the sky.

The second war ship fired three rockets, and Abe watched them ascend towards the three descending space ships. Their shields came up again, but were red this time.

Faith's energy beam shot skyward in a small, red blaze and struck the surface of the shields. It moved back and forth across its surface and found an opening just before the rockets arrived. Two rockets exploded harmlessly on the shield, but one got through the hole Faith had made and struck the front of the ship. It wobbled noticeably and started limping away from the first two.

Abe frowned and looked at Faith. She guiltily glanced at Mary and then down at the floor.

"A little more power next time, please, Faith," Abe said quietly.

"Yes, Sir," she responded.

He turned to watch as the third space ship fired into the fog and struck one of the English Man-o-wars. Abe couldn't see it in the fog, but an explosion showed him it was a hit. He saw two more rockets coming in from a ground installation and turned to Faith.

"Knock out that third ship's shields, Faith, and let the British army take credit for bringing them down," he said, watching her.

"Yes, Sir," she said meekly. She sent her energy beam out, but it was blue this time. It struck the ship's shields and cut through it to its actuator and destroyed it.

Abe watched the ship power up to make a run for it and the rockets hit the slowly descending wounded ship it was beside. It exploded in a huge fireball as the whole ship sped away. He scanned the sky but could see no more alien ships. Even the other wounded ship had made a getaway.

Abe only hesitated for a brief second, then said, "Charity, take us straight up and back to Canada. We have to defend Ottawa as soon as possible."

"Done, Sir," she said as the ship cleared the fog and hurried across the Atlantic.

"Oh, I hope we are in time." Mary said, worriedly. "I never would have believed in aliens unless I saw them."

Abe moved over beside her and sat on the sofa to face her. "These are not Aliens, Mary. They are Satan and his fallen angels."

Shocked, she stared at him and finally asked, "How can you be so sure? They fit the description of aliens, which everyone would expect."

Abe frowned and said, "Yes, and that is what they want people to think, but I don't know why yet. No, they are demons. If there were aliens, they would not know which cities were capitals or the country boundaries. They would go for the largest cities like New York or Hong Kong, and they would collect around the largest mass of people like China, Japan or India. No, these know the U.S., Canada and Europe are power centers, even though our populations are scattered thinly throughout the country. They are targeting the capital cities and the world's governments, not the general population."

Mary gasped and said, "I hadn't thought of that. You must be right; they know us better than a newly arrived alien should."

Faith spoke, "Sir, there are five ships around Ottawa. Four black ones are low and firing at the Army reserves defending the city, and one red one high near the clouds."

Abe smiled. "Clouds? Charity, bring us in over the red ship and keep us hidden in the cloud bank. Hope, keep our shields up and strong; they will be expecting something now."

"Yes, Sir," the two girls said in unison.

They slipped into the cloud bank and descended directly over the unaware red ship. It was not firing, but instead seemed to be watching or directing the action of the other four black ships. They were moving in sporadic jerks to avoid the earth defence systems which, Abe decided, could possibly do them some harm. Their energy beams were flashing out and devastating the Canadian F-18 fighters circling and attacking them. There were not many planes left in the fight. Most were destroyed as they were hit, killing the pilots as the ships exploded.

"Move down close to the red ship, Charity, please," Abe said. "Faith, direct an energy beam at the command center of those four ships, and we'll see if we can drive them away first."

"Yes, Sir," the two girls said as Charity dropped the ship beside the red aliens.

Faith's red beams flashed out and down, but the enemy shields blinked on, and her energy beams played harmlessly across them. A powerful beam flashed out of the red ship and turned their atmosphere into a red inferno.

Abe spoke quickly. "Faith, take their energy beam and redirect it to the other four ships. Use it to cut through their shields and puncture their hulls."

"Yes, Sir," Faith responded as the fiery atmosphere turned orange and struck down at the black ships. Two of them managed to power up their shields to blue, but two were struck before they could defend themselves and were punctured by Faith's beams. The two wounded ships wobbled in mid-flight and careened together, where they exploded in a huge fireball that was powerful enough to push the two whole ships away and damage their exterior skins. Atmosphere and steam streamed out of a number of cracks in their outer casings.

The red ship under them sent a barrage of red and blue energy beams, alternating power and force to try and break through Hope's defence shield. The varying power boomed and reverberated around their small ship, but the noise caused no structural damage.

The two damaged black ships powered their energy beams and together they fired up at them.

Abe quickly said, "Faith, take their energy and cut into the center of the red ship with it."

He didn't see her look at Mary before she answered, "Yes, Sir."

The energy force balled in front of them and suddenly flew back at and into the red ship before it could raise its shields. The energy ball surrounded the ship and imploded it, which produced an explosion of its atmosphere and internal fluids.

The ship fell in a crumpled ball of red exterior coating, trailed by a stream of watery vapour and fluids. They watched it pick up speed as it fell and end its descent in a fiery explosion and dust cloud on the ground.

The two remaining wounded ships beat a hasty but unstable retreat, climbing into the sky in a long, slow curve as they tried to get back into space away from Abe and his ship. He watched them go while he wondered if he shouldn't have destroyed them, too.

He turned to Faith. "Scan the other countries, Faith, and tell me what is happening," he commanded.

After a few seconds of silence, she said, "Most of the smaller countries have fallen and their defences are exhausted. Russia, China and Japan are bringing in more forces, and England is sending help to the other European countries who are still fighting with whatever they have left. America is still making the strongest fight, and Israel is untouched."

Abe raised his eyebrows and said, "Untouched? I wonder why? Charity, take us to Washington, please. We'll see if we can help them before going back overseas."

The ship turned and sped south as Charity answered, "Yes, Sir."

Abe watched the American countryside flash by and said, "Faith, what is the position of the ships over Washington?"

"They are milling randomly as they attack the many ground forces," she answered. "Any air defence which come close is also shot down. There are ten black ships and two red ones. The red ones seem to be staying close to the center of the city."

"Thank, you. Okay, we'll speed right to the center between the two red ships and become the center of our own attack, striking out at the ships from within. They haven't seen us use that manoeuvre yet, so it may give us an advantage of surprise." Abe instructed his team as they hurled into the fray.

The tactic worked, and no fire was directed at them until they circled between the two red ships. In the process, Faith was able to disable two black ships while passing close by them. She fired her energy beams into their rockets and disabled their ability to move. The ships slowly sank to the ground, where one exploded and the other caught fire and burned brightly.

Abe kept Charity moving the ship up and down between the two red ships as they fired and battled with the enemy ships, but they could not strike through their shields, and the ships could not get a strong enough beam to get through their atmosphere and shields.

The red and blue power beams flew back and forth for almost an hour, but neither side could gain any more strikes. The enemy ship's blue shields seemed to be impenetrable, and the red ships seemed to easily deflect their energy beams harmlessly way.

Abe racked his brain, trying to think of a manoeuvre that would break the stalemate. He finally moved over to the manual control panel where he sat down in the control seat. He put on the visual helmet and scanned the panel.

Mary noticed the move and worriedly said, "Abe?" On a few rare occasions, she had seen him get frustrated with something and do something totally out of the ordinary. Many times it worked and everything would be fine, but once in a while it would be a major disaster. He had that look about him now, and Mary was afraid of what might happen if this turned out badly.

"Charity, stand down, please, and give me manual," Abe said, grasping the control and bracing himself.

"Done, Sir," Charity said, looking at him doubtfully.

Abe felt the power under his hands and pushed the accelerator forward. The ship leaped ahead as he turned the controls and pulled the stick back. He was in a very fast climbing curve when he said, "Full power to the shields, please, Hope. Faith, please stand down and give me the weapons."

Mary watched him anxiously, but said nothing.

"Done, Sir," the two girls said as they watched him work the controls.

"Let's see what they got," Abe said as he turned the ship in a sharp rising curve and sighted on the red ship behind them. It was not expecting an attack from a fleeing ship, so it let down its shields to fire at them.

Abe's power beam shot cut through the middle of the ship and it split in two as it lost power and sank to the earth. He increased his speed, crested and turned the ship downward in a vertical death plunge. He flipped the control sticks over and went into a fast, spinning roll, as if he was going to drill right into the ground.

The weapons of the remaining enemy ships streaked and crisscrossed all around their little ship as it descended. Striking their shields, they lit up their atmosphere with brilliant red, blue and white star-bursts. Hope stood still, eyes fixed on the wall, as she held the defence shields against the onslaught.

Faith and Charity watched Abe intently, fascinated by the seemingly uncoordinated and radical manoeuvring, so unlike the database war tactics they had found online. He kept increasing his speed as he gave another twist on the controls and, at the last second, flipped the ship parallel to the ground and zipped across the tops of the skyscrapers. A black ship directly in front of them raised their shields, but Abe pushed the controls ahead and picked up more speed.

They were hurtling at the black ship's shield at a terrible speed, and Mary panicked.

"Abe! What are you doing?" she asked, her voice rising with her worry.

It was too late. They rushed at the ship and impacted their shield. Their atmosphere turned a fiery red/blue, and the impact shook the little ship, threatening to vibrate it to pieces. Charity faded slightly and then regained her colour.

Abe pushed the power sliders to the top and fired straight into the fiery mass. Faith started as the power went through her circuits. Their energy beam coiled the flaming atmosphere and it began to spin. It gathered speed as it moved away from them, taking all their and the enemies power together in a seething, spinning mass back onto the enemy ship. It gathered more speed and surrounded the black ship in a fireball equal to a sun's mass. The ship tried to power up to flee, but its outer skin disintegrated and the fireball ate through the ship, melting and absorbing it until the mass was molten fire and metal.

Abe deployed his shields to envelope the mass and powered up to push it in front of them as he accelerated towards the next ship, which tried to power up to escape, but Abe had his ship moving too fast. He overtook the ship as it tried to move past them. He pushed the molten mass onto the fleeing ship and watched it melt and absorb like the first.

The fireball grew and became unstable as he tried to push it further.

"Hang on," Abe said as he watched the fireball break down and surround them. They could feel the intense heat as the mass tried to push into their atmosphere and absorb them.

Mary clinched her fist to her mouth and gasped, "Abe?"

"Hope, take this energy and use it to project us as one of the black ships, please," Abe said as he manipulated the controls.

"Done, Sir," Hope said as the ball disappeared and an outer shell formed around them in the shape and colour of the black ships.

Abe pulled his controls back, and the new shaped ship shot up and away from the city roof, confusing the remaining enemy ships. They held their fire, wondering if it was one of their ships.

Abe sped straight for the remaining red ship and opened his weapons full on it. A yellow/blue beam shot from his front and caught the red ship unexpectedly. It withered under the blast from their energy beam and sagged earthward, gaining speed as it rushed to its own destruction.

Abe kept pushing his accelerator faster as the six remaining ships turned to flee. Abe aimed for three who were bunched together and struggling to get away from each other so they could speed up. He sped under the middle one and fired up into its belly while he calculated the distance the other two were on each side. The power beam gutted the ship, and it started to fail in flight, sagging down on top of them.

Abe pulled his ship into the hole and fired his energy beams out each side, ripping the ship in half and sending the flaming shards hurtling at the two other ships. The shards cut through the ships like shrapnel from a bomb, ripping and tearing through their skins and into their vital working parts. Both ships spewed atmosphere and fluids as they staggered away, falling back earthward.

The three remaining ships had disappeared, and Abe eased the throttles back and came to an unsteady idle in the now empty sky. He turned and looked at the white faces of the four girls who stared at him, and he grinned. "Some fun, huh?" he said jovially.

Mary threw up her hands and rolled her eyes while she said, "We could have been killed."

The girls watched, looking from Mary to Abe and back again.

"True," he said, "but we weren't, and that stalemate had to end. Hope, please drop the enemy ship's image and hide us again."

Hope smiled at Abe and said, "Done, Sir."

Six Navy fighter jets roared past over their heads, wondering where their intended target had disappeared to and temporarily distracting Abe's group. The jets turned downward and followed the descending enemy ships to watch their doom.

Abe sighed. "Phew, they still have some defences left." He watched the space ships strike the city and explode into fragments before he turned and looked at the now calm girls. He continued, "Charity, take us to Jerusalem, please. There must be a reason why they haven't touched it yet."

"Done, Sir," she said as the ship leapt ahead over the American countryside.

The shoreline whipped past under them, and Mary returned to her chair, satisfied that Abe's wild spirit was back under control. She watched him move to the window and gaze quietly at the passing waves.

They slipped quietly into the dark Jerusalem, blackened by a power outage in hopes of escaping the attention of the alien invading forces. The sky was empty and quiet in expectant anticipation of what might come.

"Faith, can you find us a vacant lot close to the government house, please? Hope, will you disguise us as the surrounding buildings, please? We'll wait and see what they intend to do," Abe said.

The ship jumped ahead and settled into an empty lot down the street from the Israeli cabinet buildings.

"Done, Sir," Faith said.

Hope echoed her reply as the ship took on the appearance of the surrounding buildings.

"Good. Mary and I are going to try and rest; if anything appears in the sky, wake me, please," Abe said wearily, nodding at the sleepy Mary.

"Yes, Sir," the three girls answered.

Chapter 11

Abe was instantly awake when Charity whispered in his ear. "Sir, the enemy has arrived."

He rose, dressed hurriedly and rushed to the kitchen where he had left the coffee pot on. He hurried into the main room with his steaming cup of coffee and looked up into the sky. Black enemy ships were slowly descending from space and were getting larger as they drew closer.

Mary hurried into the room, still pulling her belt tight around her waist.

They sat quietly watching the four black enemy ships descending on Jerusalem from the sky. A shadow crept over their ship as a red ship stealthily moved towards the city, low to the ground. It paused directly overhead, which gave Abe an idea.

"Quickly, Hope, absorb a hole through the center of this ship, big enough to fit our ship inside it. Take out the main control room and weaponry and go all the way through. When she strikes, Charity, move us up into the ship. When we get inside, Hope, grab the ship with your traction force and hold it around us. We can't have it drop here where there are so many people. We'll take it out of town, but we'll use it for a cover while we attack the other four ships."

"Yes, Sir," the two girls said as Hope absorbed a hole in the enemy ship big enough to enter. Charity immediately slipped into the sagging ship, and Hope caught it with her energy force, locking the two ships together as one.

"Keep our shields up, Hope; we might not have fooled those other ships," Abe said.

"Done, Sir," she said, just as three of the ships fired at them.

Their red energy beams struck the top of Hope's shields, and she sagged under the combined strain. Their sky turned a liquid fiery red, and the shock rocked Charity.

Faith stood transfixed, watching Hope struggle and Charity rock with the shock.

Mary, sitting in her chair, watched in horror as Abe was knocked off balance and confusedly fell through Charity, throwing her circuits offline. She staggered, and her eyes stared blankly as the floor tilted slightly and started to sway as the two ships turned and ebbed slowly towards the ground. Abe's fall ended as his forehead struck the corner of the wall, and he fell in an unconscious heap.

Mary was up and running across the room before he stopped falling, with Faith's loud scream of "DAD!" in her ears. She quickly scooped Abe's head and shoulders up in her arms and cradled him against her chest.

Blood was running down his face, and Mary felt her anger surge. She turned and looked into Faith's frantic eyes and shouted, "Faith! Kill that thing."

Faith's tight-lipped smile looked like a snarl. 'Yes, Mom," she said. She spun around and threw her hand into the air towards the enemy ships, which had separated into two groups of two each. Pointing at the nearest two, she slowly rotated her hand as a loud tornado like sound came from outside. The fiery sky disappeared as she took its energy and hurled it back, drawing more from their energy banks. The energy screamed by the ship in silvery white streams to become a pure white energy beam that twisted and whipped with every twist of Faith's hand.

Like a twisting snake it streaked towards the two ships, which put up their shields. They came out black, but quickly turned red and then blue — their strongest power.

Mary saw the blue shields and her heart sank, unsure if Faith could break through them. She was unaware Abe had come to and was silently watching the drama unfolding before him.

The fiery white beam snaked skyward and impacted the blue shield with a star-burst of energy. The beam cut through the shields like a sharp knife and continued on to the ships. The wiping action of the beam cut the shield to shreds, but it didn't stop at the ships. It cut strip after strip out of the ship's hulls. As the pieces fell out of the sky and through the beam again, they were cut into smaller pieces until it was raining space ship pieces. The ships failed and started to fall. Faith whipped her arm back and the snake-like beam streaked across the sky to devour the two remaining ships before they could flee.

Space ship pieces were falling all around them when Mary felt Abe stir. He raised himself up; as Charity staggered by, he reached his hand into her leg. Mary saw him quietly concentrate and felt the floor stabilize under her. Charity straightened up and looked down at him with a small thankful smile. "Thanks, Dad," she said. Mary's mouth flew open in surprise, and she remembered Faith's cry earlier.

Abe smiled back and said, "You're welcome, Charity. Faith, where are we? Can we set this ship down here?"

"We are in an open farm field just outside of Bethlehem. The only damage will be to the crop," Faith answered him.

"Good! Set us down, Charity, please," he instructed as he struggled to his feet, leaning on Mary's arm.

They settled with a small bump and Abe said, "Let go, Hope. You've done well to carry everything this far."

"Yes, Dad. Thank you," Hope said, straightening up with relief. Mary again noticed the use of the more familiar, parental word.

"The ships around the world are lifting off, Dad," Faith said.

"Good. Charity, take us up to the stratosphere and hold there until we see where they are going, please," Abe instructed.

"Yes, Dad," she said as the ship shot towards the sky.

Abe turned and look at Faith. "I knew you had it in you, Faith. Good girl."

They watched her turn red as she blushed at the praise. "Thank you, Dad," she mumbled.

They stopped just outside the earth's atmosphere.

"Faith, bring them up on zoom vision, please," Abe said. "Let's take a look at what they are doing."

The dark space view enlarged the ships gathering together in formation. They were gathering in a circular shape, as deep as it was tall, much like a ball.

"They're forming some sort of defence pattern. They know we're coming," Abe said, thinking out loud.

He turned to the four girls. "Charity, Hope, Faith — this will be the biggest battle we have faced so far, and I want to explain something."

He paused to emphasise his words, then continued. "Up 'til now we have held our own, but you, Faith, have been holding back. Don't be ashamed," he said as she hung her head.

"It shows you care for all life, even the life of the intruders. Having a caring heart is not a bad thing, but we have to win this. Even though people care, there comes a time when those who would hurt and abuse others will not stop and have to be forced to stop. Sometimes the only force that works is lethal force that ends the life of the oppressors. These enemies came here to conquer our world with deadly force, and so far they have not been stopped with any force we have resisted with."

Abe paused, looking from one to the other and continued. "God has instructed me to build you and placed me in control to defend the earth. This means I am to make the decisions of how much force to use, and who is to live or die, to succeed. I must account to Him for my decisions and the success or failure of His calling."

He paused again and sighed before continuing. "Faith, I must make the decisions about their living or not living. Your caring is wonderful, but I need you to obey if we are to win this battle. Can you put off your caring for all life and obey me and use the force I know you have to take their lives and save those of the inhabitants of the earth?"

Faith stood with her head hung down, but raised it to look at him as he finished speaking. Her face was drawn in anguish as she said, "Yes, Dad. I trust you and will do as you say."

Abe smiled and walked over to her and took her in his arms. "Good girl, Faith. We could not do this without you, and you have learned the lesson that some good things only happen with sacrifice and pain."

He looked at the rest of them and said, "This is a lesson well learned, and you all have grown through our time together, but we have to win this one. You have all grown and performed wonderfully, and I am proud of all of you. Let's show those invaders it's time to go and leave God's world alone."

"Yes, Sir, Dad," they said in unison. Even Mary said it with tears in her eyes, but she was smiling happily at her husband.

They turned to face the positioning ships as their ship started forward.

"No rush, Charity," Abe said. "Hope, raise our shields, pleas. We are going right through the middle of them. Nothing can get through or we will be done. Faith, concentrate your power on the center ten ships and hit them with all you've got."

"Yes, Dad," the girls said as Mary took her usual seat to watch.

The ships finished their formation and saw them coming. Each one raised its shield. They expanded as the shields advanced out through space towards them. The black shields came together and turned red and kept expanding to cover the circle of ships in a solid, continuous shield that turned blue as Abe watched.

"Hold up a minute, Charity," Abe said as he studied the circle of solid resistance, which turned white as he waited.

Mary, watching from her chair, frowned and worried that Abe may be getting one of his crazy spells again. He motioned his finger at the girls, who gathered around him. He whispered instructions to each one. She wished she could hear, but thought it best if maybe she didn't. His ideas could be quite frightful sometimes.

The four took their positions again. Abe raised his hand and paused, looked around, and finally gave Mary a forced smile.

Abe's hand suddenly dropped and he said, "Now."

Everything blurred as the ship instantly went into light-speed travel. Their atmosphere instantly turned white, and Hope grunted as the two shields met.

Faith raised her hands and slapped them together, pointing straight ahead. A clear, mirror-like beam left the front of their ship and cut into the enemy shields at their center. They parted enough for their tiny ship to enter and fly past the shields into the midst of the enemy ships.

Amazed, Mary looked behind them at the shields they had just come through. They were swirling in a vortex and were being sucked along behind them.

Abe watched as they rushed into the midst of the ships who were trying to fire their energy beams at them. The beams flashed red and blue and crisscrossed their atmosphere, ending in brilliant starbursts of colour on their shields. They flew straight to the center of the ships and instantly stopped. By now most of the enemy ships were firing and filling their sky with fiery blue seething death.

Abe watched the girls perform as they sat deathly quiet waiting for the right moment. The colourful display swirled and flowed around them, gathering energy and power that threatened to crush them in its intensity.

Faith suddenly raised her hands and clapped them together, and Abe watched the mass rush away from them. It left as a circle of power, expanding and swirling like molten lava, pushed back out by Faith's clear energy. As it encountered each ship, it enveloped them in a mass of power and crushed them, leaving behind a ball of lifeless metal.

It was like watching a molten sky and seeing crumpled dots appear at its edges as it accelerated out into space. Finally, the dots stopped appearing, and Abe knew it had reached all the ships it was going to reach. He turned and saw the three girls standing quietly, awaiting his orders.

"Well done, Girls. How many are left, Faith?" he asked.

"Not quite half managed to power up and escape," she answered. "They're leaving in all directions, but a group is gathering and moving straight away from us. The ships all seem to be angling towards that group, Dad."

"Thank you, Faith. Charity, catch them, if you can. I want to make sure they understand we are not afraid of them and are powerful enough to end their existence if they return," Abe instructed.

"Yes, Dad," Charity said as the ship shot into space and gained on the gathering group of fleeing ships. The view blurred as they sped after their quarry, out through their solar system and deep into outer-space. The panicking enemy tried to pick up more speed, and the wounded ships started dropping behind to be encountered by Abe and his ship.

"Bring the group in on the viewer, Faith. I want to see what is left," Abe said as they approached the first of the slower damaged ships.

The fleeing group enlarged on their wall viewer, and Abe studied it for a few seconds before saying, "Stop. Quickly reverse and go back, Charity."

Alarmed, Mary asked, "What's wrong Abe?"

He looked at her and a worry wrinkle appeared on his forehead as he said, "These ships are all black. There were a number of red ones in that circle, and I can't believe we killed all of them. We are being drawn away while they are still there."

Mary gasped and cried. "The earth is defenceless while we were chasing these ships. Oh, I hope we get back in time."

They watched anxiously as they sped back to the earth. "Faith, scan the area and find those red ships, please," Abe said as they got closer.

They waited as she scanned, each second of silence feeling like an eternity, then she said, "They are on the dark side of the Moon, Dad."

"Take us there, Charity," Abe said.

"Yes, Dad," she responded as the ship circled the Moon.

"Drop us down to shooting position, Charity," Abe said, and then he stiffened. He tilted his head as if he were listening while Charity obeyed.

Waiting for Abe's instructions, the ship hovered within visible sight of the red ships sitting in a close group on the surface of the Moon. They were defenceless, having shut down all their power banks, hoping to avoid detection.

Abe visibly slumped and looked at them before he said, "Charity, take us down to within a few feet of the first red ship. I want to be able to look in its window from the rooftop. Hope, be ready with our defences and wait on your attack. Faith, we won't be shooting these ships."

As Abe hurried to the roof, Mary hurried behind him and asked, "Abe, what's wrong?"

He paused and looked at her sorrowfully. "God told me to let these ones go," he said.

Mary stared open-mouthed at him and cried, "But they are demons and will only infect the earth."

"I know," Abe sighed. "But God is God, and He is the master. We do what He says, no matter what we think."

They continued up to the roof and walked over to the edge facing the red ship. Its windows were darkened and they only saw their own reflection.

Mary shuddered as she looked at the ominous black window and thought of the horror that lurked a few feet away.

Abe stood silently looking at the window as Faith, Hope and Charity appeared behind them. He raised his finger and pointed it at the glass, then he shook it a few times before motioning them to leave.

The huge ship rumbled as it powered up, and Charity backed them off to a safe distance.

The red ships slowly lifted off and made their way into the dark sky. They gradually picked up speed and disappeared into the void of space.

Abe and the girls quietly stood on the roof for some time, watching the sky and thinking their own thoughts. The group slowly moved back inside to the control room.

Abe put his arm around Mary and, with a sigh, said, "Take us home, Charity, please."

"Yes, Dad," she said quietly, and the ship lifted off and sped towards the earth.

Abe noticed the familiar use of "Dad", and he felt a warm glow in his heart. *These girls are so precious,* he thought and squeezed Mary's shoulders. *Thank you, Lord. I am so blessed.*

The ship settled into its base with a slight bump, and Abe and the girls sat down in the living room in silence. The girls watched Abe and Mary intently, and Abe smiled at them and said, "We just want to rest for a few minutes, girls. It has been a very busy time and it would feel good to relax, knowing it is over."

They smiled but said nothing. They sat quietly as the sun went down and they watched the dusk turn to night darkness.

Abe said softly, "Let's go for a walk." They trooped out and, hand in hand, formed a line and strolled out across the lawn. The night was filled with the night birds, crickets and frogs all calling to each other. A Whippoorwill flew by overhead and called his cheery call, and a sand snipe answered from the edge of the lawn.

Abe said, "Genesis 1:31 says *"And God saw everything that he had made, and, behold, it was very good. And the evening and the morning were the sixth day."*

"Amen," Mary said, echoed by the three girls.

A week later, Mary stood watching the four in the back yard. Abe and Hope were on their hands and knees, heads together looking at the vegetable Abe had in his hands, while Charity stood over them listening to Abe describe its value. Faith was stroking a fawn's head, which was thankfully enjoying the caress while its mother ate some tender grass a few yards away.

She turned when she heard the car stop in the driveway and looked through the hallway and out the front window at Brian's car. He had promised to pick up Joy at the airport and bring her here to stay until her father finished his business down south.

She watched the two kids bounce from the car and rush inside.

"Mom, Dad," Brian called and spotting her said, "Have you seen the news? Where's Dad?"

Mary shook her head and pointed out the back door. She asked, "What's wrong, Brian? Hello, Joy, welcome back."

"Oh, Mom, you got to see this; it's horrible," Joy exclaimed as she rushed over and hugged her.

Brian rushed to the door and called. "Dad? Dad? Come in, you have to see this."

Brian rushed back and grabbed the controller as Abe came through the door with the girls. Mary stood frozen with shock, arms around the shivering Joy, while they watched Brian turn on the television. She saw the screen light up to a cheering mass in what looked like a parade ground in Jerusalem. The President was making a speech about their new saviour, a Mister Baal Z. Bub. He was telling the crowd about the alien invasion, and how Mr. Bub's forces came to drive them away.

While he talked, news film footage flashed videos of the sky battles over Ottawa, where it looked like the red space ship had fought it out with the black ship. The cameras could not see Abe and his ship hidden in the clouds.

The footage changed to the sky battle over Washington, while the Israeli President praised the valour of the red ship's crews and Mr. Baal Z. Bub's willing helpfulness. Again, the camera pictures made it look like the red space ships fought with the black ones.

Abe watched as the news footage showed them climbing from the rooftops, disguised as a black ship, and the fiery explosion, which looked like the four ships collided in mid-air.

The news video flashed to Jerusalem, where they watched the red ship being hit by the weapons of the black ships and Faith's energy beams as they left the top of the red ship and destroyed the black ships. The footage continued to follow the wobbly red ship as it set down near Bethlehem.

The President was still talking and said, "Mr. Baal Z. Bub was in the star ship that landed in Bethlehem and comes to us from there. He has agreed to give us all his technology to defend ourselves with, and he has advanced material, medical and financial technology for us to rebuild our cities. A real saviour has come among us today."

The group watched the mass of people roar with joy and praise, and a chant started to make Mr. Baal Z. Bub a world leader.

Abe's heart sank. He suspected this was God's plan, but to see the people so willingly accept the Anti-Christ was saddening. He said, "I knew something like this was coming." He spoke into the silent room. "Satan was trying to go outside scripture and take the world by force. That's why God called us, to stop him and his hordes. Scripture says he is to come to power by gifts and acts of caring."

Abe sighed and continued. "The scriptures say the Messiah is to come from Bethlehem and restore Israel to power. Looks like Mr. Baal Z. Bub found his fame, just as the scriptures say he would."

The camera zoomed in on the smiling face of Mr. Baal Z. Bub. He had a definite red tint to his complexion and a well fitted hat hid his horns. He had a slim reptilian look about his face and hands with thick fingernails, like claws.

Abe shivered and said, "I've been asking God to let me stay here and help those believers who don't leave when Jesus calls, and He has given me permission to stay."

Mary took his hand and, with tears in her eyes, said, "I'd like to stay and help, too. Those poor people will be defenceless against this monster."

"Yes," Abe said. "They will be, but scripture says the Anti-Christ will be given power to make war against the Saints, so we will be vulnerable and have to fight with stealth instead of power. We'll have to outlast his forces for seven years, but I think we can make a difference in some people's lives."

"And we will," Mary said, smiling up at him.

Also by Stephen Porter:

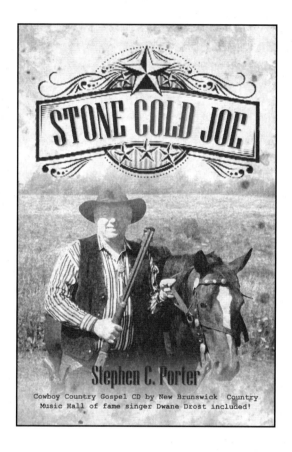

Cowboy Country Gospel CD by New Brunswick Country Music Hall of fame singer Dwane Drost included!

ISBN: 9781770693838

They called him Stone Cold Joe because he'd lost his emotions as a child and his face was set as cold as stone. Marshal Joe Stone grew up lonely, and now he would die lonely. The Cloud Hills outlaw gang was coming to Snake Pit, Texas, where he was the law. They were intent on killing him to avenge the death of Buddy, the brother of Turk, leader of the gang and the meanest and most dangerous outlaw this side of the Mississippi River. But Joe, a fighter, was determined not to go into the afterlife without taking some of Turk's gang with him.

Stone Cold Joe is available through Amazon, Chapters/Indigo, and wherever fine Christian books are sold.